LOST ISLAND RAMPAGE

GUSTAVO BONDONI

SEVERED PRESS
HOBART TASMANIA

LOST ISLAND RAMPAGE

Copyright © 2021 Gustavo Bondoni

WWW.SEVEREDPRESS.COM

ISBN: 978-1-922551-90-0

CHAPTER 1

Sked landed on the roof with a slight scuffing sound. He released the carabiner holding him to the line and listened until the sound of the helicopter disappeared into the night. Even though the chopper was supposed to be stealth tech of the best, and that the sound was muted, he was glad they'd chosen dark, overcast night for the incursion.

He looked out over the side of the building, tensely waiting to see if any of the antlike security people ten floors below suddenly sounded an alarm or began to roll out anti-aircraft artillery.

Satisfied that he'd gotten in unobserved, Sked turned his back to the waterfront of Xiamen and studied the flat expanse around him. The roof looked just like the ones on all the other office blocks on Xiahe Road: scattered air conditioning units and vent chimneys, a few pipes and silver insulation that felt rubbery underfoot.

But this building and its blue-glassed twin ten meters away were anything but normal office blocks, despite their blue mirrored glass and their corporate logos in the lobby. They belonged to the Ministry of State Security, and they were one of the places where the Chinese government stashed embarrassing prisoners.

Actually, only one of the buildings was a prison. The other was an office block full of signal intelligence people, and even at three in the morning, it would be full of operatives at work. That meant if the Buddha had sent him to the wrong tower, he was going to have to answer a lot of truly uncomfortable questions which, whether he told the truth or not, would land him in a cell beside Akane. That would probably qualify as the world's lamest attempt at a rescue, ever.

He decided not to think about that. The Electric Buddha was a colleague who wouldn't intentionally steer him wrong. Yes, his information often came with strings attached, and they were granted when they served additional purposes beyond just helping out, so you had to be on the lookout for when the other shoe dropped. But the data was always solid. The only question was who else would be benefiting from this particular mission.

In the end, it didn't matter.

The door was a beast, of course, but the Chinese were still thinking in terms of brute force. They reasoned that anyone who decided on an airborne assault would be military in philosophy. Hence the armored door.

That was a mistake. He pulled out his laptop, a device with enough power to brute-force the Pentagon's password systems if he so desired, and plugged it into the keypad's inlet port. The fact that it even had an inlet port was another sign that the Chinese thought of this as a fortress to be stormed rather than an asset that could be assaulted electronically. That the Buddha had known about the deficiency was a good sign.

The keypad didn't put up much of a fight. Less than ten minutes later, the foot-thick door swung open on beautifully oiled hinges to reveal a staircase painted in innocuous grey and complete with anti-slip strips on the steps.

Sked wondered if the Ministry was concerned that an invading paratrooper might slip and hurt himself on the way in and sue them.

Concentrate, he told himself. *Don't get cocky because security on the rooftop was crap. Security on the rooftop is always crap. It's the guys inside you need to worry about. And the guys inside are very, very good at what they do.*

He inched down the stairs and, three floors later, hit his first alarm point. From here forward, there were cameras and motion sensors in every hall and every stairwell.

Time to take them out.

Security inside the building was way too tight to attempt anything as things stood. Try hacking these cameras while the building was working to spec and you'd set off every alarm between Xiamen and Beijing. So, it was a good thing they'd been planning this particular caper for a week.

"Blow the cable," he subvocalized into the microphone implanted in his jaw. Then he sat back and waited.

Out in the street, one of the Buddha's other friends, someone Sked had never met and would never meet, had taken a perfectly legitimate work crew from Xiamen CCGT, a local utility company, and done some repair work on old cabling a block away. Unbeknownst to any of the other workers, one transformer unit had an extra coil made of high explosives.

In response to Sked's command, it exploded, cutting power to the building and leaving him sitting in the dark.

But only for a second. The emergency lights flicked on, the cool greyish glow illuminating the hallway.

Sked moved quickly. He had seconds, perhaps a minute or two, before the generator kicked in and the building was back on regular power. When that happened, the cameras would come back online as soon as the system rebooted, which wouldn't take long.

He sprinted to the nearest camera, unplugged the two cables leading into it and plugged them into two devices. The data cord went into his laptop, while the power supply went into a high-power quick-discharge capacitor he'd brought for precisely this purpose. Then he waited for the lights to come back on.

As soon as they did, he commanded his laptop to try to get through the security for the camera system. It probably wouldn't work, but it was safe to try, as any alarms or system instability would be attributed to the power outage causing one of the cameras to malfunction as opposed to enemy action. And in attempting to get into the system, his programs would keep the security people occupied, trying to get things running well again.

Additionally, if things went really pear-shaped, he would order this particular camera to show some truly alarming images which could conceivably distract the bad guys and buy him some time.

But if he had to use that, he was probably screwed.

Once that was done, he hit the power button on the capacitor and sprinted towards the next stairwell. He had five seconds.

Behind him, lights blew out and cables popped as the capacitor discharged hard. It wouldn't take out the electricity in the building, but hopefully, knock out a couple of floors' worth of circuit breakers.

In the stairwell, he removed his black jumpsuit to reveal a set of grey coveralls topped with a matching grey cap which he pulled down over his face to conceal his extremely out-of-place occidental features.

Then he pulled a screwdriver out of his pocket and walked down the stairs. It wouldn't fool anyone he encountered, but it might be good enough for the cameras, especially since the coveralls had been stolen from a laundry load and matched the ones the maintenance team in the building used precisely.

He just hoped the guys watching the cameras weren't too diligent and that they accepted the implied story: the initial power outage had damaged something which had blown out when the generator came online. And now someone was checking it out, poking into things with a screwdriver. It should work.

Sked reached the twenty-second floor, five stories below the roof, and two below his artificial blackout, and supposedly the place where he would find Akane. He emerged from the stairwell and found himself in a dimly-lit, carpeted enclosure. A row of empty desks stood between his position and the floor-to-ceiling windows.

Anyone looking in from outside would think it was just an office building.

But from where he was standing, Sked could see the truth. A false interior wall separated the visible outer layers of the building from the concrete inner core. There was another door set in that core, and the intelligence told him that it wasn't going to be opened with a keypad cracking program.

Fortunately, he'd come prepared. He returned to the stairwell and, using his screwdriver and a hacksaw, he removed the handle on the stairwell side of the door and closed it. Security would need a battering ram to get it open because it was five centimeters of steel. Unhurriedly, he placed small explosive charges on each of the elevator doors.

There. The disguise had served its purpose and he was ready to act. He removed the bulky coverall, and pulled a final series of explosives out of his pack. This suite consisted of a long explosive cord as well as shaped charges for the contour of the door and a big, unsophisticated bomb for the lock. He hoped it would be enough.

He placed the explosives, went around the nearest concrete corner and put plugs into his ears. Then, pausing only long enough to remove the automatic pistol from the holster at his hip, he hit the remote control detonator.

The building shook around him and the noise thundered, even through the earplugs.

Sked didn't pause to marvel at the explosion. He was in motion, around the corner and, noting with a grin that his demolition consultants had completely overdone the explosives, ran through the ragged gap where the door had been.

Dust clouded everything within the prisoner enclosure but Sked was ready for it and made a beeline for the guard post. He needn't have bothered: both guards were down, one with blood pouring out of his nose, the other with his neck twisted at an unnatural angle. Sked decided that shooting them in the head as insurance would be a waste of time and bullets and headed down a corridor that wound its way in a square around the concrete core of the building, towards the cell blocks.

His objective was the first door on the right and, since the lights were still on, he simply walked up and removed the physical bolts holding the steel panel in place. No fancy hacking was ever going to open these doors—the Ministry was too smart for that.

He pulled it open and peered inside. It was dark, so he looked at the wall beside the door and flipped the switch he found there.

The lights illuminated a block three meters square. A cot in one corner held a thin woman with short, dark hair. Her hands were over her ears, and she whimpered.

Gently, he pulled one of her hands away. "Akane?" he asked.

She didn't respond, just whined and tried to put her hand back.

He tugged harder. "It's me, Sked. Listen to me. We've got to get out of here."

An eye opened and she squinted at him. "Is… is it really you?" Her face was bruised, and a long thin scar, not deep and not quite healed, ran down her right cheek.

"Of course it's me. Who else would I be?"

"What are you doing here?"

"Getting you out. Can you walk?"

"I… don't know. Help me up."

He put his shoulder under her arm and helped her to her feet. After a couple of tentative steps, he realized it would be quicker if he carried her.

He took her in his arms and swallowed back a curse. He wasn't a huge man—the paratroopers he'd trained with back in the day could have thrown him through a wall without breaking a sweat but Akane weighed next to nothing. Even less than usual. He went as quickly as possible and let her back onto her feet when they reached the outer window looking out over the harbor.

Behind him, a rhythmic thumping shook the area. The guards were trying to break down the stairway doors.

"We need to go quickly," he said, looping a harness around her waist and pulling it tight.

"Go? Where? The elevators are back there."

"The elevators are booby trapped. We're going that way." He pointed at the window.

"What?"

But Sked was already moving. He put a harness around Akane's waist—it was clipped to a similar harness he was wearing—then shot the window five times and, picking up Akane, sprinted at the collapsing safety glass. He was relieved when it popped out of its frame under their combined weight and headed toward the ground below.

Twenty-two stories wasn't a high altitude for a jump, so he deployed the chute immediately. Only two things mattered now: they needed to get across Xiahe Road and the imperative necessity to land in the water. If they made it, security shouldn't be able to reach them in time.

The distance from the wall of the building to the harbor wasn't long, maybe forty meters, but they almost didn't make it across the chain link fence that separated road and water.

Sked only realized he'd been holding his breath when the fence floated beneath them with three scant meters to spare. No one had fired a shot at them yet.

The water was as cold as a commissar's heart, and the shock made Akane struggle, but he held onto her and said: "Quiet. Stay still."

This part was the hardest, because he depended on others for it to work. They knew where he'd landed... now it was a question of whether they would be picked up. If not, at least Sked knew what the cell that awaited him looked like.

A splash sounded in the dark water nearby and Akane gripped him harder. "Is that a shark?"

"Shh," Sked whispered as something large rose out of the water beside them.

"Did someone order a cab?" a British accent asked moments before a beam of light blinded them.

"Cut the comedy and throw us a rope," Sked replied.

"No need for that. One second." The object came closer and Sked felt it bump against them. "There's a set of molded footholds right beside you." The light illuminated them.

"Can you climb?" Sked asked his sodden companion.

Akane nodded and he pushed her onto the fiberglass hull of the submarine, and then kept helping her up the stairs.

"Did I say you could touch my butt?" she asked from the darkness.

Sked smiled. She must have been starting to feel better, must have been accepting that she had actually been rescued and wasn't going to spend the rest of her—possibly very short—life in some clandestine jail while the spies decided where to dig her unmarked grave.

"We don't exactly have a lot of time here," Sked replied. "You hurry or I'll push."

"All right. You can push. But just this once."

The next few seconds felt like an eternity as he waited for the bullet to hit him between the shoulder blades. Surely the security people had managed to get their act together by now, and would be taking a bead on them?

But he didn't die. As soon as Akane had disappeared down the hatch, he dove in after her.

"Dive!" he yelled.

"I will, but submarines work better when they aren't flooding," the man replied and closed the hatch behind him. "We can't exactly carry a large crew in here, you know. So I need to close doors and do the driving myself."

Sked studied their new surroundings. The hull that had seemed so enormous sitting in the water next to them actually enclosed a cramped space, barely wide enough for them to squeeze through.

"Take a seat," British guy told them. There would be no exchange of names or pleasantries on this trip. "We're heading due south. Next stop, the Philippines."

"Why south? Isn't Taiwan nearer?"

"It is, but the sea between the mainland and Taiwan is crawling with Chinese Destroyer Captains whose one wet dream is that they'll spot a submarine in the water and get to drop a depth charge or two."

"All right. How long?"

"At least twelve hours. Fourteen is more likely. These drug submarines were built for stealth, not speed."

"Drug submarines?" Akane asked, her eyes flicking around the dimly-lit, white-painted interior.

"Yeah. Bought this one at a DEA auction in Texas. They were selling it for scrap, to recycle the motors and stuff, and they'd drilled it full of holes to keep people from using it as a sub again." He shrugged. "It seemed easier to patch the holes on this one than to build a new one, so I bought it."

"Man," Akane said with a light in her eyes that spelled trouble, "when this is over, contact me, will you? I'm easy to find online. We have got to talk. There's so much potential…"

"We'll see," the man replied without taking his eyes off the instruments.

Sked smiled. Akane was a reasonably major player in his circles, a hacker whose ability to get the job done was matched only by her tendency to cause massive collateral damage and piss people off. The caper that landed her in a Chinese jail was just the latest in a career of ever-increasing mayhem that was never going to end well.

The guy at the helm had obviously heard of her and wanted no part of the legend.

"You got any food in here?" Sked asked.

"Yeah. That cooler over there."

Akane beat him to it. "I could eat a horse," she said.

Sked smiled. Yeah, she was going to be okay…

As long as he could get her somewhere safe, which, unless he planned to stay underwater for the rest of his life, was not going to be easy. The Ministry of State Security was her biggest enemy, but it was only one of them. Combined, there were few holes the people hunting her couldn't reach.

But there was nothing he could do about it now. None of his electronics would work until they surfaced.

**

The boat they'd transferred to was an old fishing trawler owned by the same British Captain, and containing a South American crew. But at least they were on the surface and in range of a cellular network.

The phone was a cheap disposable with a Korean chip. Unconnected to anyone or anything that had to do with Sked. It would take a monumental act of bad luck for someone to be monitoring it, especially since the call was made on the Philippine cell network.

"So, you got her out," the Buddha said when he called the one-time number he'd memorized. "I would have bet anything against that. My money was on both of you being shot in Tiananmen Square as public nuisances."

"And yet you let me go ahead with it. Some friend."

"You weren't going to let me talk you out of it, so I decided to do what I could to improve your chances. I'm glad it worked."

"I need a place to lie low."

"With her?"

"Of course."

"Not easy. She's on a lot of people's hit lists. But..." there was a pause, something very unusual with the Buddha. "I think I have something. And you don't even need to get on a plane."

"Talk to me."

"North Sentinel Island."

"Never heard of it."

"Not a lot of people have. It belongs to India, but it's off the coast of Myanmar. It's actually mostly administered by the natives, except for one tiny resort they tolerate in exchange for certain things they can't get themselves. Metal knives and such. It only opened a couple of months ago... but the agreement seems to be holding so far."

"Wait. Tolerate? Holding so far? I get the sense that these natives aren't exactly welcoming of outsiders."

"Full marks. They've been totally isolated from the world and never allowed any outside contact until this resort. They even killed a bunch of missionaries a few years ago. You might have read about it."

"If I did, I don't remember."

"Anyway, it's perfect. No one will ever, in a million years, look for a pair of rogue hackers there. Hell, it doesn't even have an internet connection."

"Sounds like heaven."

"Does a bullet in the head sound better?" the Buddha asked.

"No."

"Then let me talk to the Captain."

CHAPTER 2

The video showed dinosaurs attacking a group of Eastern-European-looking farm buildings, knocking the inhabitants—presumably the farmers by the looks of them—around and feeding on their bodies. The shots were amateurish, jerky, cellphone footage.

A sudden jump cut showed another set of creatures advancing on a man with a gun who'd taken cover behind a low rocky wall. They flushed him out and a second shooter, unseen in the image, shot him. His head exploded in a spray of red mist.

Then came the important part. The three dinosaurs sniffed at the body, grabbed a couple of quick bites and then kept moving in formation towards... the video didn't show it, but Jermaine Jakes assumed it was another target. He stopped the projection with an angry stab at his remote.

"The Russians," he growled into the darkened boardroom, "are so far ahead of us it isn't even funny. Not only do they have large carnivores that can function well on land, but they've also somehow got the creatures' mental functions developed to the point where they can coordinate with human troops and," he pounded on the extremely solid and expensive wooden table for emphasis, "ignore edible flesh lying right in front of them. How long until you can get me something like that?"

He slid his finger across the screen of his phone, which had the effect of raising the level of illumination in the room. Then he glared at his C-suite, the top people in the company he'd create. "This tech is marketable, effective. How much longer until we have something like this?"

Sabrina Williams, the woman in charge of ZooDef's labs cringed in her seat. "Two years," she replied.

"Two fucking years? The market will be gone by then. Fucking *gone*. Do you understand what that would mean? We're all out of jobs and with zero possibility of ever getting a new one. We'd be radioactive in the industry, and any of our names on a prospectus would send the venture capitalists running for the hills. Why are we so far behind?"

Williams straightened. She wasn't really a whiner; the emergency meeting—and its contents—had caught her by surprise and now that she'd had a second to gather her thoughts, she responded: "We weren't behind. Not until just this instant. We're moving as fast as possible. And we've been faster than anyone else so far."

"Evidently, we weren't faster. We were slower and didn't even know it."

"My team has kept up on the bleeding edge of published science in the gene edition and custom animal field. We're fifteen years ahead of the bozos trying to de-extinct the heath hen. We worked back from a chicken genome to get to what we have now, beating every crazy timeline you threw at us."

"Someone has obviously been working on the quiet."

"That," she responded coldly, "is not my responsibility."

The words earned her a glare from Dieter Ratzenberger, who she'd just thrown under the bus.

Jermaine wasn't feeling generous. He hadn't reached his current position by being generous to those who failed.

"Dieter, care to illuminate us?"

"I'd need to analyze the footage. Where did this come from? Is it related to that tabloid story a couple of days ago?"

"You'd better believe it. But this didn't come from some two-bit journo from a fashion magazine. This came to me through the bank."

Everyone knew what that meant. Jermaine was ZooDef's CEO because of his position at LichtenBank, the company footing the bills. The first black man on the board of the three-hundred-year-old finance powerhouse… and therefore the one who got all the messages that came through Africa.

Of course, this one had come directly from Russia, but neither his C-suite at ZooDef or any of the Bank directors would be informed of that… he wanted them to think his niche was very limited. His ambitions demanded it; there were advantages to catching everyone by surprise.

But if ZooDef failed, that was all moot.

"Then it's real?"

"Utterly so. You need to step it up." Dieter was the best at what he did, at least in the private sector. Unfortunately, what he did was to gather information on stuff buried deep in the most secret levels of government programs, which meant that the very best of all were not available on the open market. Defense and Intelligence were the only two areas where the best of the best actually did work for certain governments. The only place where he couldn't buy the talent he needed. It was frustrating, but a good manager had to work with what he could get.

"Unavoidable," Dieter snapped back. "Not even the Russians know what most of their secret projects are up to. Russia's a mess."

"A mess that directly affects the future of this company. I need to know who, what, where, and how, and I need it yesterday."

Dieter stood. "I'll get right on it."

"Wait. I suspect you may get another assignment before we're done here."

Dieter raised an eyebrow but sat.

"Sabrina," he said, turning back to his head of research. "I need to catch up to these bastards, and I need to pass them. We need to be ahead in a short amount of time. If I know how Russian programs work in this new capitalist era, they'll keep the best of their research to themselves, but they'll sell the second-tier stuff to the highest bidder. Pretty soon, every two-bit African warlord and wannabe terrorist is going to have their own pet toothosaurus and we'll be out of the market." He paused and looked around the room. "And that would be the end of the company, so I'm giving you carte blanche. What do you need to catch up in the next three months?"

"I..." she swallowed and gathered her thoughts. "I can have the Compsognathus ready to sell in two months, if you let me test them. Our specimens are locked in the sub-basement of the Tucson Campus. I can't develop them if I can't see what they're doing. I need to see them working under real conditions."

"Your Compsognathus are tiny," Jermaine replied. "I don't want something the average citizen can kick into the next county. I want something the size of your Giant Mosasaurus, but I want it to work on land."

"Well, you're not getting that in three months," Sabrina replied. "What we may be able to get is a slightly larger version of the Compsognathus. The reason we went with those is that they showed a tendency to hunt in packs. I can have a batch of bigger ones ready in a week. Twenty of those working together could truly ruin someone's day, especially if they need to get through human-sized openings. It's not perfect, but it could be marketable. But to test it out, I need to see them in action. Outdoors, hunting real prey. Smart prey."

"You want us to do field testing. Kill humans?"

"Do it somewhere out of the way, but yeah, that's the only chance we have to study their dynamics. And while we're at it, I want to test the Mosasaurs, too. They're not worth anything stuck in those tanks. I'm pretty sure anyone who wants to wreak havoc at sea will want one."

"We've had this discussion before. Land attack is where the market is at."

"Let me test. We can jump the market, maybe. What do we have to lose at this point?"

Jermaine took a deep breath. He wanted to slap her down, but she was right. They were at the point where his preferences no longer mattered. Any chance to get a marketable product out there before the market disappeared needed to be explored.

"All right. Dieter, find us a good place. Land and sea. I want ten candidates on my desk in an hour. I'll choose the right one."

He left the meeting, letting his senior-most people find their own way back.

***

Sabrina gazed into the tank. It was dark down here, fourteen floors below ground level, and the tank was only illuminated by weak floodlights from above, to simulate the inky depths of the ocean.

She couldn't really see what was inside, but she could sense the movement, the play of shadows inside the green water.

No one who didn't know what the tank held would have believed there was anything in there... unless they thought, looking at those same shadows that it might be a submarine, or something equally large.

Sabrina knew better. She'd built a whale-sized predator that, if released into the ocean, would rule the seas by the simple expedient of might making right. A blue whale with proportional teeth. Something that would eat sharks for snacks.

Though not actually dinosaurs but reptiles, Mosasaurs were as varied as any species of dinosaur, with forty different subspecies recorded in the fossil record. But these were special Mosasaurs.

They were really, really big ones.

Bigger than the biggest on record, and as big as the genes permitted her to go. If she tried to expand these monsters any further, she was going to need to bend too many parameters away from the Mosasaur base code and twist it into something even more exotic.

She'd planned that for Phase II.

Unfortunately, her well-paced plan, built to be challenging while delivering wonderful results, had just been thrown out the window by some cowboys in Yekaterinburg. Now they were in full emergency mode, trying to get to market without worrying about product development.

But... silver linings.

"Hey there, babies." She often spoke to the beasts in the darkness. "You're going to be let out. You know that? I don't know where yet, but you'll likely have to wear your collars." They'd been experimenting with using shock collars to keep the monsters in the right area of their tanks, as a rudimentary guidance system. "But that's okay, isn't it? It will be worth it. Real sea to swim in, real fishies to eat. You'll like that, won't you?"

She believed the creatures could hear the vibrations from her voice even down there in the huge tank. The sides of their heads had enormous membranes which she suspected were ears, but much more sensitive than anything in the sea today, attuned to catch vibrations from hundreds of miles away.

Of course, she hadn't been allowed to research it more fully. Jermaine wanted answers for land warfare problems, not long-distance underwater communications questions.

One of the shapes brushed against the thick plexiglass, a shadow darker than the water around it. She imagined being in the water with something that size, and her mind recoiled from the image. Just being safely behind the specially designed partition, rated for three times the force one of these creatures could theoretically exert against it, was enough to make her feel like a tiny prey animal in a world that belonged to this monster.

But the feeling passed. She wasn't prey. She was mother.

She watched with love and pride until a persistent vibration in her jacket made her fumble for her phone. She scowled when she saw it was a message from Dieter and, after reading, growled. "Where the hell is North Sentinel

Island? Sounds like something cold as hell in the Antarctic Circle."

She googled quickly and smiled. Not bad. Not bad at all. Dieter was still a jackass who'd dropped the ball in the worst possible way, but at least he had decent taste in tropical paradises.

Sabrina turned back to the tank and purred. "Fancy someplace warm, my babies?"

***

"Stop!" Tim Ruggers yelled at the idiot driving the truck.

Well, driving might be a bit of an overstatement, as the term appeared to imply that he might actually have sufficient control of his vehicle to avoid an obstacle on occasion.

"What?" the guy yelled back.

"You're about to destroy a wall. Have you done this before?"

"Fuck off," the driver replied. "You want to try? What kind of asshole builds a loading dock in a maze?"

"We're nearly there," Tim replied. The man might not be the next Andretti, but he did have a point. The tortuous nature of the underground logistics area was legendary even among the good drivers. He pointed to a closed loading door. "That's the dock you want. Number seventeen."

"Finally," the trucker said.

As soon as the trailer was stationary, Tim jumped onto the dock and hit the code on the door, which lifted slowly. When it was waist-high, he slipped through the opening.

The containment units were right where he expected them. Unlike the truckers, who had been hired from a supplier, his own logistics team was 100% professional: they got things into place on time.

This load was going to San Diego, where it would board a ship to somewhere in the middle of the Indian Ocean off the coast of the Nicobar Islands, and to await further instructions once they arrived. It was a strange assignment, but he was used to that. He'd hardly blinked when Jermaine had ordered him to hire a ship with the capacity to unload her own containers, including oversized and overweight ones... and given him a blank check with which to do it, then told that if it wasn't available in two days, he would need to start printing resumes.

Only luck had kept him employed. The owners of the *Stern Liberia* had agreed to screw over other paying customers and delay their shipments for a couple of months in exchange for a metric crapton of cash.

Tim had delivered the crapton. After all, it wasn't his money.

The storage units he was loading now weren't oversized. In fact, they were the size of twenty-foot containers. Unlike standard cargo carriers, however, these were worth about a hundred thousand dollars each. Inside each one, contained in a honeycomb pattern that made efficient use of the space while leaving room for pipes and wiring, were two dozen cage-like enclosures for the little dinosaurs Sabrina's team had been building. Each creature was kept in a state of semi-torpor by some kind of sleeping gas that circulated through the container. They were the size and weight of a large turkey.

His job was to get them aboard the ship, get them halfway across the world and then unload them at some unknown point without killing any of them or letting them drop into the sea. Just about the only baby-sitting duty he didn't have to perform was to feed them, as Sabrina was sending people along to do that bit.

This was the last load. He signaled to the man driving the forklift to advance into the truck... slowly. Then he'd guide the driver out again.

He didn't actually have to guide the truckers himself. He could have delegated that menial task to any one of the several lower-ranked people present, but he wanted to think for a while before he got back to his bigger headache.

Moving the dinosaur would be a logistical challenge, but it was nothing compared to those shark-lizard things with huge teeth in the tanks. Those were the size of whales and weren't built to be moved around.

Except that Jermaine wanted them on the ship with the lizards.

And if Tim told him no, then Jermaine would just fire him and find someone willing to do the job.

So he was thinking about it in the loading bay, waiting for the eighth construction crane to get into position before they started the sling lift. While each creature could be lifted relatively easily, you needed to make certain it didn't crush itself under its own weight on the way up, and that meant multiple points of suspension. And getting all that working and then landing the thing into the specially constructed transport tank… was the stuff that logistics managers' nightmares were made of.

And then the extra wide load had to cross the two hundred miles between Tucson and San Diego.

Yeah, guiding a trucker with no depth perception was a five-star holiday compared to that.

***

The salt sea breeze caressed his skin and Dieter snarled at it. This wasn't his habitat. He didn't want to be there. He hated the outdoors in general and the ocean in particular.

But this time, he had little choice in the matter. Jermaine was pissed beyond even the usual hard-edged corporate impatience he usually displayed, and when the boss was in that kind of mood, heads rolled.

To keep that particular fate at bay, he'd joined the expedition taking the specimens to North Sentinel Island, even though he had other work to do—he needed to continue to unravel the knot that hid the Russian agency in charge of developing the creatures from the videos—and despite the fact that the putative leader of the mission was that unbearable obsessive Sabrina Williams.

That Sabrina didn't like him was not a worry. Sabrina didn't like anybody and most people didn't like Dieter. But the fact that she was utterly focused on her animals could be a problem. There were important questions that would need to be decided on the way, and not all of them would be solved by increasing the glucose drip on cage seventy-four.

At least the logistics side of things would work out. Ruggers was good at what he did, even if he was terrible at hiding just how amusing he found the power dynamic between Dieter and Sabrina. He seemed to be in a constant state of snigger.

An alert on his phone brought Dieter back from his reverie. Someone had dug something up and sent a series of data files.

He read the summary and groaned. It was even worse than he'd expected. The Russians had been working with a North Korean geneticist who'd defected for the money.

Worse, the man had apparently defected again. Having gotten what he needed from Mother Russia, he'd gone freelance and was busy contacting rogue states and terrorist organizations to sell the stuff Jermaine had seen in the videos. Dieter suspected that his boss had gotten the video from one of the potential clients.

Of course, he couldn't ask where the data had come from. If he did that, Jermaine would just smile enigmatically and say: "I was under the impression that knowing that kind of thing was your job."

The most galling thing was that he'd be right.

Dieter spent the next hour reading the information. He wrote a five-line email with the salient points on it and sent it off to the CEO's office. Then he sat down and thought who might have a tip on where he could contact the sellers. He'd need to pass himself off as a potential buyer, of course, but that should pose few problems. One of the major reasons he held his job in the first place was the multiplicity of aliases and alter-egos he'd set up precisely for this kind of thing.

He opened a secondary laptop quarantined from his real one, and opened the Tor Browser. Then he signed into one of the darknet chatrooms as Karl Stuttenberg, an aging former member of Baader Meinhoff who kept his hand in the game as a liaison for aspiring revolutionaries in Europe.

Now, the question was which of his information brokers he should contact for the data he needed.

In the end, however, there was really only one name, one person on the planet that could purvey this kind of thing quickly and, most importantly, discreetly.

The Electric Buddha. The only guy with all the answers. He'd even been the one to suggest North Sentinel Island.

Dieter began to type.

Outside his cabin, the port of San Diego began to move as the colossal ship gently slipped its mooring. He paid it no particular attention. As long as he had an internet connection on board, it made zero difference to him whether he was on land or at sea.

At least professionally, which was the only part that mattered. His personal preferences were less than irrelevant.

CHAPTER 3

Cora Gimenez observed the two bunnies sunning themselves on deck with one eye, while keeping her other on the weather. A storm at sea was not much of a concern for the former Marine sergeant, but the unlimited stupidity of her billionaire boss' onboard guests was.

Much as she thought the silly little groupies to be a waste of protein and space, it was her job to keep them alive.

"Yo, Barbie dolls," she called out to them.

They didn't even raise their heads, so she walked up to them. She was tempted to toss the frigid contents of the bottle of water in her hand over their heads for ignoring her until she realized they were both wearing earbuds from which music could be heard even a few yards away.

She relaxed. They might be too dumb to take care of their ears, but they weren't disrespecting her on purpose.

Cora stood where they could see her and they both did exactly the same thing: they put their hand in front of their faces to see who'd entered their space. Both looked disappointed to see her there.

She wanted to smirk and tell them that the boys had more important things to do in the daytime than talk to them, but she suddenly felt a little sorry for them. They probably thought the people they were hanging with valued them for something other than their gym routines and implants, and they would have a serious disappointment coming their way when reality hit. The owner of this yacht and his social circle weren't soccer players. Bunnies were a pastime, but when it came time to settle down, the wives would be from good families and these girls would be a part of the past no one spoke about.

But right now, they were living the dream. She saw no need to ruin it for them. Being dumb wasn't a crime unless they made the mistake of disrespecting her.

"Hi," she said.

The women clearly didn't know who she was, but they weren't confident enough in their roles on the ship to brush her off. They sat up and peered at her. "Hi," one of them responded. "Can we help you?"

This one's English sounded Eastern European, which matched her pale skin and ice-blue eyes. The other one didn't speak, but she was a little darker—not much—and was wearing a bikini with the Union Jack on it. So Cora guessed British. Her Malaysian boss loved to show off with pale blondes on his arm even though he always treated them like ladies and, as far as Cora knew, never took a bunny to bed. The women who achieved that honor were always upper-class Malaysians or Singaporean women. But he thought blondes made him look powerful to the occidental men he hung out with, so that was what he was seen with. That wasn't politically correct, but his checks had never bounced and he'd always treated Cora with the utmost respect... which, in her book, meant he could run around with whoever he felt like.

"I'm sorry to disturb you," she said. "But there's a storm coming."

They peered in the direction she was pointing.

"You think we should get inside?" Union Jack said, her accent confirming her origins as being lower-class England.

"It's going to get a bit bumpy in a few minutes," Cora replied.

That earned her a smile from Eastern Europe. "Thanks for letting us know," she replied. Implied was that Cora could have let them get drenched.

Now Cora felt guilty. Had it been a question of a light rainfall, she probably would have let them take a surprise shower. After all, the temperature was not going to be enough to drive them inside, even just before a rainfall; it was always hot in the Indian Ocean except during the Monsoon... and even then it was still mostly hot. She'd only warned them because this one was going to be quite the toad-strangler and she didn't want them overboard if the sea got rough. The paperwork would have been horrendous and Tam, Mr. Lai's lawyer would probably have made Cora fill it all in.

She decided to be nicer to the bunnies from then on. There were eight of them on board, two for each of the young men accompanying Lai on this particular trip. As far as Cora knew, they were not prostitutes in the usual sense of the term, but girls who'd been offered a chance at a champagne and luxury cruise with people they'd met at a party and who'd thought it sounded like fun.

Now she did smirk because she knew exactly who slept where. They might not be prostitutes, but they had... modern morals.

But then again, she'd spent the past fifteen years among soldiers. She had nothing whatsoever against people getting laid whenever they could.

Cora watched them disappear into the nearest door, but she didn't follow them in. This was the kind of weather she loved, and the 500 foot yacht wasn't going to be overly disturbed by the storm, even if it pitched a little.

So she stood her ground, staring into the teeth of the darkening sky, daring it to try to sweep her off the deck.

She scanned the suddenly black sea, noting the tactical situation—a habit she would likely never break—and saw some kind of container ship in the distance. The only sign of land was a smudge near the horizon, too small to be mainland of any sort, so it must have been one of the islands they occasionally stopped off at for the local party scene.

Maybe, as Head of Security, she should have known exactly what their position was, down to the last second of latitude and longitude, but that was another habit she wasn't going to break any time soon: it was the Captain's job to transport the Marines to where they needed to be. Once there, the Marines kicked ass.

Cora had extended her scope to include what happened onboard the *Vanarisa*, but that was it. She'd ask where they were when they arrived.

The first drops fell on her face and the wind picked up.

"Come on. You know you can do better than that," she said.

As if rising to the challenge, the wind obliged, driving fat drops into her face.

Her smile widened. "Better, but I think there's more."

Within minutes, the rain pelted her and the thunder of drops hitting the sea surrounded her. The world disappeared behind a grey curtain, cutting her off from everything that didn't belong. She inhaled deeply and simply enjoyed it.

Ironically, the sea didn't look like it was going to get rough any time soon. The wind wasn't quite strong enough for that, even though the shower did justice to the latitude.

She could barely see the water beside the ship, but they weren't about to sink.

Just as she realized that the waves weren't going to knock her into the sea—and that she'd had no real need to save the bunnies—and relaxed, the ship jolted to one side and lifted almost out of the water.

Only her lightning-quick reflexes—still sharp at thirty-eight—kept her from taking a swim. One hand snagged the railing as it flew below her.

When she realized what had happened, Cora was hanging by that one hand, pain radiating out from her right shoulder, which had borne the brunt of the impact. She quickly brought her other hand to grasp the railing and pulled herself up.

"You're letting yourself go," she said after struggling more than she expected to regain the deck. "That wouldn't have been so hard in basic. Now, let's see what the hell is happening."

The ship felt a little slanted, listing to one side. Not serious yet—it would not even be noticeable to anyone not attuned to ships at sea—but if they were taking on water…

She ignored the door that the bunnies had disappeared into and sprinted towards the bow. Lai's crew were competent, if taciturn. They kept themselves to themselves and seemed to feel that they were somehow above the rest of the billionaire's employees.

"What's happening?" she asked the Captain. He was a dark-skinned Frenchman from one of the Caribbean Islands who'd gotten bored of driving cruise ships.

"Not now."

"Yes, now. Do what you need to but tell me the status."

"We're sinking," he replied with a scowl.

"You're shitting me."

The man actually took his gaze off the instruments to give her a withering look. "I don't joke about things like that. I'm not a Marine."

Cora wanted to ask him how the hell he'd managed to hit something in the middle of an empty ocean, but it wouldn't have helped her do her job, and that was the only thing she cared about presently. She nodded. "How long?"

"If the damage assessment is accurate… two hours."

"Can we get to the island over there?" She pointed in the general direction of the landmass she'd seen earlier, now obscured by the sheeting rain.

"North Sentinel? We might, but it will be close."

"Is it safer to keep the people on board or to take the lifeboats?"

"I think the best course would be for me to stay aboard with a couple of sailors and for the rest of you to take the lifeboats. Take the starboard and port boats. Leave us the stern dinghy, just in case."

She knew what he was saying, and she'd been around enough sailors to know what he wasn't saying. She held his gaze. "It's your call, Captain. You need to give the order."

He sighed. "Abandon ship," he whispered.

"Yes, sir." If they all made it, she would ask some pointed questions. But right now, the man was in a bad place.

She sprinted off to find Lai. He was standing outside the main stateroom, buttoning up his pants.

"What's happening?" he asked.

"We need to get off the ship," she replied. "I need everyone off in fifteen minutes. Anyone in there?"

He smiled. He knew she tolerated any indiscretions he might indulge in as long as they didn't stop her from doing her job. "I was just having a nap. It's empty."

She didn't insult him by looking, just nodded and headed to the next room.

"Can I talk to my Captain? This yacht is worth a certain amount of money, and I'd like to know what's wrong with it."

"Of course, just be at the starboard lifeboat in ten minutes."

"Yes, sir," Lai replied. But he said it grimly. She supposed even billionaires hated to lose hundred-million-dollar boats.

She got on with it and within ten minutes, everyone on board had arrived at one of the two lifeboats, standing unhappily in the rain. Fifteen people to a side, which was perfect: the boats could take twenty each.

"All right. Don't worry about your stuff. The crew is driving the ship towards the same island we're heading to. They should have enough time to get there, and then we'll assess the damage and see where we go."

"Can't we just go with the ship?" one of Lai's younger guests asked.

"No. If it sinks, I want us well away. Now get in."

She would have loved to do what the executive suggested and not have to deal with the whining, but the Captain, whatever his shortcomings, was right about one thing: they were definitely taking on water, and the ship was now listing a lot more noticeably than before.

The lifeboat looked more like a luxury minibus, complete with rumbling diesel engine, than a stark survival unit. It was attached to the boat by an automatic clamp and winch assembly that could be lowered automatically from within the lifeboat itself.

They were barely settled when she gave the sailor who'd be driving them the order to release the clamp. Her passengers consisted of the important people—Mr. Lai and his employees, as well as some of the sailors—while the first mate had the rest of the crew and the bunnies in the other lifeboat.

The first thought that occurred to her when they landed in the water was that this little boat moved around quite a bit more than the yacht. The same seas that had disappointed her just moments before were not tossing the smaller vessel around like a toy.

Still better than the CRRCs they made her ride in the Corps. Those bounced around like a son of a bitch.

"Let's see if we can keep the other lifeboat in sight," she said. "I'll feel much better if I can keep an eye on everyone."

The sailor nodded and started to push the throttle forward when Cora yelled another order. "Wait. Stop. I want to see this."

So instead of pulling strongly away from the yacht, they drifted past, moving barely faster than the ship itself.

"What the hell is that?" the sailor said.

The hull had been stoved in on the side facing them, a deep dent running almost ten meters of the length of the ship. That, at least, was consistent with the possibility of having run into something: a rock or some other vessel.

But that was the only evidence consistent with a collision. Above the dent, the hull looked like it had been scratched by a cat—if a cat could tear through metal composite sheet. Long gashes streaked along the ship and, in one place the metal hung in a fold, as if it had been torn away.

"How can that happen?" she asked the sailor, who was staring wide-eyed at the broken vessel.

"I have no clue," the man replied. "I suppose it must have caught on something."

"I didn't feel anything catch or snag," Cora replied. "Just the initial impact that almost threw me overboard." She rubbed her shoulder as she said it, remembering the wrench.

They observed in silence, creeping ahead of the mega-yacht until Cora slapped her palm against her forehead. "Damn. The other lifeboat. I forgot about them completely and they probably went on ahead. Speed up. Let's see if we can find them."

They searched in the rain for thirty minutes, but the downpour persisted, so Cora told them to head towards the island. The lifeboat had a functioning GPS and she wished that the builders had also thought to install a radio or satellite phone capability.

At least the other lifeboat should also reach the nearest island.

"North Sentinel, right?" she asked the sailor.

"Yeah, though we might be better off heading for Andaman. It's a little farther away, but there are a lot of people on it."

"How much farther?"

"An hour. Maybe a little more in this sea."

"No. Stay the course. Let's get to land first and see what we can do from there. Maybe we can repair the yacht well enough to limp wherever we need to go next. There has to be someone on North Sentinel who can help us."

"There's a spot on my map, the Lost Island Hotel and Beach Club. It's on the east side of the island, but we can go around."

"Let's aim there."

The yacht was completely out of sight, no one had cell coverage, and the island was nowhere to be seen. Only the GPS allowed them to navigate.

"We should see the island soon," the sailor said.

"Don't hit it," Cora replied. "I'm really not in the mood for a swim while trying to keep this lot from drowning."

The sailor turned pale. "What was that?" He pointed at the water behind Cora.

She turned. Nothing but sea and the grey curtain of rain. "What?"

"I thought I saw something. A head coming out of the water."

She tensed. "What? Like a person swimming?" Had the other lifeboat overturned, even though the seas were relatively mild?

"No… like a monster. A huge whale, too big to be a shark."

"Just get us onto the island. If it's a whale, it probably just came up for air."

"I guess." The man didn't look too convinced, but he turned his head back to the controls.

It was a good thing, too. The wind began to gust and the breakers near the island were getting quite a lot bigger.

"Maybe we should go around a little further away," the sailor said.

"I don't think so," Cora replied. "That storm looks like it's getting worse. Just beach us here."

The trip onto the beach was nearly enjoyable. Once they got aligned right, the waves that had buffeted them helped them ashore and they rode one final breaker onto the beach. As soon as they grounded, Cora felt a weight come off her shoulders. This boatload, at least, wouldn't be drowning on her watch.

"Don't run up the beach just yet," she called to the passengers who were standing. "We need to haul this boat up the beach a bit. If it drifts off and there's no one on the island, we're stuck here for good."

They had just survived possibly sinking out at sea, and still had a bit of a hike in front of them before they could even be remotely considered safe. But if she knew human nature, there would be someone griping in 5… 4…

She wasn't surprised that it was one of Lai's young executives who started grumbling something in a language Cora didn't understand but assumed to be Malaysian. But before she could tear him a new asshole, Lai himself stepped in and gave him a dressing down that, even though she couldn't understand the words, was very, very clear in substance. The executive lowered his head and sprang into action, pushing with the best of them.

And the best of them was Lai himself. The man might be a billionaire now, but she knew he'd come up through the ranks of the Malaysian oil industry, starting off as an oilfield engineer before starting his own companies with the knowledge he'd gained there. She already knew he'd lost none of the work ethic—the hardest part of her job was simply keeping up with the man so that either she or someone from her security team had eyes on him at all times—but now he proved that living a life of luxury hadn't dulled his passion for getting his hands dirty. He pushed as hard as the rest, harder than most.

Once, after a long, hot push, they got the boat above the visible tide line and tied to a tree, she turned to him. "You would have made one hell of a Marine sergeant," she said.

Lai smiled and bowed. "Coming from you, I know that is a serious compliment."

She returned the grin. "The highest I can think of. Now, how about we march these pussies across this island."

"Until we're back in civilization, you're the boss," he responded.

That, she thought, was probably why this man had as much money as he did. Knowing when to delegate and whom to delegate to were critical once your organization became large enough that you couldn't do everything yourself.

She looked at the trees that abutted on the beach. They weren't happy tropical palm trees. These were thick trees, dark trees.

"All right then. Just to stay on the safe side, I say we walk along the beach. It will be wetter and a bit longer, but I really don't want to have to herd this circus through the trees."

Lai nodded and they set off.

CHAPTER 4

Mary climbed through the door of the lifeboat and into the rain. She would have preferred to take the other lifeboat, the one that the big muscular security woman would be on, but they hadn't given her that choice. Hell, they hadn't even allowed her to change out of her Union Jack bikini.

She shrugged. It wouldn't make much difference. Swimwear and flip-flops were the right attire for a tropical beach in a hot rain. For once in her life, the overdressed people were the ones in the wrong clothes.

They left the lifeboat half-beached behind them and headed towards the tree line. When she stopped dead, Jana, the only other person in a bikini, nearly bumped into her.

"Bubbles, you okay?" Jana asked.

She hated that nickname, but it had been with her ever since she'd gotten her boobs done when she was sixteen. At first she'd barely tolerated it, but later found that men found it unthreatening, and that they were a lot less likely to do macho posturing around someone who called herself 'Bubbles'. In the end, she'd gone with the dumb blonde bit because it opened doors. And in that role, she was Bubbles to the hilt.

"I thought I saw something move in the trees."

"People? We should ask them for help."

"You think people would hide?"

"They're probably just as scared of us as we are of them."

Mary laughed. "Have you looked at us? Would you be afraid of a couple of blondes in bikinis?"

Jana winked. Like Mary herself, most of her wide-eyed bimbo innocence was an act. "They probably should be."

"I'll tell the sailors." She turned back to the rest of their party, who seemed to be discussing something about what to do with the lifeboat. "Guys," she called out. "I think I see something up there, in the trees."

A dozen faces looked at her. Half belonged to the rest of the girls on the trip, who, unlike Mary and Jana, had dressed to kill before lunch, complete with platform shoes, short dresses, deep necklines which showed more than the bikinis, and jewelry. It would have been ridiculous if she hadn't been so scared. The other half were sailors, five men and one more woman, a stewardess who seemed to be making a serious effort to separate herself from whatever species she considered the female guests to be. All of the crewmembers were in white uniforms. The woman had her hair tied in a bun so severe that she could have fit it under a regular sailor's hat. That had to hurt.

"There's nothing moving," the cook said after a cursory glance.

"Well, there was something just now. I saw it."

"Probably just a bird of some kind," he replied and turned back to the argument about the ship. He was the only one that even acknowledged her comment. The rest had ignored her after the initial look to see who was making so much noise.

Mary looked back up the beach. The spit of white sand they were standing on ended in leafy underbrush. Beyond were tall trees that, to her eyes, seemed to be about four or five stories high. But whatever had moved—it was hard to see clearly in the rain—had not flown into the upper leaves, but had been moving on the ground. If it was an animal, it wasn't a bird, and it was pretty big.

And if it was a person, they were working hard to avoid being seen.

Moments later, three of the white-uniformed crew marched past her towards the jungle, followed by a straggling line composed of the rest.

She took up station beside the cook, a dark-skinned guy who spoke with a strong Filipino accent.

"What happened?" she asked.

He gave her a lopsided smile. "I got outvoted... everyone to one. I wanted to push the boat up the beach so it wouldn't get washed out by the tide."

"What for? Isn't the whole point to get us on land? Hasn't it done its job?"

He looked at the rapidly approaching trees. "I'm not sure. We might not be sinking, but there's nothing here that I'd call civilization. Spending the rest of my life on a deserted island is not my idea of a good time."

"We'll be fine."

"That's what they said. And they also think the trees will stop the rain, and that pushing the lifeboat is too much work."

"Won't they? Stop the rain, I mean?"

He chuckled. "They stop the drops, yeah. But they also channel the water, so that when it does manage to get through, you're pretty much in for a drenching."

"Maybe we should stay a few steps behind them and let them open the way for us."

"I like the way you think."

The leading group had finished walking up the full length of the spit of sand and were looking for a way into the impenetrable-looking greenery. A slight opening in the leaves was visible to their right, and they set off in that direction.

Mary heard a whistling sound. That was their only warning. The female crewmember fell to the floor with a sudden gasp.

Everyone turned to see what was wrong, but it didn't take an expert to understand. A dark wooden shaft a meter long protruded from her neck. Even Mary could tell it was an arrow.

"Oh my god," one of the girls among the leaders yelled.

Another screamed.

But Mary, a few steps behind, had already seen what they couldn't: several figures, features hard to discern in the rain, were charging towards them from the left, exposed on the beach.

"Over there!" she yelled and, barely pausing to drag the cook along, sprinted for the gap in the greenery.

She didn't turn to see if the others followed. It wasn't that kind of group. Other than Jana, she really hadn't clicked with any of the other women on board, and even if she had, she wasn't going to stop running to wait for any of these people. She kicked off her flip-flops and put on a burst of speed.

Leaves and twigs cut her face, stuff impaled her feet, but she could worry about that when the guys with the arrows lost interest in her.

And then Mary stumbled, and she knew she was dead.

The cook had other ideas. He bent down, dragged her to her feet and pushed her along the path, forcing her to go as fast as she could. She heard the rest following, crashing among the trees behind her.

A scream sounded—a male scream—and she redoubled her efforts. The opening had led them through the underbrush and then into a forest of tree trunks where, fortunately, it was easier to run.

The downside was that everything on the floor seemed to want to cut into her feet.

A couple of minutes later, she came to a clearing and stumbled, panting to lie on a bare patch of sand behind some bushes. Three more people landed next to her: the cook and two of the remaining sailors. Though she'd fallen by mistake, she realized—as her companions must have—that the place concealed her from the path they'd been running along. Desperate footfalls dashed past, but she only lifted her head in time to see one of the women on the ship moving slowly. Then, through the cover of leaves, she watched as a group of men with bows shot past.

They were dark-skinned and rotund, but too tall to be pygmies. The muscles of their arms and legs were big and rounded, not fat. And there was nothing comical about the bows they carried. Some of the arrows looked much too long to be usable, at least as tall as she was in cases, but Mary had already seen how effective they could be. They ran through the jungle with the arrows held ahead of them, somehow threading between the trees without getting tangled. They wore only a tan belt, light against their dark skin, and otherwise appeared to be nude.

Mary only realized she was holding her breath when the last of the tribesmen passed and she started breathing again, feeling the relief of air reaching her lungs.

Incredibly, she realized that they'd gotten away undiscovered.

Still, none of the people around her moved. They were all waiting for more of their pursuers to charge through, maybe someone left behind to sweep the trail for exactly this kind of situation.

After a couple of tense minutes, however, none of them did, and the sounds of the pursuit were lost in the woods. The cook stood and pulled her up. Then he turned to the other two sailors.

"We need to get back to the lifeboat and get the hell out of here," the cook said.

"You're crazy," one of the sailors answered. He was a sunburned Dutchman, blond and red. "We're sitting ducks out on that beach. We should go that way." He pointed at a ninety-degree angle to the direction the chase had taken. "We can move parallel to the beach in the direction opposite the one they came from. That way, we can move away from them without showing ourselves."

"And then what? This is an island. Eventually, they're going to find us."

"The yacht should be here by then."

"So? Do you think the Captain will be able to hold off twenty men with bows?" the cook retorted.

"He'll shoot them if he has to."

"That won't do us much good here on the island. We need to get the hell off this place and sail for one of the other islands."

"No." The big Dutchman crossed his arms. "We do as I say."

"Screw you," the cook replied. "I'm taking the lifeboat."

"It's your funeral," the bigger man responded. Then, without waiting for an answer he set out, and his companion followed him without a word.

"Stupid," the cook said.

"I'll go with you," Mary told him.

"You're not afraid of getting spiked?"

"I want to get the hell off this island."

"Good. And the tide is coming in, which is even better."

"Why?"

"Because unless it's floating, we aren't going to be able to push the lifeboat off the beach without help."

"Oh. Right. Makes sense." She hesitated. "So do we just walk down the same path we just ran up?" It felt wrong, somehow, as if they'd simply turn back time and run into the locals again.

"I think that would be best. I... I've never been in a situation like this before."

"You should come visit my family in Lambeth sometime. Would get you trained right up. Especially if you come at night."

"Lambeth... in England."

She nodded. "London, but not the good part."

He stepped back onto the path and, seeing he wasn't immediately speared, Mary got the courage to do the same.

"Ow," she said as a root found a bruise on her foot. "I might need some help."

He looked at her feet. "Ouch. I'll carry you."

"You? You're a bit small for that, aren't you?" He was about as tall as she was and thin to go with it... and he was wearing shoes, so he was probably shorter than she was in real life.

"Can you get on my back?" he responded, ignoring her words.

"I..." she tried to take an unaided step, show him she was capable of moving on her own, but the pain told her she was lying. "I'll try."

She couldn't remember the last time a guy had taken her piggy-back riding without wanting to get into her pants. And though this one might—she'd caught him looking where all guys looked when she wore a bikini—she had to give him the benefit of the doubt. If it hadn't been for this tiny little dude who she'd never spoken two words to before they got off the lifeboat, she would be in the hands of the islanders, captive or worse.

"Thank you," she whispered as the guy showed a decent amount of speed despite the extra weight. She could feel his muscles through the uniform: wiry, but strong.

"You can thank me if we get out of this," the cook replied. "Buy me a drink or something."

She laughed. "You're one of the good guys, aren't you?"

"I'm one of the scared guys."

They reached the edge of the forest and looked out at the lifeboat. It looked much farther away than she expected.

"Let's give it a few minutes," the cook said.

"Why? Do you think someone will come?"

"No. I want it to get afloat. See, the water is already almost under it. Just a few more minutes."

It seemed much longer to Mary. Hours, probably. Weeks, even. But she watched the water creep up centimeter by centimeter, concealed among the last row of bushes and jumping at every sound in the jungle behind them. Had there been that much noise when they were running for their lives? She had no clue.

"All right. We need to go now. Run for the boat. If I don't make it, hit the big red button until you hear the engine and then pull the silver handle all the way back. That will move you into the sea. Then turn the boat using the steering wheel until the front is facing the waves and move the handle forward. You got that?"

She nodded. "I'll figure it out if I need to. But I won't. You'll be there."

"Go!"

He let her go ahead and then ran behind her. Any arrows coming from the trees would hit him first. Then his presence behind her was gone. Had they killed him?

Mary tried to will herself to look, but she just couldn't do it. Every step she took convinced her that she next would bring an arrow between the shoulder blades. She began to cry, sobbing and puffing until, with a shriek, she threw herself behind the boat, hidden from the coast. She scratched at the doors, clawing at the handle until she got inside.

Then she crawled inside, carefully keeping her head below the glass, out of sight of the animals with the bows and arrows.

She found the button the cook had told her about and punched it.

"Come on, you little fuck!" she screamed, hysteria threatening to overcome her. The engine fired and she reached for the handle.

Before she made it, the door was yanked open and two people crashed in, knocking her violently to the floor. She screamed.

Then she felt the boat reversing into the sea, catching on something and then moving again. Then it turned to face the waves.

Mary opened her eyes to see the cook, sweating and wide eyed, working the lifeboat controls.

She looked beside her to find that the second person was the crewwoman who'd taken the arrow to the neck.

"You stopped to get her?"

"I had to check."

"Check what?"

"If they'd killed her."

Mary gasped and stared at the woman beside her. She was pale, bloodied and had a fucking arrow through her neck.

But she was breathing.

"You can come out from there now," the cook said.

But Mary couldn't move. She couldn't do anything but laugh hysterically. She knew she was out of control, but she couldn't stop. It went on for quite a while until the cook cut the engines and knelt beside her.

"Are you all right?"

Mary managed to get herself under control. "You asked me for a drink," she said. Then she started laughing again. It was worse than marijuana laughter... she just couldn't stop. Not for the life of her.

"Yeah, so?"

"I was just wondering what you'll ask of her if she survives."

His own laugh was just a dry chuckle. She, on the other hand, still couldn't control the guffaws.

***

When she recovered, they began a slow navigation around the island.

"What are you doing?" Mary said. "Let's get the hell away from here."

"I'm checking to see if anyone made it back out of the jungle," the cook replied.

She didn't argue. She wouldn't be alive if it wasn't for him. In her book, that meant he could do whatever he wanted.

"What about her?"

"I don't know. We're moving in the right direction for Nicobar, so it's not as if we're losing too much time. And it might be worth it. At least now that the goddamned rain's stopped, we can see again."

It was true. Minutes before, the beach beside them had barely been visible. Now it felt like they could see clear across the ocean.

"Look!" Mary said. She pointed to the beach a few hundred meters ahead.

"Who is that?"

The cook squinted. "Looks like Behrend and Sundeep."

They drew closer, and Mary saw that the two men—the crewmen who'd hidden from the pursuers with them and then gone in a different direction—were running along the beach as fast as they could go. Every few steps they looked into the trees to their left, as if looking for something.

"The natives must be after them," the cook said. "Maybe if we swing close, they can swim to the boat. I wish this thing could go faster."

The two runners were still more than a hundred and fifty meters ahead of the lifeboat when numerous small forms emerged from the greenery.

"What are those?" Mary said.

"Damned if I know."

They were brown, birdlike creatures, waist-high. They walked on their hind legs like chickens, but were way too big to be farm birds. They were muscular and leathery, with no feathers visible from where they sat.

They were also much faster than the men they were following.

The runners must have realized that at the same moment Mary did, because they stopped and turned to face their pursuers. As the distance between them closed, Mary saw that the front of the blond man's uniform—she assumed that must be Behrend—was covered in blood.

The creatures were upon them instantly. Somehow, standing next to people made it even more clear that these weren't birds. It wasn't just the size, but the way they moved. Mary remembered seeing chickens running in a farmyard beside an A-road on some trip with her parents, and these moved differently. Instead of holding their wings out for balance, tiny arms hung in front of them and they balanced perfectly on the balls of their long feet.

"Those things are so thin the guys are gonna box 'em to pieces," the cook said.

The first one to get too close proved him right, as the big blond sailor kicked it so hard it flew through the air and landed in a heap.

"Right on!" the cook exulted. "Can't this thing go any faster?" He tried to open the window, but it was a sealed unit. You needed to open the door to get it open, and that had a security clasp. "Get that open and yell at them to come towards us," he told Mary.

She tried to comply but, after a moment, found herself staring at the scene on the beach.

The creatures—they looked like walking lizards to her now—had surrounded the men and were circling warily. None of them seemed to want to share their companion's fate.

The door popped open, surprising her. She'd been fumbling at it blindly while she watched the scene unfold. "Guys!" she yelled.

Either her voice failed to carry far enough or the men were too preoccupied to acknowledge her.

The standoff lasted another couple of seconds, and then, as if some invisible signal had been sent, every one of the creatures around the sailors attacked at the same time.

It was no contest. The two men stood only a moment before they were buried under the onslaught through sheer weight of numbers and bodies. Mary heard a long, drawn out scream which cut off suddenly.

"No!" the cook shouted. He pressed the silver bar forward, but the lifeboat chugged along at the same sedate rate it always did. It was built for luxury and safety, not speed.

Mary watched, mesmerized, as the creatures moved back from the two men, eyeing the immobile, bloodied figures warily, as if to make sure they weren't going to do anything unexpected. Even from where she was sitting, Mary could tell that Behrend and Sundeep were beyond heroics. Sundeep's wide-open, terrified eyes, told her that he wouldn't be doing anything ever again except haunting her dreams forever.

"What are you doing?" she asked the cook.

"Trying to get close enough to save them," the man replied. They were thirty meters from the place the two men lay.

She put a hand on her arm. "They're dead."

"No, we can still…"

"They're dead." She wanted to say his name, for emphasis, to comfort him, something. But she realized she didn't know it.

The creatures, convinced that they were safe from their victims, moved. They began to feed.

"Let's go," Mary said softly. "Let's get out of here."

"Fuck," the cook replied, and pulled his shoulder from under her hand. "Fuck this all."

But he steered the lifeboat back onto a course that would take them parallel to the beach.

CHAPTER 5

Sked opened the door to their cabin and realized that everyone staying at the resort seemed to be on the beach.

Akane, standing beside him, blinked several times and glowered into the bright sunlight. "What the hell happened to the rain?"

"You know how these tropical storms are," Sked replied. Akane hated being out in the sun even more than he did... and he was a night owl and an indoors person. Still, the two weeks they'd been at the resort had transformed her. The deathly pallor was gone from her cheeks, and she'd even managed to get past the sunburn phase to where her face and body were even starting to take on a light gold tan. Combined with the weight she'd regained and the complete unavailability of anything stronger than rum on the island, it was the first time he'd ever seen her looking healthy. Health made her stunningly beautiful.

"Want to take a dip?" she asked.

He raised an eyebrow. "I want to see what everyone's looking at."

Their fellow holiday-makers were standing in a loose circle on the white sand, looking at something lying by the sea. Sked couldn't see what it was.

As they approached, one of the employees of the resort, dressed in white shorts and a blue t-shirt, was trying to move a rotund man and his wife from the scene.

"Please, sir," the lackey whined. "We're dealing with this."

"Have you notified Mumbai?" The man had a deep voice with a clipped British accent. Even though he seemed to be in his mid-sixties, the young man speaking to him was never going to be able to budge him by main force or gentle persuasion. The Englishman was a full head taller and at least fifty kilos heavier than the employee. And Sked knew—from conversations over dinner—that the British gentleman was a former SAS Colonel. He almost hoped the people at the resort attempted to get physical. The man would toss them all into the sea.

"Our local law enforcement station isn't in Mumbai. It's in South Andaman."

"Well, when are they coming?"

"They aren't. We sent the boat and a couple of our boys to talk to them and show them pictures. But I know what they'll probably say: it was either a shark or an accident, and that they'll log the incident and tell us to keep the body on ice until we can send it over. They don't get too worked up over people who die at sea. Not even tourists." He shrugged as if to say it happened all the time, and he wasn't going to get too worked up that it had happened on his watch as long as people moved away.

"That's no shark bite," the man said.

By now, Sked and Akane had reached the edge of the crowd and looked down to where everyone's gaze was focused.

The first thing Sked saw was a large jet ski.

Correction. Half of a large jet ski.

It looked like it had been torn in two, with the back half discarded.

Again, he corrected himself. The vacation they'd taken was dulling his first impressions. The jet ski didn't look like it had been torn in half; it looked like it had been *bitten* in half.

Then he realized no one was looking at the jet ski so he craned his neck to see what they were looking at.

That's when he saw the body. Even in his current condition face down on the sand, Carlo was unmistakable: deeply tanned skin covered the bulging shoulders and back muscles of a man who spent good chunks of his day in the gym. His legs, Sked knew, were equally impressive.

But those legs were gone. Everything under the man's kidneys was gone. This time there was no room for confusion: he'd definitely been bitten in half. Sked could see the teeth marks... although he didn't know what kind of creature would have teeth that size.

"Damn," Akane said. "He was the best looking thing on the island. I wanted to ask his girl if they wanted to swap for a night."

"What?"

"Kidding," she replied with a smirk. "You're cute when you get jealous."

Under different circumstances, he might have responded, but now, all he could do was marvel that Akane could banter while half a guest was lying in the sand, entrails stretching all the way into the sea. He'd seen his share of corpses—working around the fringes of the law made for some interesting professional interactions—but Akane was cold, really cold.

Of course, he'd seen plenty of evidence of that before.

"Besides," she went on, "it doesn't look like his little pocket Barbie is among the gawkers. She was probably the appetizer for whatever munched him. So the swap would have been dead on arrival."

That was a good point which nobody seemed to be talking about. Sked stepped into the circle. "Has anyone seen his girlfriend?" he asked.

An elderly German woman, who always seemed to be the first on the beach just after dawn and the last to leave in the evening, spoke up: "They went out together, early in the morning. I saw them take the vehicle. He pulled it all the way to shore himself. Strong fellow."

"And she didn't come back?"

"Son," the big Colonel said. "You're looking at everything that came back. I'm afraid the girl is dead."

The resort employee tried again. "Please. We'd love to get this cleared up with the respect the man deserves, but as you can imagine we can't move him until we get instructions from Andaman. Please."

Sked moved away, but not because he cared what the resort told him to do. As far as he was concerned, a resort that didn't warn its guests that there might be dangerous animals in the water didn't deserve his obedience. Besides, he didn't like the resort itself. There was something strange about it: the place was a fortress, with the borders not only fenced off but fenced off with the kind of fencing that would slow down an infantry division. The fence was twenty feet tall, topped with razor wire and three levels thick. He'd seen more inviting borders around North Korean military installations.

More tellingly still, it stretched into the sea nearly a hundred meters out. The resort was either really concerned about something getting in or about its denizens getting out. Sked wasn't sure which, yet.

The reason he moved away from the dad man was that he'd seen something out of the corner of his eye. In the distance, a tiny dot approached the beach: a boat of some sort.

He strode over to the spot where the boat would likely land, wondering if the guy they'd sent to Andaman could have gotten his answer already. But as the vessel approached, it soon became apparent that this wasn't the ship the resort used to ferry visitors and supplies from the larger island. It was a smaller vessel, shaped like a British canal boat but made of fiberglass instead of wood.

Interesting. Shipping, other than the employees and guests headed for the resort, was forbidden to approach within five nautical miles of North Sentinel Island, so whoever was aboard the boat was defying the Indian Navy... something that boat didn't look big enough to do. Not for long, anyway.

The boat hit the beach without stopping, and a guy inside wrestled with the door as Sked ran over.

"Is there a doctor here?" the guy shouted.

"I suppose so," Sked replied. "Luckily, I haven't had to ask." He turned to see the rest of the group approaching now that they'd noticed the boat. The resort employee who'd been trying to get the Colonel to move led the charge. "Is there a doctor on the island?" Sked asked him.

The man ignored him and rushed up to the boat. He grabbed the driver's shoulder and shook.

"You can't be here," the man said. "This island and the water around it is off limits. I need to ask you to leave."

"We have an injured woman aboard," the man responded. Sked now saw that there was a woman with him, a blonde in a British flag bikini. She looked so healthy that he made a point of not staring at her; he didn't want Akane to get mad.

"That makes no difference to me," the employee said.

"It makes a difference to me." The speaker was another man in the blue polo shirt of the resort employees. This guy was in his forties and Sked hadn't seen him before. Dark and with a black mustache, he seemed the stereotypical Indian man, right down to the British accent. This island was getting more and more English by the minute.

"Go back inside. I make the decisions here."

"You're just the manager of this resort. I took an oath to protect human life, but none to the resort." He turned to the man in the ship. "Who is injured?"

"She's in here. I'm too scared to move her."

The doctor climbed aboard and came out, dusky features pale. "Get me some towels and a bucket of warm water. And a saw."

"You're fired," the manager said. "Now get off that boat. I'm sending you back on the next supply ship."

The Colonel shouldered past the manager and looked inside the boat. Then he turned back, redder than a ripe apple, took two steps towards the manager and hit him with the most beautiful uppercut Sked had ever seen. It snapped the man's jaw shut and then launched him through the air to land on his back with an audible thump.

That done, he rubbed his hand and turned to the other blue-shirted people present. "There's a woman in there who really needs medical help. If any of you try to stop the doctor from helping her, or are just too slow to jump when he says frog, I'll make you regret it, male or female or any of those newfangled genders they have now. I don't discriminate. Now, you heard him. Run."

They ran, and Sked moved in to see what had caused Colonel Volcano to erupt. For the second time since finishing his nap, he got a gory show: a woman inside wearing what had once been a white uniform which was now covered in blood. She had something stuck in her neck, and the doctor was listening to her chest.

"Is she actually alive?" Sked asked.

The man looked up. "Yes. But only by luck. This missed the major arteries and the spine. The problem will be getting the arrow out without causing further damage."

Left unsaid was the fact that further damage looked likely to kill her. Leaving it in looked like it would kill her, too.

Sometimes Sked was glad he wasn't a doctor. "Is there anything I can do to help?"

"Yes. Stand there and if anyone tries to make this boat move, beat the living daylights out of them." With that, the doctor pushed past and ran to a hut outside the reception area, sprinting back a moment later with a handful of tools, just as three other blue shirts arrived with buckets of water and towels.

"Rita, I'll need help with this one," the doctor said.

A young woman carrying an armful of towels nodded and brushed past Sked.

With no further orders, Sked just stood there until the guy who'd been driving the boat climbed out to join him. "Do you think they'd object to getting us something to drink and maybe some food?" the guy asked.

"If they do, I suspect they'll have to deal with the Colonel," Sked responded with a smile. "What happened to her?"

"Natives."

"Where? There aren't any other islands nearby."

"On this island."

Sked nodded. That explained the fences, anyway. "Didn't know there were any people living here."

"Did you know about the killer dinosaurs?"

Sked swore under his breath. In almost any other circumstances, he'd have told the man from the boat that he should get his prescriptions checked after a comment like that. In a more charitable mood, he would have told him to lie down because the stress was getting to him.

But not now. Just before the operation to liberate Akane from the Chinese cell, the Electric Buddha had hired him to infiltrate the email system of an employee of a corporation that had been developing the gene editing knowhow to create exactly what the guy described. Worse, he suspected that the hack was purchased by one of that company's competitors... so at least two organizations were building dinosaurs, probably for defense purposes.

Suddenly, the Buddha's insistence that Sked lie low on North Sentinel Island looked less like an inspired choice and more like one that had been thought out long in advance. In the best of cases, Sked was there as the Buddha's eyes on the ground in a place without internet.

Worst-case scenario was that having Sked murdered by a bunch of militarized dinosaurs was a good way for the Buddha to tie up loose ends.

The worst part about it was that, when this was over, he couldn't just walk up to the Buddha and beat the crap out of him... If there was one player in the hackerverse that absolutely nobody could pin down—although several had tried—that player was the Electric Buddha.

***

Two hours later, Sked opened the door to the cabin he shared with Akane. It contained a double bed, which served to support their cover story: that they were a married American couple. Of course, Akane knew he was always willing to live that reality and, after making him sleep on the couch a couple of days, she finally invited him into bed.

She looked up from an old paperback she'd pulled out of the resort's scanty bookcase.

"We should have waited a few years before coming here," she said.

"Why?"

"Because these places never buy books. They just put the ones their guests leave behind on a shelf somewhere and hope for the best. This resort is too new to have accumulated anything decent."

"I guess you're right," Sked replied.

Akane sighed. "So how is she?"

"Doctor says he has her stabilized. Not sure what that means in this case, as we moved her into his office, which looked like something from an old movie. Not exactly a high-complexity operating theater for a critically injured woman."

She looked at him, long and hard. "You actually care, don't you?"

That caught him off guard. "Of course. Shouldn't I?"

"You wouldn't have, once." She got off the bed and leaned on the desk beside the window. "It used to be us against the world, remember? Our crew and anyone along for the ride were the only people that mattered. You'd have died for any of us. We'd have died for you. And fuck the rest of the world. So what happened?"

Sked sat heavily on the chair beside the desk. "I'm not sure you'd believe me if I told you."

"Try me. I've seen some crazy shit."

"Not this crazy."

She waited in silence, eyes scanning him, moving up and down and side to side in that way she had.

"I'm not the guy you used to know." He watched her face to see if there was any reaction.

"That's what I just said," she replied.

"And that's not how I meant it. I'm literally not the man you first met. Brown. HappyHack. Fredling. Whatever he was calling himself when you met him, it isn't me."

She raised an eyebrow. "Don't tell me you've found religion."

"Not at all." How to explain? He decided to blurt it out. "Something happened to Brown on one of his missions. As far as I can tell from my very fragmented recollection of that period, someone downloaded another mind, my mind, onto the one that was already there. We fought for control. Brown lost."

"So who are you?"

"It's pretty confusing. But I think my name was Luca. I used to be a personal trainer."

"A personal trainer?" She laughed. "Sorry, I can't really see that."

"The memories are muddled. It's like I have one man's thought patterns and another man's memories and skill set. I know it sounds crazy. Hell, I would think I'm crazy if it weren't happening to me and I didn't know that I'm not crazy."

"Well, crazy people never know they're crazy." She stared out the window for several seconds. "Was this just before Hong Kong?"

"Yeah. I don't know how I managed to get home. If you hadn't been there…"

She nodded. "You were in bad shape."

"I didn't know who I was. I didn't remember anything about what I'd done before that trip. You showed me the ropes and then it all came back in a flood… but not my real memories. I got Brown's memories."

"You *are* Brown."

"You need to believe me on this. I might act like Brown and remember the things he did and knew, but he's not me and I'm not him. I don't remember how they did this to me, and I'm not sure where, even though I remember trees, a jungle like the one around us."

"You never mentioned trees when we were putting you back together."

"It only occurred to me after we reached this island. The trees, the humidity… I don't know. *Something* jogged my memory."

"Don't you remember where you were?"

"Not remotely."

"And your passport…" she let the words die away. She knew as well as he did that in their line of work, passports were either not used at all or used once and discarded.

"No help. Hell, I don't even have one under my real name. But I'm starting to think this happened in Central America."

She shrugged.

He went on. "But you want to hear something interesting?"

"I dunno. Every time someone tells me something interesting, I end up with another price on my head."

"That's because you run off and either steal or sabotage the interesting thing they tell you about. Just listen, this one shouldn't get you in trouble. You know those people on the lifeboat?"

"What about them?"

"They say the island's crawling with killer dinosaurs."

"Oh, come on. They're probably drugged out of their minds. I mean, how else do you manage to shoot one of your friends in the neck with an arrow?"

"I think they're telling the truth."

"That's..." she gave him the fisheye. "All right. Spill it. What gives?"

He explained about the Buddha and the gene labs.

"What else?" Akane said.

That startled him. He hadn't thought there was anything else. But now that she mentioned it.

"I think I remember something. Something about the place where they overwrote my mind. The guy who did it..."

"What about him?"

"I think he was in the crazy animal modification game. I think there were monsters there."

Akane rolled her eyes. "You know what I think? I think you went to some party somewhere, you went on one bad trip after another and now you've got your brain so fried that you're confusing your nightmares with reality."

"You know I don't do that."

"Lately, I don't know what I know about you. Changing your handle to Sked out of the blue, suddenly growing a conscience you don't need. Just about the only thing you treat the same as always is me."

"You sound jealous that I'm being nice to others for a change."

"No. I'm wondering if I can still trust you."

CHAPTER 6

Jana cowered in the makeshift cage. The natives had stripped off her bikini and she feared the worst.

She was surprised that they hadn't done more than stare at her and poke her with spears while they'd pushed her inside the wooden stockade which they'd tied with grass-like leaves. It looked like the leaves wouldn't hold against a determined attempt to escape... but she decided not to test that while the villagers were about. If they left her inside, an opportunity might arise when they went to sleep.

Only a handful of the men and a couple of equally naked women remained in the clearing they'd dragged her to. The men were either older than the ones that had tracked her down or mere boys, not even into puberty. But it made little difference: the spears they held would cut her to ribbons. She'd already seen what had happened to Isabel.

No. She wouldn't think of that. Not now. She could mourn her companions later, once she survived the ordeal.

"Listen," she said in English. "This is some kind of mistake."

The tribesmen chattered among themselves in a language she'd never heard. In fact, she'd never heard anything like it, not even in the cosmopolitan melting pot of Prague, one of the places in Europe where east truly met west. This language didn't consist merely of words but of clicks and gutturals she couldn't even follow, much less understand.

In her experience, though, everyone spoke English... or at least one of them would. Even in the smallest Czech village, there was always someone who had some English, and he was the one the villagers would come and get when some clueless tourist misread their GPS and got lost. She knew because she'd been the one for her own hometown, a tiny farming hamlet near the Austrian border.

But either these people really didn't speak any English or they pretended not to.

Jana reflected that if she'd murdered a bunch of tourists, she'd also pretend not to be able to understand a word anyone said. Everything would be much more convenient that way.

She knew they'd killed them. She'd seen them dragging the bodies away, stripping them down and...

No. She wasn't going to think about that.

"Let me out!"

The tribespeople ignored her and went about their business, which seemed to consist of inspecting the clothes they'd removed from the dead. Jana watched a bloodstained white uniform passed from hand to hand as the women made appreciative noises... just like her mother and grandmother would have done after a market day.

Except her ancestors wouldn't have killed anyone for their prizes.

"Please, let me go!" Though her voice filled the clearing, none of the locals paid Jana any heed.

Suddenly, they disappeared. She didn't even see where they went. One minute the clearing was filled with all the natives who hadn't been part of the ongoing hunt and the next... nothing. They hadn't even made any noise she could hear. It was like they were all ghosts.

"Hey! Where'd everyone go?"

Though being the prisoner of murderous natives was not something she would have chosen for herself, the suddenly empty clearing was spooky. Even the birds and the insects had gone quiet.

Something cracked in the distance, the soft sound of a twig breaking which, in the silence, sounded like a gunshot.

The noise brought Jana back to her senses. The islanders were gone, which meant that she had an opportunity to get out of the cage. She attacked the grass tying it together.

It was much tougher than it looked. The natives obviously knew what they were doing.

It wasn't, however, indestructible, and after rubbing it against the wood of the pole, she managed to wear through a single strand. With a little more play in the structure, she was able to wear down the next one a bit quicker. She needed to hurry—who knew when the islanders would be back.

She looked out to see if anyone was returning.

"Oh God," she whispered.

The clearing was full of animals that looked like dinosaurs. Small ones, even smaller than the velociraptors from the first Jurassic Park... but dinosaurs. She couldn't believe what she was seeing.

The top of their heads barely reached her waist, but there were a lot of them. She retreated from the door of the cage, moving as quietly as she could to the back.

They must have heard her. Small mouths with disproportionately large teeth began to snap at the stockade. The little monsters pushed against the walls of the cage. One, behind her, managed to get its head in through a gap between the floor and one of the fence posts. She stomped the snout with her bare foot… but wasn't able to smash it. At least she had the satisfaction of watching it pull out with a shriek.

Now, however, her own work was conspiring against her. The frayed grass ropes holding the stockade door together creaked and strained.

"No," Jana breathed as the door popped open. She tensed for the onslaught.

For a moment, nothing happened other than the occasional face peering into the enclosure.

Then three of the creatures stormed in at full speed.

Jana covered her face, but none of them hit her there. She felt fire rake across the back of her leg and fell to the ground, unable to stand.

Teeth tore her hand away from her face and she saw a mouth snapping closed on her neck.

As the blood flowed onto the dirt, and the light in her eyes dimmed, Jana's final thought was that she was going crazy.

She was sure the dinosaur that had torn her neck was wearing a collar.

Hooked to the collar, she was certain she saw a webcam.

Before she could process that, the lights went out forever.

***

The bodies were fresh, but a black cloud of flies took off when they approached.

"That isn't good," Cora told Lai. "Let me go look."

But when she approached, the Malaysian man matched her step for step. She raised an eyebrow. "You sure you want to do this? It doesn't look pretty, and probably has nothing to do with us."

"I may be getting old," Lai replied, "but my eyes are better than most people's. And they tell me that those bodies are wearing a uniform identical to the one the sailors on the *Vanarisa* wear."

Cora sighed. She hoped he hadn't noticed, and that it might be coincidence. But now that he'd said it, she knew they would be the men from the ship. She wasn't superstitious, but the fact that her fears had been uttered meant they'd come true. Any Marine could tell you that.

The corollary to that truth was that she'd failed. People she was responsible for had died on her watch. That Cora hadn't been anywhere near the action meant nothing; her decision to evacuate had been the root cause of whatever happened—and she'd find out what that was if it was the very last thing she did. And once she was done, her resignation would be on Lai's desk as soon as they got back to civilization.

The two men. Lens Van Rijn and Khatri were barely recognizable. They'd been torn to pieces by…

By what? She looked around, trying to read the footprints on the sand. It was too churned up, but whatever had done this had emerged from the woods, and there were a buttload of them. Her hand unconsciously went to her hip, where for a decade and a half, her sidearm had resided.

To her surprise, she found it there, which startled her just as much as not finding it had when she'd first returned to civilian life. She remembered putting it there before boarding the lifeboat, thinking it might come in handy if they ran into a dangerous animal.

She'd been thinking along the lines of shooting a crocodile if they came on it—or whatever—but now it looked like the only thing she'd be able to do with a sidearm would be to make a lot of noise and try to scare off the pack of whatever was in those woods.

Still, the gun felt comforting. She turned to Lai.

"I recommend we stay on the beach, but if you don't want to follow my recommendations anymore, I would understand."

"We'll stay on the beach," Lai said. There was neither accusation nor absolution in his gaze.

They gathered the rest of the group and walked past the grisly remains. It was interesting to see how the executives kept their eyes straight ahead, pretending there was nothing to look at, while the rest of the crew stared. More than once, the first mate made as if to speak.

"Don't worry," Cora said. "I'll make sure someone recovers them and gives them a proper burial." She knew it would likely be her last official act as Lai's Head of Security.

They trudged along for a few hundred meters more. Cora kept her eyes on the forest the entire time, occasionally glancing backward. If there was anything ahead, the people with her would see it.

Lai held up a hand. "Wait."

Cora's hand went to the holster again. It was incredible how quickly the old habits returned. "What?"

"Can you smell that?"

"Smell?" She wasn't expecting that, but she sniffed the air and was suddenly hungry. The faint odor of burning wood and cooking meat reached her over the scent of sea. It was a relief: she'd expected Lai to have discovered more decomposing bodies of their shipmates. The wind was coming from inland, which meant that the smell likely had the same source.

"Decision time," Cora said. "Do we keep walking and eventually arrive at the resort or cut into the woods and find the people having the barbecue? My vote is the barbecue, guys, because I'm not certain how far we need to walk to reach the resort or how safe this beach is. But I'm also not sure walking into those woods is a good idea."

"Let's go," Lai replied. Then he held up a hand. "And no, I won't hold it against you if it's the wrong choice. Listen, I hired you to use your experience and your judgement to keep me and my people safe. You've done that so far, and I can't really expect anything else. This isn't the time for you to have a meltdown, we need you more than ever."

She nodded and nearly saluted. "Thank you, sir. I'll do my best."

"That's what I expect."

They turned towards the greenery bordering the beach and found a path through the undergrowth that got wider as they entered the trees. "Well, someone is using this anyway," the sailor who'd been driving the boat noted.

"Yes, but I'd like to scout ahead to see that the way is still clear. Does anyone know how to shoot one of these?" She held out her gun and the sailor took it.

"I was in the Philippines Navy," he replied. "I know my way around a handgun."

"Good. Don't shoot unless you absolutely have to and if things go to hell, climb the trees. A lot of ground predators can't, although, to be honest, I have no clue what might live on this island. Either way, at least you won't get swarmed by major numbers."

She set off through the woods, moving as silently as she could but knowing that any recon Marine would have laughed at her.

Hopefully, whatever was out there wouldn't be as good as a recon Marine. Few were, human or animal.

The path wound between the trees for about fifty yards as the crow flies—the distance was longer on the sinuous path—until it came to a sandy bowl surrounded by trees. The clearing was about fifty yards wide and occupied by several naked people she assumed were the villagers native to the island. The smell of meat cooking was stronger there, strong enough to make her drool, but something, some sixth sense, kept her from calling out to them.

What was it? What was wrong with the scene? The only thing she could point out was that the people around the firepit were not dressed in civilized fashion. Most of them were butt-naked wearing nothing but a tan belt around their upper waists.

But that wasn't it.

Then she spotted the pile of sticks—bows, arrows and a spear or two—on the ground behind them. Had her subconscious seen the weapons?

Probably not. There was something else she wasn't quite focusing on. Something that had to do with the firepit the crowd was milling around.

A couple of the natives shifted and she got a clearer look at the meat on the spit. It was a good-sized animal, but there was nothing surprising in that. The bodies on the beach had already confirmed that there were large predators present. And large predators had to eat something.

She was about to go talk to the islanders when two of the men got their shoulders under the spit and shifted it to another pair of forked sticks stuck into the sand. This had the effect of moving the meat around ninety degrees so it was head on to Cora's position.

"Holy shit," she whispered, and backpedaled away without thinking. The action of moving the spit had positioned the barbecue so that its head was directly in front of her.

She found herself looking straight into the open mouth of one of the bunnies. Her expression told Cora that her death had been painful, and she wondered if the villagers had even bothered to kill her before impaling her onto the stake and cooking her alive.

The islanders were cannibals.

Or at least they were when they were able to get meat from outside the island.

She shook her head and attempted to focus. The first order of business was to get the hell out of there.

No, she thought grimly. The first order of business was to document what she was seeing. Her cell phone might not be connected to the network out here, but she always kept it charged because that was where she kept her daily planner and work schedule. So she filmed thirty seconds of footage, enough that there could be no question about what was happening.

The woman cooking over the open fire—fortunately not one of the bunnies she'd spoken to on the ship, the ones who'd been so polite—had saved Cora's life. If she hadn't been slowly roasting to show the world what the natives did to people, Cora would have shared her fate. The least Cora could do was to take back proof of the end that had befallen the woman. Perhaps some justice could be meted out, although from what she'd heard, this island was beyond civilized law.

Though every fiber of her being was screaming at her to get the hell out of there, Cora forced herself to complete the video and then backed slowly the way she came.

But Murphy's law is never far from soldiers, and she stepped on a branch she didn't see and the crack sounded across the clearing.

Enough. She didn't wait to see how the cannibals reacted, and sprinted down the path to the beach.

"Run!" she told the contingent waiting there.

To their credit, no one questioned the Marine bowling in their direction and the group set out at a dead run in the direction she was pointing. Most of them seemed to be in good shape, and even Lai could pick them up and put them down. She ran up to the sailor who'd taken her gun and held out a hand.

The man gave the pistol back.

"Keep them running along the beach. I'm going to take the rear and make sure we aren't followed."

The guy nodded, and Cora fell back. At the very rear of the formation was the guy who'd tried to get out of pushing the lifeboat onto the beach. No surprise there, but though he might be a jerk, she didn't want to lose any more people on her watch.

"Come on. You really don't want these guys to catch you," she said.

That resulted in a slight increase in speed which lasted for all of ten steps.

"Wimp," she said under her breath, but fell back further behind him. Any future deaths that befell this group would happen over her own corpse, which at least would save her the indignity of having to resign.

The beach curved around an inlet and she could only see about fifty meters back, which meant that their group, for the nonce, would be out of sight of any pursuit. Hopefully the islanders would simply eat the meal they already had.

The soldier in her, however, reminded her that things never worked that way. If she didn't see the natives coming it was because they were moving along a shortcut through the woods that would let them cut the group off up ahead.

Spurred on by this, she headed to the front again. Other than a couple of stragglers, the others appeared to be, by some unspoken agreement, keeping formation up ahead. She caught up and passed them, ignoring the pleas to wait up as they went around yet another corner in the sand.

She almost ran into the fence.

Cora stopped and whistled. It was the kind of enclosure you put up when the bad guys might try to drive a cement truck through it: sturdy and really tall, with no gates in it.

On the other side was a recreational beach that would have been at home in any resort on the planet. From where she was standing, she could see a volleyball net and an octogenarian couple walking, their feet just getting wet.

The fence extended into the jungle—it had been erected by someone who knew what he was doing, because the trees had been cleared ten meters away from the fence. No one would be able to climb over a tree and just drop in.

It allowed her to see that there were no openings in that direction, which meant they needed to go around it on the seaward side.

"Out into the water," she ordered. "We're going around the fence."

Again, Lai didn't hesitate even for a second.

Again, most of the group followed the old man's lead.

And again, the dipshit exec who'd just arrived balked. "We should call those people over there…"

"There's no time for that," Cora replied.

"I don't think…"

She leveled the gun at his head. At this range, she might miss the precise center of his forehead by a millimeter to either side, no more. "Get moving," she said, as she cocked the gun.

He moved.

When they were about halfway along the fence, seventy meters into the sea, someone at the resort spotted them. By the time they reached the edge, half-swimming, half-grabbing the fence itself, the second lifeboat from the *Vanarisa* arrived to pick them up.

Three minutes later, they were on the beach.

Lai turned to her and nodded. "You got us out," he said. "But now I need to know what that was all about."

Cora nodded back. "You're not going to like it."

"I wasn't expecting to."

CHAPTER 7

Sabrina watched the video. She watched it again, focusing on the eyes of the woman. There was a naked fear in that gaze that got her thinking.

She wondered if that was the way humans—and their hominid ancestors—looked when cornered by a saber-toothed tiger. That look of sheer terror must have been the very last expression on the faces of millions of unfortunates before mankind managed to dominate the natural world.

She watched the clip again.

A blonde, eyes so wide that the iris nearly disappeared in an expanse of white. Slack-jawed utter terror. This one wasn't even screaming... she must have accepted death as something inevitable, something natural. Her hands weren't moving, not even when the other Compsognathus tore into her stomach.

As a biologist, Sabrina knew that animals often stayed perfectly still to avoid detection by predators. Sometimes it worked. But this was something different; this woman knew she was caught. She had nothing to gain with staying paralyzed, everything to gain by fighting until her final breath, but she just sat there passively as the dinosaur calmly ripped her throat out.

Absolutely fascinating.

Best of all was the final shot before she died. Sabrina was convinced that the woman looked straight into the camera. It was like looking into the eyes of the dead. Wonderful.

This video was so much better than the other one. The two men on the beach had stood their ground and been overwhelmed, but there was nothing intimate about it, just the violent death of combat. They'd been swarmed by a dozen of her creatures, and died in an instant.

She watched that video again, in case she'd missed something, but no. It was just as boring as it had been the other times she'd run it, relieved only by the sense of satisfaction inherent in her creatures working effectively and proving what she'd told Jermaine: the modified Compsognathus were wonderful at tracking and attacking unarmed civilians. They'd dropped those two easily, immediately, and suffered only one loss. It was even better than she'd expected, and when she got them bred to attack all together without sending a test subject out first, even those small losses would be minimized. It would take some work—identifying genes that drove behavior was much harder than the ones that defined physical characteristics—but she would manage.

Besides, she had time to tweak; the creatures could go on sale immediately as they were. They were more than effective enough for the job.

That was all well and good, but her interest wasn't commercial, it was professional. The video of the two men falling to her pack was nowhere near as interesting as the one of the woman in the cage. That one showed the potential as a psychological weapon of the resurrected dinosaur.

In a world where social media ruled supreme and people would go utterly bananas over a virus that only killed a tiny fraction of those it infected, a bunch of dinosaurs running about should cause a most satisfactory effect to study mass-panic dynamics. Germaine would love the fact that, as a terror weapon, this product could be used with maximum effect even if the real death tolls were very small.

It was Jermaine's job to get the best price he could for it. But it was her job to develop the creatures so that they would give the best effect.

In that sense, the video of the woman was pure gold. It was intimate, almost a study in a psychiatrist's office. Sabrina smiled as she watched the video again, letting the woman's expressions play out in slow motion and wondering if that was what her own face had looked like in those interminable sessions when they tried to cure her of... well, the doctors had had their own fancy names for it, but, in essence what they wanted to do was to remove her personality and drives from her mind and replace them with those of the very people she detested, the sheep who lived in a constant state of fear and who needed to control the rest of the population—not because they cared about others, as they claimed, but because by controlling everyone else, they would make their own world safer for themselves.

Fortunately, Jermaine had saved her from all that. He'd told her that he'd read her psych reports and that he didn't care that she was at least a sociopath and probably a psychopath. He told her he believed in separating the artist from the art and what she did on her own time was her own affair, as long as she got results.

Well, the woman's face in this video was most certainly a result.

It was a moment shared between them. They say everyone dies alone, but Sabrina felt she participated in this woman's death, in the pain and the acceptance.

There was also an aspect of mystery to the video. This was a Caucasian woman, not one of the islanders they'd studied. There was no reason for her to be there in the first place.

And she was naked and appeared to be locked in a primitive cage. The first minute of the video showed the outside of the enclosure quite clearly: wrist-thick poles stuck in the ground held together by cords of some kind. She had expected to find an animal inside, the native's food.

Instead, there was a naked blonde. That was a surprise, to say the least.

She stood and stretched, feeling a headache coming on. The footage was jerky and jumped around a lot, as one would expect from a bunch of cameras mounted on the necks of darting dinosaurs.

Sabrina needed to go for a walk on deck, to clear her head and maybe talk to some of her team.

The late afternoon sky showed no sign of the earlier rainstorm. The sun beat down hard and she allowed herself to bask under it for a few moments as she stared out over the blue sea and wondered where her big beauties were. The Compsognathus were working out quite well, but her true love would always be those sea monsters. Magnificent beasts that didn't need to attack in packs.

"Hello, Sabrina," she turned to see who it was and smiled when she realized it was one of the researchers Jermaine had attached to the project.

"Hello…"

"Carmen," the woman replied. "I'm in analytics."

"Ah, yes. I remember now. You developed the echo-tracking implants on the Mosasaur." The sea monsters were too big for collars to work, but they had to be tracked somehow. The team had developed a system that screwed into the Mosasaur's bones from outside the skin. The monster probably felt the half-inch-wide screw as something akin to a mosquito bite. "That was great work."

The researcher smiled uncertainly. "Thank you. I was just going to see you about that. We had some weird readings a few hours back, as if the female sample had come into very close contact with a large ship of some kind."

"How close?"

"Impact at least…" she hesitated. "The creature may have attacked the ship."

"Ah. Have you been able to identify the vessel?"

"Mr. Ratzenberger has been working on it. He came around just now to say that the only other boat in the region is a huge pleasure yacht called *Vanarisa*."

Sabrina shrugged. It meant nothing to her. "Thank you."

"Since I was on my way, the other analysts asked me about the Compsognathus video. Is that downloaded yet?"

Sabrina nodded. "Some of it. I'll send you the first few minutes as soon as I get back to my cabin."

The woman wandered off, and Sabrina wished the rest of the ship's crew knew what was actually going on. It would save her hours and hours of removing the interesting stuff from the footage. Unfortunately, all the junior members of staff had been told was that the small dinosaurs were going to be released onto an uninhabited island. They actually thought they were two hundred miles further east than they really were… and that the land off to port was a small uninhabited speck. They would freak out completely if they knew the test was being done on live humans.

It was a nuisance.

Then she smiled. A pleasure yacht was a good place for a blonde to have originated. She had cameras on the Mosasaurs, too, and it might be a good time to see if they'd transmitted anything interesting.

If she could prove that they'd already sunk a ship… then this would end up becoming a most productive day.

Sabrina scuttled back to her quarters and, pausing only long enough to send the analysis team a few sanitized videos of the Compsognathus herd doing nothing very interesting, she sent one of the drones out over the ocean to see if she could get a signal through to the recorder on the female sea monster.

No, she corrected herself. *Not the sea monster. She has a name, and that name is Kali. And the male is called Shiva. If I start treating them as interchangeable, I'll start thinking of them as expendable. And they're not. They're my babies.*

Even the Compsognathus that died on the island is one of them, although he was one of dozens. Unless I treat them as individuals, I'm no better than the rest of them. No better than Dieter or Jermaine.

The drone hovered over the area where they were keeping the monster contained, a few miles out from the island.

Now, there was little to do but wait. The military drones, on the heavy-duty batteries, could hover for about 45 minutes, so she programmed them to relay, with one drone always over the target area while the rest recharged. Sabrina also programmed the system to sound an alarm if the footage began to come through. The underwater cameras were designed to film only when there was something at least human-sized in range. Otherwise, they'd gather endless hours of Kali swimming or Shiva eating tiny fish.

She dozed for nearly two hours before a persistent beeping noise annoyed her enough to open an eye.

"I must have been really tired," she mumbled when she saw the time. "I could sleep another eight hours." But when her addled mind realized what the alarm meant she shot out of her bunk and nearly fell reaching her computer. "Show momma what happened," she said.

And the system did. Sabrina watched, enthralled, as some kind of ship came into view, the rumbling of its engines discernible even in the awful audio of the underwater recording.

She smiled as she saw the Mosasaur react to the unwanted intruder in exactly the way she expected: violently. The camera suddenly accelerated towards the hull of the ship and, from the camera's vantage point, Sabrina watched Kali's head slam into the bottom of the ship. Then, moving upwards towards the water line, slam the vessel again and again and again.

"Careful, sweety," she whispered. "Don't hurt yourself."

But the Mosasaur kept attacking even after it reached the surface, using its claws to excellent effect along the sides of the ship before it lost interest in the one-sided battle and swam off in some other direction.

Her grin was ear-to-ear now. Even if the ship hadn't sunk, the potential here was enormous. The video clearly showed how Kali had attacked a huge item, something they hadn't been able to test or even really to imagine in the holding tanks in Arizona.

And if the ship sank… jackpot.

She picked up her phone and did something that would normally have been distasteful to her, but which she now did with something almost approaching enthusiasm.

"Dieter," she said once the connection was made. "It's Sabrina. I need a favor. Two actually. I need you to find out where that ship you tracked earlier is now… and I need you to watch these videos I'm sending you. I think Jermaine is going to have a good day."

***

Harold Tse grinned into the wind, hot even in the night. The Zodiac Futura Commando, so new that the smell of rubber overwhelmed the scent of sea, cut through the waves like a well-sharpened watermelon chopper through bare skin. At this rate they'd be on the island in minutes.

He made a mental note to thank Cheng back in Philadelphia for suggesting the electric outboard motor. It was utterly silent, but powerful enough to move them quickly.

"Light," the man next to him said.

Harold didn't like this man. But he didn't have to. The man represented Beijing… whether that meant government or Triad, he hadn't asked, and it wasn't his place to know. The only important thing was that the man was there to observe, and would not take part in any of the violence. When the mission was complete, he would report back to his masters and that report would pretty much seal Harold's fate within the larger organization. Being out in a backwater like Philadelphia meant that he didn't have much exposure to the big operators in Asia.

Of course, he also knew that the main reason for his presence was that he was expendable. Losing a mid-level boss from Philly wasn't going to hurt the organization too much.

But failure wasn't an option. He'd brought his best three men along, two of them former soldiers—one from the US Army, the other a British-Chinese expat—and his most experienced hitman. They would be prepared for anything the target might have waiting.

Harold turned back to the guy driving the boat. Limey Han was rock-solid and knew how to handle watercraft. "Can you bring us to shore about three hundred meters from that light?"

Han nodded and gave a fraction of a turn to the tiller.

The intelligence had tracked their quarry, a hacker named Akane who'd stolen a fortune from the Triad operation in Macau, all the way to Andaman. There, several witnesses had spotted them boarding the boat to a resort. This resort.

Unless they had another submarine waiting for them, this was where she remained; a sitting duck with nowhere to go but six feet under.

The moon was out and Han had no trouble beaching the boat in the soft turf. Then, as the observer observed, the four men from Philadelphia picked up the inflatable boat and lifted it to the tree line. They wouldn't be spotted prematurely.

The main problem with the mission—the only difficulty at all, in fact—was that, though the insertion had to be done by night to avoid being spotted, the actual hit was going to have to wait until morning. The resort consisted of a dozen identical cabins and this was probably the only hotel in the world which didn't have its reservation system online. Apparently, you arrived and chose the cabin you liked from the ones available.

That meant that they either had to identify the quarry beforehand or risk discovery while bumbling about in the dark.

He'd dismissed Crazy Eddie's suggestion that they just kill everyone until they happened to find the right cabin. No need to make unnecessary enemies… and even less to make unnecessary headlines. His superiors wouldn't like that at all.

"Did you see something, boss?" Mike Zhen asked.

"Where?"

"Behind us, something breaking through the water."

"No," Harold replied. "It was probably a dolphin or something. We're not here to watch dolphins."

They moved slowly along the beach, just outside the tree line, inching towards the resort. Even in the moonlight, they weren't used to doing their work in the wilderness. Harold stumbled over a root and barely caught himself before hitting the ground.

He laughed at himself. He was a city boy, not some kind of jungle commando. Unlike so many people in Philadelphia's underworld, Harold didn't see himself as a freedom fighter against the ills of a system that had mistreated him, but simply as what he was: a man who followed a family tradition reaching back as many generations as he knew. His branch of the Triads wasn't something built in the past decade, it was an integral part of the community, and it supplied services that might otherwise be lacking…

His clients were no longer immigrants just off the boat. That was his grandmother's generation. They were integrated into the fabric of American society. Some had assimilated fully, even taking spouses that weren't Chinese. Some spoke no language but English.

Nevertheless, even the most Americanized came to Harold when they needed a special service that couldn't be bought from Amazon, grateful to find discretion and understanding. His business was built on trust, not the ability to field a militia in a jungle.

Even Crazy Eddie and his watermelon cleaver had gratifyingly little work to do. Violence was bad for business, and bloody headlines were bad for careers.

So this mission was way outside the usual parameters, nothing at all like what they were used to.

The group's approach was less than elegant, but he wanted to get a feel for the place while the moon was still out. It would help them the following day.

Something darted out of the foliage. Small and sleek, it was hard to see what it was, even in the moonlight.

"Watch out," Eddie said. The warning was just in time. Harold rolled to the side and felt air rush over him.

Limey was less fortunate. The animal that missed Harold slammed straight into his stomach, and he let the air out with a loud grunt.

"Everyone get over here," Harold commanded. "Turn on your flashlights."

The lights, like the Zodiac, were military-grade and the animals disappeared without Harold ever managing to get a look at them. He bent over Limey. "You okay?"

Limey held a hand over his stomach. "I'll live. I got a deep gouge, but nothing too serious." He pulled himself to his feet. "What the hell was that?"

"Damned if I know," Harold replied. "But it seems to be afraid of the light. Can you walk?"

"Yeah."

"Let's get moving, then."

As they headed off in the direction they'd been moving, Harold stole a glance at the observer. Was the man impressed that they'd persevere? Disgusted at the fact that a mere animal encounter had almost wrecked everything and thinking that they were all a bunch of bumbling amateurs? His face made it impossible to tell.

One thing was for certain. With the beams of their lights burning through the jungle, no one looking this way would ever miss them.

Crazy Eddie walked over, close enough to whisper without the rest of them overhearing.

"They're still in the forest," Eddie said.

"Who?"

"Those critters. And there are hundreds of them."

Harold shone his light where Eddie had indicated. "I don't see anything."

"Trust me, they're around."

With that, he pulled his watermelon chopper, a flat, straight blade, out of his specially tailored scabbard and took point again.

Harold swallowed. "Keep moving," he told his team.

CHAPTER 8

Akane led him by the hand into the woods beside their cabin, but Sked knew her too well to expect this was a romantic assignation. She was a strictly indoorsy kind of woman, although she wouldn't care if "indoors" meant the bathroom of a rave club full of sweaty people, as long as there was a roof over her head.

A bug-filled jungle would not be her style, no matter how fragrant the wind or romantic the chirping of the nocturnal creatures. Ever.

When she led him to the fence that divided the resort from the rest of the island, illuminated along its length by strong floodlights, he wasn't in the least bit surprised or disappointed. The night was still young... and besides, he was curious as to what she thought she was doing.

"What do you think?" she said.

"I already told you what I think. I think the fence is a smart move, considering that there are aggressive natives and genetically modified dinosaurs on the other side."

"It doesn't raise any suspicions?"

He scratched his head. "Not really. Should it?"

"Think for a second. How was that woman attacked?"

"With an arrow." He grinned at her and waited. This was where Akane was mistress of all: figuring angles. She might be rash, irresponsible and prone to taking other people's stuff without asking, but up until the point where the theft was discovered and the victim sent well-equipped thugs after her, Akane was utterly brilliant. Underestimating the consequences of her plans had never stood in the way of setting them successfully in motion.

"And do you think that fence would stop an arrow? Of course not. So why aren't the pygmies or whatever is out there shooting the guests full of holes and reclaiming their land? I mean the presence of the fence indicates that this area no longer belongs to them, right?"

"I guess..." Sked snapped his fingers. "Maybe it's to keep the guests inside so the natives can live in peace."

"Probably. But do you think you need that kind of a fence to keep the Colonel's wife in here?" She peered up at it. "Hell, I don't know if you could climb that one."

"I can do it, but I'd need to be seriously motivated. If I had the choice, I'd rather swim along the seaside and go around it."

"And the natives have boats. And the resort has a jet ski."

"Not anymore."

"Don't be a smartass." She looked back at the fence. "So why the hell is it here, and, since it's not to protect the guests or, really keep them inside, who put it here?" She pointed to the rear section of the resort. The fenced resort area extended five hundred meters into the forest—they'd walked the perimeter of the fence—but there were no paths through there, and no apparent reason for the enormous area. Maybe the developers were speculating on increasing the number of cottages as the resort got more popular... but that would mean that the beach between the fences would become overcrowded. It didn't seem to make sense that anyone would fence in such a huge area for not useful reason. "Don't you wonder about the heart of darkness behind us? The resort isn't using the land, so what's in that jungle?"

Before Sked could answer, a gunshot sounded in the trees beyond the fence. Then another, and running footsteps could be heard coming their way. Sked raised an eyebrow and the pair hid behind a tree to see what would come out of the woods.

"Over there," Akane whispered. She pointed to the fence a hundred meters away, close to the shore. "People."

Three men ran desperately in the direction of the resort. The leader hit the fence head-on and fell back. The remaining two shone their flashlights into the darkness. One of them fired.

"Save your ammo until we can see them," the other one shouted.

Akane and Sked raced along the path that bordered the fence on the inside of the trees. Seconds later they were twenty meters from the men.

"What do we do?"

"Those guys are Chinese," Akane replied. "And look at those tattoos. They're here for us."

"What are they shooting at?"

As if in answer to his question, several small dinosaurs walked into the illuminated fringe between the trees and the fence. They looked exactly the way the Marine woman who'd come in with the big group had said they did, which corroborated the story the guy from the first boat had told. Seeing them in the flesh made little difference other than to remind him just how small they were.

It didn't matter though. These were obviously pack hunters, and the guys at the fence would run out of bullets long before the dinosaurs ran out of pack.

"I've got an idea. Stay here." Sked pulled the cap he used for being out in the sun from his pocket and fit it low over his forehead. Then he approached the men at a jog.

"What are you doing?" he asked in English, trying to imitate the Mumbai accent of the folks who ran the resort.

One of the men turned to look at him, eyes wide. "We need to get inside. Where are the gates?"

"No gates on this wall. Too dangerous. Someone might leave it open and let the cannibals in."

Sked personally didn't believe the woman's story about the islanders being cannibals; she'd probably been too scared to see clearly, Marine or no Marine. But it was way too good a story not to use in the current situation.

"Who are you?" the guy asked.

"I'm Jocko, and it's my night on perimeter duty. If you want in, you'll need to climb."

"We can't. Those things will grab us if we do. We already tried, further that way... which is why there's only three of us left."

"I can help you there," Sked replied. "Can you get your guns over the fence? If you can, I'll cover you as you climb."

The man seemed to be about to argue, then shrugged and turned to his companion. He took a moment to heave the gun, underhand, in a high arc that flew precisely into Sked's waiting hands.

"Throw the other two over," Sked said. "I don't want to run out of bullets at a bad time."

Another man followed suit and when Sked raised an eyebrow, the first man simply shrugged. "Eddie doesn't believe in guns."

Sked suppressed his shudder as he watched the glint of the floodlights off the straight blade of the watermelon chopper the third guy held up for his perusal. He'd lived in Asia much too long not to know the kind of damage the Triads regularly did with those.

"All right. Climb. I'll cover you."

The men did and, as soon as they turned their backs, some of the bolder animals proved that they'd been telling the truth. They charged immediately.

Sked wasn't an Olympic-quality marksman, but he was pretty good. He got the leader of the pack in the breastbone and was relieved to see it fall over. He'd been afraid that these bastards would be impervious to bullets. Either because of thick leather covering or enormous bones, but it appeared that they could be hit.

The second shot was less successful, as the dinosaur he hit only stumbled and got back up.

He would have preferred to take head shots at the things, but he didn't dare: he'd read somewhere that dinosaurs had thick skulls shielding tiny brains. Besides, the heads were smaller than the bodies, and in the uncertain light and with all the bobbing and weaving the monsters were doing, he was pretty sure he'd miss if he tried.

So he blasted another one in the chest. This one fell over and stayed down.

Meanwhile, the three Triad killers had climbed about six feet up the wall. Sked suspected there was an alarm sounding somewhere in the resort, and that a guard would be around to see what was happening, probably quite soon. Sked preferred to disappear before those men arrived.

Convinced that the dinosaurs couldn't climb using those ridiculous arms, Sked let the next one arrive at the fence. It tried to climb using its hind legs and a combination of arms and mouth, but it was a hopeless proposition. It fell back and glared at Sked.

He shot it in the head, just to see what would happen.

It fell back but, only a couple of seconds later, it got back up, shaking its head angrily. It was missing an eye and the bullet had carved a gash along the grey-brown skin, but the thing stood there looking angry and a little confused. Sked moved back from the fence a bit to give the men a little room, but that beady black eye followed him, as if trying to memorize the one it blamed for causing it so much pain.

Akane materialized beside him and took the second gun. When the Triad men finished their arduous climb—they turned to find both weapons trained on them. Six eyes immediately focused on Akane.

"You," spat the one who'd been talking to Sked earlier.

"Hands up," Akane said. When they complied, she continued. "How do you want it? In the head?" She brought the gun up. "In the chest?" Akane brought it down a bit and then continued. She smiled. "I think I'll shoot you in the nuts, just to watch you bleed out knowing you'll die as less than a man."

"Stop it," Sked said. "No one is shooting anyone. Not yet." He eyed their three captives. "Not unless you do something stupid."

The look the three guys gave him made the dinosaur look downright friendly.

"Now," Sked said. "You guys don't sound like you're from Shanghai, so maybe we can understand each other. I assume you know who we are?" The one who'd been talking, the leader, nodded. "And we know why you're here."

Sked's original plan had been to keep them busy until resort security showed up and then hand them over to someone who owned cable ties before disappearing back out into the great wide world, hopefully better hidden than they'd managed this time around.

"Now, we don't want to be killed, and I assume you don't want to die, either."

"Not particularly, but it probably wouldn't make much difference," the Triad man said. "If you shoot us now, you're probably going to save us a good deal of grief."

"What?"

"We lost our observer," the leader replied. "The guy Beijing sent over to see that the hit was carried out correctly got torn to pieces by those things back there. If you hadn't been there, or if we'd screwed up the killing, it would have been bad for our careers, but not fatal. This? We're dead men walking. So if you put one between each of our eyes, at least it will be a quick death. Even if that bitch shoots me in the nuts, I figure I still come out ahead."

"Just say the word, motherfucker," Akane said.

Sked smiled. "You heard her. And if you did your research, you know she'll do it, too. Your call."

The man sighed. "Dammit. What do you want?"

"First off, tell Eddie to drop his chopper. I really don't want to have to worry about that any more than I have to. That's right, kick it over here." He bent to pick the watermelon knife off the floor and hefted it. Vicious thing; no wonder the Triads loved them. Then he turned back to the leader. "You know who I am but I haven't had the pleasure. Why don't we start with introductions?"

"I'm Harold, he's Mike and you've already met Eddie."

"You don't sound Chinese."

"We're from Philly."

Sked chuckled. "Wasn't expecting that one. Now, the only reason I haven't let Akane here shoot you is that we have a bit of a situation."

"You mean apart from your dinosaur infestation?"

"That's part of it, of course. But it gets worse. We think there might actually be cannibals on this island. Or at least natives who don't like us much. As you can tell by that fence, the truce between the natives and the resort is a bit iffy. We think it's breaking down." He paused. "Also, some of the people back at the hotel think there's some kind of monster in the water, but I just think they drank too much punch during the resort bingo night."

"I saw something, too," the guy named Mike said. "Behind us, in the water. It was big, but not big enough to catch our Zodiac."

Sked's interest surged. "You have a Zodiac? How big?"

Harold glared at Mike but, after Sked waved the gun encouragingly, he replied. "Six-man unit. So eight people at a pinch. Nine if the extras are kids." He shrugged. "The guy who sold it to me said we could load it up with whatever we could fit onto it and it wouldn't sink or slow the boat down too much. Not sure if that's true."

"Pretty much," Sked replied. "Those things are awesome. It's a real one, I assume, not some second-rate knockoff for the wannabe warrior trade?"

"The real thing."

"Good. Because we need to get as many people as we can off this island, and we just don't have the boats we need to do it right now. How far from here did you leave it?"

"A couple hundred yards."

"Good." Sked waved the gun. "I need you guys to march back to the resort. Stay where I can see you. You already saw that I can shoot this thing. I don't want to shoot anyone, but if you run, I can probably hit you before you take five steps. Akane tends to aim for the head if she can't shoot you in the balls."

The three men nodded glumly and trudged in the indicated direction. Once away from the fence, Sked breathed easier.

He'd played dumb with Akane earlier, drawing her out to see what she was thinking, but he agreed with her 100%. The fence just didn't work for him as a protection for the resort, either. Her idea that there was something in the empty jungle behind the hotel area was probably the right one.

And if that were true, it meant that there were people watching the fence... and he suspected he didn't want to meet them.

Or maybe he did. Because if there were people watching, and they didn't think that three guys with guns being chased by a pack of dinosaurs isn't enough to merit coming over for a look... then whatever they did consider a threat was probably an awful thing.

"Keep moving, guys," he said as they emerged from the wooded path into the first of the clearings where the cabins lay. Sked had brought them along this path so he could stash them inside the room he shared with Akane and avoid awkward questions, at least until he could think of a good story.

Once inside, he sat the men on the bed and left Akane to cover them while he went off to get some rope. The jet ski had been tied to the dock, which meant that there would be some unused cord over there.

The night was dark and muggy. The moon had set a few minutes before, and there was no wind to speak of. The beach was lit by torches, which had seemed romantic when they arrived, but now just macabre, disrespecting those who'd died on the island and the woman fighting for her life in the infirmary. Shadows flickered here and there, giving the impression that things moved on the beach.

One thing didn't move, though. The Colonel was standing, toes in the water, staring out to sea. He faced in the other direction, but Sked got the feeling that, despite this and the distance, the old man knew exactly where Sked was and what he was doing.

He cut the cord and hurried back to the cabin, hoping Akane hadn't shot anyone in his absence.

She hadn't, so he tied them up. Mike and Harold seemed resigned to their fates, but Eddie gave him chills. The man looked at him with a slightly amused expression as if thinking that a real professional would have killed all three of them already. It was a face that said that staying alive was fun because it meant that Eddie could come after them and carve them to pieces at his leisure.

Still, Sked maintained his posture that he wouldn't kill anyone unless it was completely necessary. He avoided Akane's gaze, though. He knew she disagreed, and she didn't have to do what he told her, so it was best that it didn't become an issue.

"Okay," the man named Harold said. "Now what?"

"Now we come to an agreement," Sked replied. "I think you guys, given your... specialized skillset might be able to help us out here. Other than a couple of people—a former Colonel and a big Marine girl who looks like she could bench press the lot of us—I don't think anyone else is going to be of any use in defending the resort from what I think is about to hit us."

"And you want us to help? How do you know we won't just kill you the first time you turn around?"

"Yeah," Akane echoed. "I'm interested in that bit, too."

"I trust any Triad member who gives his word to keep it. I've played the game all over Asia, and I've never seen anyone back away from it. Do you guys value your honor in Philadelphia?"

"Of course."

"Then we have nothing to worry about. I call a truce. You promise not to move on us, and to help us get the hell off this place and I give you your lives."

Harold glared at him. "No can do. I've sworn oaths that are more important than this one. If my superiors ask me to kill you later, that's what I'm going to do."

"I thought you said they were going to kill you."

"They might. But that's their choice. I'm not breaking the oath."

"Kill them now," Akane said. "He's still working for the Chinks. He'll put a slug in the back of your head as soon as you turn around."

"Wait," Harold said. "How about we hold the truce until everyone in this room is off the island?"

"We'll need a couple of days after that to disappear. How about we hold it until you get orders to break it?" Sked countered.

"How about someone tells me what is happening here?" a new voice, deep and ragged, inquired. "No, don't turn around. Just lay the weapons on the floor very slowly."

Sked complied and, keeping his hands up, turned to face the man who'd interrupted them.

"Hello, Colonel," he said, amused to note that the man wasn't even armed. He had only *sounded* armed to the teeth. "You may be able to help us out."

CHAPTER 9

"I don't care what you might need the ship for," Cora said. "I have an injured woman I need to get to Andumar, and the lifeboat belongs to Mr. Lai, not to the resort. You should be thankful that he allowed you to send one of your people along in the first place." She glared at the manager.

The little man looked like one of those little jackasses that have to have their own way every time, and the fact that someone had given him a position of relative importance had only made him worse. He was the kind of guy, were he not protected by the outrage of a society that frowned on such things, whose lights she would happily have punched out. A large purple bruise on the bottom of his jaw, and swelling spreading across half his face made her think that someone had beat her to it. Maybe that Sked guy, who spoke the lingo and walked like a special forces soldier, even if he didn't quite look the part.

"I insist that you allow us…"

"Go away, little man," Cora said. "Send one of your people if you like."

He turned a beetroot shade of red, but went nowhere.

Mr. Lai had already shepherded most of his people into the lifeboat, after first authorizing the removal of six seats—two entire rows—from the craft in order to accommodate the stricken woman. The doctor said that she should be all right to transport, but she didn't look all right to Cora. Anyone who'd looked like that out in the field would have been given immediate Medevac, even behind enemy lines.

So that left nine seats on the lifeboat. The first was taken by the sailor who'd driven them over. Two more went to Cora and whoever the resort sent. The other six were filled with Lai's young executives, by the old man's order: he charged them with making contact with the company and getting aid, as well as trying to locate the yacht, of which there had been no further sign since they abandoned ship.

That left the cook and the surviving bunny, as well as the remaining soldiers and Mr. Lai himself to wait for rescue.

"Are you sure you don't want my place, sir?" she asked Lai.

He shook his head. "No. I need someone who can kick ass if necessary on the boat. You're the only one who qualifies. If someone panics—and those six are the most likely candidates—you can subdue them physically, which is something I can't do."

"They'll do whatever you say."

He shook his head again and for a moment, Cora could see his age in his features. "Only until they get scared. Once that happens, what their boss says becomes secondary, and they become panicked herd animals. I don't think these guys are physically brave in the least."

"You could leave one of them behind."

This time he laughed. "That would land me on the front page of every newspaper in Malaysia." He made air quotes. "Billionaire abandons employees on cannibal-infested island. Would do wonders for my image. No. It's best that I stay here. Hell, if the cannibals and dinosaurs leave us alone, I'll try to get some rest."

She didn't like it, and would have preferred to keep him in her sight, but she had her marching orders, and she wasn't about to start disobeying at this point in her life. "Yes, sir." Cora turned to the manager. "Have you chosen the employee, yet?"

"Yes. I'm coming."

"Don't you need to be here to run the resort?"

"They'll be fine without me." He didn't meet her gaze. "I'm the best one to speak to the authorities."

Yeah, sure, Cora thought. *You're not fooling anyone, you little chickenshit coward.*

But she didn't say it and just nodded and motioned him in ahead of her. It was easy to see why some men engendered the loyalty that Mr. Lai did while others had bruises on their chin.

They'd already pushed the lifeboat to the edge of the water, so it only took a few more tugs by the people left on shore to get it afloat.

The sailor at the helm gently steered the prow into the tiny breakers and accelerated into the water.

Cora turned back and spoke to the doctor: "How is she?"

"Weak, but steady. If he can do it without things getting too rough, it would be best if the man at the wheel gave us all possible speed."

"I'll talk to him, but I know from our earlier trip that this isn't a fast boat."

"Do what you can."

She turned towards the front again, not because she needed to face the sailor to ask him about the ship's performance but because she hadn't liked the look in the doctor's eyes. He wasn't optimistic about the woman's chances, but he didn't want to say it out loud. She'd seen that look in a medic's eyes only once, out on a training exercise in the Pacific with the Nimitz carrier group.

A sailor had fallen from a mast onto the deck of the deployment ship she was stationed on, right when she'd been on loan to the ship's Navy crew for the glamorous duty of sorting through garbage. The guy had landed on a generator twenty feet away and impaled himself on an exhaust port or something.

He'd been alive when she reached him. Alive when the Navy boys working her detail had helped her pull him off the equipment and onto the floor, and alive when the medics arrived to wheel the man away on the stretcher.

The medic, when he thanked her for acting quickly, had worn the same expression as the doctor in the lifeboat.

After her shift, she'd gone up to the infirmary and learned that the sailor had died shortly after arrival of multiple massive internal injuries.

It hadn't surprised her in the least. After that, she'd found the medic and gotten drunk with him. It seemed the right thing to do.

She took a couple of minutes to compose herself before speaking to the man driving the lifeboat. He confirmed what she already knew: the leisurely pace they boasted currently was as fast as the boat could go. It would be a long trip, made longer by the stress of having a woman on board who desperately needed them to move faster.

"Don't we have an emergency beacon?" she asked the sailor.

"Yes. But those are only for ships in need of immediate relief."

"This counts. Hit the beacon. I'll take responsibility for any nautical crimes we may be committing. Hell, if the Indian Coast Guard sends anything faster than this, we'll be giving her a better chance."

Lai trained his men well. The guy just nodded, released a plastic rectangle meant to keep the beacon from accidental activation and mashed a big red button.

She turned back to the doctor, surprised at how far the island seemed. They'd made nearly half a mile.

As she opened her mouth to speak, the words caught in her throat, making an "aaaaah" sound. Her face must have shown her utter shock as well, because the doctor raised an eyebrow and turned to see what she was looking at.

What she was looking at were teeth the size of her legs framing a mouth like Carlsbad Caverns.

Cora did something she hadn't done in years. She screamed. It was a gut reaction, the primate inside her suddenly released, and she stopped as soon as she realized what an un-Marine-like sound she was uttering.

Her yell served as a warning to the others in the boat that something was very, very wrong.

The quickest to react was the executive who'd been giving all the trouble. He glanced over his shoulder, saw the gaping maw, full of water and beginning to close, and dashed for the front of the lifeboat.

A split second later, when he was halfway across the distance between them, the boat began to tilt backward and the rest of the passengers began to react. Most of them never got out of their seats before the boat tilted back and threw them towards the rear window and the open mouth.

But the man who'd moved first wasn't about to give up. He threw himself forward and reached for Cora's outstretched hand. She grabbed his arm in midair, pulling him slowly towards her as she fought gravity.

That was when the world became a maelstrom of noise and water.

As Cora watched, the teeth closed around the boat, tearing through it like it was made of paper, and allowing foaming saltwater to enter from all over and swamp her. Just before her head went under, she gagged on the smell of rotting fish.

The wall of water buffeted her around and she went down. Her mind barely had time to register what had happened before the waves took her down: something, some unimaginably colossal thing, had bitten the lifeboat in half. Only the man driving, Cora herself, and another one of Lai's executives had been on the right side of the bite.

Now she was underwater with no idea which way was up.

She panicked for a second, but then she realized her training had already taken hold: she was breathing out, just enough to keep water from filling her nose. That meant she was upside down.

There. She got herself righted and tried to open her eyes. That stung like hell and she wasn't able to get a good bearing on where she was—the sun was always up, but had she actually spotted it?—but still, she swam towards where she thought up was. She was aware that her body might be getting its signals crossed, but there was nothing she could do about it except to keep swimming. As long as water wasn't trying to get into her nose, she wasn't heading towards the bottom.

Or was she? She'd been going for longer than even a decent dipping at the hands of the monster should have accounted for. Normally, she wouldn't be too worried about hitting the bottom, but they'd been out pretty far when they got hit. What if the bottom was a mile away?

Her lungs burned, more a sign of her near-panicked state than a sign of having been in the water too long.

Also, there was something wrong with her right hand: it wasn't moving through the water the way she was expecting it to. It was dragging along as if it had been mangled. The weird part was she didn't feel any pain. *Probably the adrenalin*, she thought.

All right. She was probably going to die, so she tried opening her eyes again and forced herself to keep them open. No sun in sight, so she turned the other way. Still no sun.

She was damned if she was going to drown without a fight. She kicked hard in the direction she thought was up. Three seconds, four seconds. She had to breathe.

She felt weakness begin in her legs…

Her head broke through the surface.

Cora breathed. She would have cried for joy, but that would have meant breathing less, so she breathed and breathed. For a moment, she didn't care that there was a gigantic monster in the water with her. She didn't care that she had a half-mile swim ahead of her. All she wanted to do was breathe.

And she did. It felt better than anything she'd ever experienced.

Unfortunately, she was a Marine, and the personality traits that had made her a good one—combined with the training she'd received at the hands of even better ones—didn't allow her to simply enjoy the feeling. She needed to assess her situation and see how to solve it.

First off, she was still in deep shit. No way around that. The dunking and lack of air hadn't done her stamina any good, and a half-mile swim hadn't been fun even back when she was trained to within an inch of her life. She didn't know the sea or currents around the island either, which just added to the joy.

Secondly. She had to check that arm. It was dragging along in the water. She turned to look, expecting to find a bloody stump where her hand had been.

She found a bloody stump, but it wasn't hers. She was still holding the hand of the man who'd jumped for her in the lifeboat. The hand, most of the forearm... and nothing else. That was what she had been dragging along.

"Yuck," she said and pried the dead fingers off her before throwing the arm out as far as she could.

The action galvanized her. She turned to the island, aimed for the resort and, silently singing an obscene Marine marching song in her head, she swam.

And swam, and swam. The island looked like it wasn't getting any closer.

She'd done this before, though, and knew how it worked. She put her head down and swam some more.

This time, when she looked up, the shore was visibly nearer.

But there was something else. A dark point just in front of her bobbed up and down. Had someone else survived?

It would be the one bright spot in the unmitigated disaster that was the end of her professional career. Now, she couldn't even save the ones that were in her sight. She wondered if the Foreign Legion accepted people her age... or whether she would have to join one of the mercenary organizations in Africa. She was tough, but those units were hell on women.

She swam towards the black point. She didn't think about the massive ugly in the water with them. If that thing decided it needed a light snack after chomping the boat, there was nothing at all she could do to stop it. She didn't know what it was, except that it was neither a fish nor a whale. Its skin looked more like the smooth leather of a giant crocodile... but that wasn't it either.

It didn't matter. What mattered was that she needed to get back on land. Water wasn't her element and while the creature might be able to walk on land—where it would be formidable indeed—at least Cora knew how to defend herself there.

So she swam.

To her surprise, the dot didn't get closer. Whoever was swimming out there was as good as she was and keeping his lead. She didn't expect that of the executives, but it would have made sense for the sailor driving the lifeboat to swim well.

Eternal minutes later, arms and legs afire, she was helped onto the beach by the Colonel and the guy who called himself Sked. As soon as her body was fully out of the water, she collapsed onto the floor beside the other swimmer, arms and legs burning.

It was the doctor.

For a moment, dismay warred with disbelief. Dismay that the people she was paid to protect had died. Disbelief that anything in the back half of the lifeboat had survived to tell the tale. She'd seen the teeth snap shut. That was it. It had to be it.

She was still panting hard, but she sat up, just to prove that Marines were tougher than doctors—even than this doctor, who seemed to be indestructible—and caught his eye. "How the hell did you get out?" she said. "I saw you die."

The man didn't answer immediately. He got on all fours and then, with difficulty, onto his knees. "Lactic acidosis," he grimaced. "I barely made it."

"I was right behind you. If you'd gone under, I would have gone after you."

"You barely made it out yourself. But to answer your question, I saw myself die as well. The teeth..." he shuddered. "I was saved because a piece of one of the seats caught between two of the teeth. I grabbed it and held on when it swallowed everything and everyone else. So when it opened its mouth to chomp the rest of the boat, I was still in the mouth. I got the hell out of there and swam away as fast as I could."

"Did anyone else make it?"

He studied the sand before raising his head and holding her gaze. "I'm ashamed to admit that I didn't check. I just swam for my life."

She suddenly realized she'd done the same. Of course, in her case it was mostly because she hadn't known which way was up, but after getting out of the water, she hadn't even thought about looking for other survivors. "Yeah, me too," she said. It hurt like hell to admit it, but she wasn't one to run from hard truths.

The doctor's gaze never wavered. "You didn't have a patient to think of. I did."

Anger flashed. "I was responsible for everyone on that lifeboat. They're all dead, except for you. And that was no thanks to me."

"Enough," the Colonel said. "I saw what happened out there. Irene and I were walking along the beach and we saw the whole thing. No one could have predicted that monster, and no one would have been able to do anything. Just surviving and getting back here was superhuman. So stop pretending to be more noble than you are and pick yourselves up." He gave Cora a glare that she knew well. Hell, it was the kind of look she'd used on noobs in her unit until she retired. "Get up, soldier."

It hurt like hell—something she suspected the Colonel already knew—but she got up. She even stood at attention. Had she been up for inspection, the man would have had no cause for complaint.

"With all due respect, sir, I was responsible for those people. And it's not just moping. I failed completely and everyone's dead."

"Yes, they are. And you probably won't be keeping your job. *But none of that matters.* The job isn't done yet. You can feel sorry for yourself when it is."

"Yes, sir." She nearly saluted, but caught herself. She wasn't a soldier anymore, even if the old man was playing on her training. She wouldn't give him the satisfaction of a complete victory.

But even as she walked off to confront Lai, she smiled. That old bastard of an officer knew exactly what to say to her. She'd heard he was SAS, and by his age, he would have been a young commando in the middle of both The Troubles and the first Iraq War. He'd probably seen a thing or two in his time.

Lai was unrecognizable, his gaze fixed out beyond the horizon.

"I'm sorry, sir. I tried."

He shook his head and focused on her. "I know. I never thought... monsters. Real ones. I'm glad you got out."

"I wish I'd gotten the rest of them out. I know you valued them."

"I know you didn't like them, but they were bright men. They had futures. Some of them had young families. They were my next generation of managers, the people I was going to trust to run my companies so I could take a rest."

"I'm sorry."

Lai chuckled, a little of his former personality returning to his face. "You are the only person I've ever met who would blame themselves for losing people to Godzilla."

"I trained to fight stuff much more dangerous, and smarter than an overgrown fish, sir."

Her boss' recovery was complete. He looked at her with a piercing gaze. "Back then you knew what you would be fighting," he replied levelly. "So now that you know, what's the plan?"

"You mean my plan for dealing with armed cannibals, hungry chickensaurs and Godzilla water monsters?"

"Yes. That and finding out who put them here so I can get revenge for this."

"That's all you want from me?"

"Even if you resign, you still work for me until the end of the month. It was in our agreement."

How the hell he could remember what he'd signed with every single one of his people was beyond her, but if he said it, it was true.

"I'll need to think about it."

"Hurry," Lai said. "I suspect we'll be needing that plan before long."

"I think I'll talk to the Colonel," she replied. "And to that Sked character. He knows more than he's saying."

"Good. I'll let you get to it."

***

Sabrina played the video again. She watched the colossal jaws close over the lifeboat and tear it to shreds. It was marvelous to see, but she was concerned about Shiva's stomach. That was a lot of fiberglass to digest.

Even so, Jermaine would be ecstatic. You couldn't create better publicity than this. She'd been disappointed that the

Vanarisa hadn't sunk after all, and that it was still afloat a few miles off the island, caught on a sandbar where her beasties couldn't reach it. But the drones had confirmed that it wasn't going anywhere for the time being. The crew had lashed a lifeboat to the side to keep it steady and a couple of men were attempting to make repairs.

They could deal with the yacht later. In its current state, Shiva or Kali would make quick work of it.

In the meantime, they also needed to deal with the people on the island. If they were killed by the dinosaurs, they served as actors in company commercials, albeit unwilling ones.

If they survived, they were witnesses.

Jermaine had been very clear on that: there could be no witnesses.

But that, too, was a problem for another time. Right now, she wanted to watch that lifeboat die again. And then she'd watch the footage of the Compsognathus killing that woman in the cage.

"Yes," she whispered.

That clip was lovely. Even better than the one with the Chinese men in the dark. Pity that some of those guys had made it over the fence.

She relaxed in bed and selected the next one to watch again.

CHAPTER 10

"It doesn't make sense," Sked said.

Akane looked up. She was doing a crossword puzzle... which seemed utterly unbelievable on a number of levels. For one thing, Akane wasn't the kind of person who did crossword puzzles.

But it went deeper than that. Quite aside from the puzzle itself, Akane was more relaxed than he'd ever seen her. Normally she was taut as a bowstring just before the arrow was released. She lived at high-energy and high velocity, crashed for a few hours and then did it again. There was no halt, little pause. Even just after making love, she was thinking about the next step, staying in bed only moments after they were done, maybe to smoke something—never a joint, and never tobacco, and Sked never accepted a drag when she offered... he didn't even want to know—and then began to pace like a caged lion.

And now she was lying on a beach lounge chair doing a crossword puzzle while men sent to kill her wandered around on the beach beside her.

The worst part about it was that she knew perfectly well that their situation was precarious. Not only were the Triads a threat—albeit a temporarily abated one—but there were also the small matters of the cannibals, the dinosaurs and the sea monster that had trapped them on the island so they couldn't escape either of the aforementioned problems.

Apparently, however, that threat level was so much lower than what Akane was used to in her everyday existence that she needed to entertain herself with crosswords...

Sked couldn't begin to imagine what the rest of her life was like, and he suspected she would never let him in far enough to actually see. Their relationship pretty much consisted of getting together every few weeks to jump in bed and, on occasion, having Sked pull her out of some deadly situation of her own making. The Chinese jail had been the latest of an ever-escalating series of serious issues he'd solved for her.

For his own part, Sked wouldn't have been able to concentrate on a crossword for all the oil in Saudi Arabia.

"What doesn't?" Akane asked when it became clear he wasn't going to volunteer anything else.

"None of it. This island was supposed to be empty when the Buddha recommended it. Suddenly, it seems to have become the epicenter for everything. Armed cannibals and dinosaurs and monsters and the Triads. A yachtful of morons with a billionaire patron. Yes, I know the Triads supposedly followed us to get here, but come on, there's no way they could have tracked our escape all the way to Andaman without help. More than one person had to talk."

"The Triads can make a stone talk."

"Yeah... but the Triads weren't the ones at the back end of that trail. That was the Chinese government."

Akane shrugged. "The Triads are probably a lot closer related to the government than anyone imagines. At the very least, they have people who talk to them."

"I'm not so sure about that, but even if it's true, why would the Chinese put them on our trail? Why not come after us themselves? I'm convinced someone else sent the Triad guys here... and we weren't killed because we got lucky."

"The Buddha?"

"Maybe. But the Buddha sent us here... and he had to have known this place was about to get crowded. That's the kind of thing he knows."

"So you think he wanted us to die?"

"I thought about that... but no. He could have had the crew of the fishing boat chop us into bait if that's what he wanted." Sked looked out into the sea. At least there was no sign of ship-eating monsters out there. "No. He wanted us here for some reason. He doesn't want us dead."

"Why?"

"I suspect there's something here he doesn't like, and everything that's happened since is his way of making life difficult for whatever that is."

"I don't think the Buddha would be too bothered by a second-rate beach resort and a bunch of cannibals."

"No. He wouldn't be. And he wouldn't send us out after it either. Hackers and Triad thugs would make very little difference to a lost tribe." He paused. "There's something else here."

Akane laughed. "*More* stuff? You were just saying how ridiculously complicated this mess already is and now you postulate there's something else on the island? Are you even listening to yourself?"

Sked sighed. "You might be right. But I want to look at whatever is in those trees behind the resort. You coming?"

"What, now?"

"I'm too nervous to do a crossword."

"Wuss."

But she got up and they headed towards the cabin to get more suitable shoes. The Colonel crossed their path as they moved up the beach. "Going somewhere?"

"Into the jungle behind the cabins."

That earned them a raised eyebrow. "And why, may I ask?"

"We like to have sex outdoors and we'd rather not have an audience," Akane said. "Now, if you don't mind. We'll be back in an hour. Two if my husband here can last that long."

The agreement was that the Colonel would help keep the Triad men to their word while, at the same time keeping Sked and Akane from escaping the island. So the man wasn't just being nosy... but Sked still had to snicker at the fact that anyone would dare to speak to the bluff Englishman that way.

The Colonel turned red and said, "All right, carry on, then. But if you're not back for lunch, I'll let them go in after you."

"Tell them to bring cameras," Akane said and walked on, leaving the former special forces soldier open-mouthed behind her.

Sked stifled his laughter and followed her.

The woods were a dense tangle directly behind the cabins, so they walked along the resort's forest paths.

"Did you notice something?" Sked said. "The forest is much denser towards the middle of the empty area than towards the edges. It's almost as if they planted more undergrowth here than natural."

It was true. To their right, the trees along the path were widely-spaced and one could easily walk into the woods. On their left were vines, creepers and all sorts of ground vegetation that would require a machete.

"So let's go the way the forest doesn't want us to."

They pushed into the weeds on the left and made it a few yards. "We'll need to go get better equipment," Sked panted.

"No. Wait a second," Akane replied. "I think..." She pushed on a particularly thick clump of leaves which gave way to reveal a much more sparsely vegetated area that resembled the other side of the path. "How much do you want to wager that someone put that tangle in to stop curious people from walking in?"

"No bet," Sked replied. "I'm already convinced."

He was even more convinced when they found a well-maintained path heading deeper into the jungle.

"Not subtle," Akane observed.

"Not in the least. And neither is the surveillance." He nodded towards a tree. About halfway up the trunk someone had bolted a security camera. Wires ran down the bole and into a green tube buried underground so only one extreme was visible.

"We should probably go back," Akane said.

"No. Let's pretend to be what we're supposed to be. Kiss me."

They held the clinch for a few moments and then walked along the path hand-in-hand, superficially just two lovers out for a stroll.

"You think anyone will buy this?" Akane asked.

"Just keep selling it."

They made excellent time along the path. Not having to push through the underbrush made progress effortless. Within minutes, the path came up to a concrete structure seven or eight meters wide with a large door built into it. It was an old structure, stained with damp and with moss growing over it in places. The door, four meters wide and nearly three tall, looked like it could withstand a missile strike. Sked would have pegged it for something left over from WWII except for one thing: it had a keypad lock with the Bharat Electronics logo emblazoned on it.

"Keep walking, pretend we're not interested," he said with a smile, and goosed her just as they passed the next camera.

"You're overselling," Akane replied with a smile that said he was an utter moron.

He knew this was the critical juncture. Whoever was inside the structure would look askance at anyone investigating, and if they believed Akane and Sked had ulterior motives for being where they were, they could come out and grab them with no witnesses. But they'd most likely leave them alone: it was much smarter to ignore people who wouldn't care or even understand what they were looking at than to create questions by kidnapping tourists.

Most of the resort's inhabitants, after all, would just shrug off the structure as some old storage unit.

They wouldn't know that you didn't put a keypad lock like that one on a random storage unit.

They continued along the path without slowing or speeding up until they reached the other end, kissed a few times for effect and then pushed through the undergrowth to get back into the familiar resort forest.

"You've established that there is something strange and secret hidden back there. My question is what are we going to do about it? Are we going to grab our guns and try to invade?"

"What? No. Why would we do that? We don't know what's in there."

Akane raised an eyebrow. "We know the Buddha's interested. Shouldn't that be enough?"

"Not necessarily. Knowing the Buddha, it might be a warehouse full of old personnel records, stuff he can mine for incriminating evidence about people he wants to blackmail," Sked replied.

"But then why has everyone converged on this island? The only reason we even went looking for something is that you felt there was too much going on for it to be explained away."

Sked sighed. "I hate it when you use my own words against me. All right. So what if there's an Indian Army data center down there? You want to storm it with the guns we took from those Triad guys? Hell, we barely have any bullets left. For all we know, they could have a battalion hidden in there."

"Then what now?"

"I need to think."

"All right," Akane said. "Then I'm going to get something to eat and take a nap. See you."

She walked off, leaving him open-mouthed. They were stuck on this island, surrounded by enemies and monsters, but he had no doubt that she would eat and take her nap without being troubled in the least.

He hurried after her. Maybe she was right.

***

As it transpired, they didn't take a nap. Akane grabbed him as they went in the door of the cabin and kissed him deeply. A couple of hours later, they heard something from outside.

"What the hell?" Akane said.

"Gunshot," Sked replied.

"I thought we'd taken their guns?" The Colonel, fortunately, had let them keep their weapons after they'd explained the situation.

"Only the Triads'. I bet the Colonel has one, probably something obnoxious like a Desert Eagle. He probably decided to try to take out Godzilla with a handgun."

They dressed quickly and blinked as they came into the light.

To their surprise, the Colonel hurried past their door just as they emerged, lacking in handguns of any description. He was heading towards the northern border of the resort. He stopped when he saw them standing there, just as surprised to encounter them as they were to see him.

"It wasn't us," Sked said.

The three of them ran along the path toward the fence. Once there, they looked to the right and saw the big former Marine, the woman who'd come in with the lifeboats, inspecting a heap on the ground.

She stood when she saw them approach and nodded towards it. "One of the natives, trying to climb over. He was aiming an arrow at the German woman back there, so I shot him off the fence."

Sked noticed she was carrying a pistol, a serious-looking semi-automatic befitting of a former member of the armed forces.

"We should probably tell the management," the Colonel said.

"There were more of them," the woman replied. "They ran off when this guy fell, but they weren't happy."

As if to underscore her words, an arrow whistled out of the trees, clanged against the fence and fell short of their position, fletched shaft quivering in the sand.

"We should get to cover," the Colonel said. "Immediately."

They sprinted to the nearest cabin and watched the fence from behind its wall. The Colonel beat them to the place. He could still run, although he was puffing when they arrived.

One of the blue-shirted resort workers was moving in the opposite direction and Sked grabbed him as he passed, bringing him to safety.

"What's going on?" the man sputtered.

Sked recognized him as the guy in charge of the bar in the afternoon—a young Thai with a great sense of humor. And a guy always willing to tell a guest when they'd had enough to drink. A good man. "We need to get everyone off the beach and bring them together behind that cabin. Can you do that?"

"Sure, but why?"

"Islanders are attacking."

"Attacking?"

"Just do it. We'll explain to everyone together."

The guy wasn't the manager—that worthy had been chomped attempting to save himself when the lifeboat was attacked—and that might actually have been a good thing. He didn't argue, didn't bluster or try to tell them that they weren't in charge; he just set off in the direction of the old woman sunning herself by the shore.

Sked chuckled. She'd been the target of the original arrow, and the Marine girl had saved her with a very loud gunshot... but the woman didn't even appear to notice anything untoward was going on.

Three men appeared from behind the cabin. Sked tensed when he recognized the Triad criminals from Philadelphia.

"What the hell's happening? We heard gunfire."

"One of the natives tried to climb the fence." Sked pointed to the Marine, who had broken cover and was standing on the beach looking at the fence. "She shot him."

"That woman?"

"Yeah. Apparently she was a Marine and now works security for a rich guy," Akane said.

"Looks like she could kick the shit out of all three of us."

The woman walked back to where they were standing. "I don't need to kick the shit out of you," she replied, showing that her hearing was much better than any of them had suspected. "I have a gun. By the way, the name's Cora. Cora Gimenez. And I wasn't just a Marine, I was a Marine sergeant, which means that I'm one of the meanest people you will ever meet. And from this moment on, you're all going to do exactly what I tell you to, unless the Colonel over there prefers to take command of this island."

"What?" one of the Triad guys, Mike, said, spitting into the sand. "No way, bitch."

She moved quickly. A second later the offending man was down on the ground with Cora kneeling on his chest, her fist cocked to strike again.

"I'm sorry, I didn't quite catch that," she said.

The man chuckled. "I thought you weren't going to kick the shit out of us."

That actually got a laugh. "I said I didn't need to. I never said I wouldn't do it just for fun." She looked at the rest of them. "I have a feeling I don't have time to train the people here, but you need to understand that following orders saves lives. The Colonel and I are the only ones here who have seen real combat."

"That's not entirely accurate," Sked said. "I've deployed on some umm... unofficial missions."

"How unofficial?"

"Let's just say that if governments were involved, they wouldn't want me telling you so. But I know my way around both the command structure of small-unit covert operations and the kind of equipment they use. Urban and jungle."

She rolled her eyes. "One of those. All right. Anyone else?"

No one spoke, so she got up and helped the Triad guy to his feet.

"Then let's go talk to the rest of the guests."

***

Cora looked over the faces in the crowd and sighed. Keeping these people alive on an excursion to a suburban mall would be hard enough... if the natives actually kept coming.

They would. Murphy's law guaranteed it. And if the islanders were smart, they'd come at night.

"All right. Listen up. We're in deep trouble, so I need everyone to pay attention. First off," she turned to the staff. "Is everyone here?"

The people in the blue shirts counted heads, conferred amongst themselves and finally one of them, the guy who'd been with them before, spoke. "It's kind of hard to know for sure, because we don't know exactly how many people came in on lifeboats, but we think so. All the guests are here for sure, and so is the staff."

"Thank you." She'd already done the headcount of Lai's people, and the ones that weren't dead were accounted for. The bunny in the British bikini was there with the cook as were the sailors who hadn't been involved in the doomed escape run.

She nearly teared up to see the blond girl and the cook. Of the people she had sent on the other lifeboat, she suspected these were the only two who'd survived. And she was glad that the English girl had been one of them—Cora suspected that she hadn't had an easy life, and the whole party-sex-kitten act was her way of getting out of a bad situation.

Not every poor girl could join the Marines.

"The natives tried to get in here earlier. They will try again, and if they do, they will kill every last one of us and then they will cook us and eat us."

An American woman, fiftyish and with blue-tinted hair, spoke: "How can this be? Are you saying that they built this resort knowing it was surrounded by cannibals?"

"I have no idea, ma'am," Cora replied. "I think the manager might have known, but he isn't around. Anyone else have any ideas?"

The blue-shirted guy who'd been elected speaker for the staff shrugged. "Not a clue. We just work here."

"Well, this is unacceptable," the woman said. "You should just speak to the natives and apologize for coming here in the first place. This is the kind of abuse of native rights that leads to this kind of thing."

"Sure," Cora smiled. "Feel free to do that. We'll wait for you here."

"What... No, I mean..." Beside the blue-haired woman, Cora was amused to see her husband trying to pretend he didn't know her. Their domestic life must, she thought, be interesting.

"No one here was present when the initial talks with the natives happened so, since you kindly elected yourself human rights monitor, please go ahead and negotiate on our behalf."

"I meant someone else should do it."

"Of course you did. But since that is the dumbest suggestion ever, I would ask that you shut the hell up now."

"I don't have to listen to this."

"No, you don't. So leave. But I won't let anyone who stays with me lift a finger to help you when the natives come. I'm sure they'll find you tasty."

"The staff has to help me."

"The staff have to try to stay alive. You are less than irrelevant."

"You can't talk to me like that."

That was it. Cora took a step forward and looked down at the obnoxious lady. "If I hear another word from you, I'll beat you senseless and leave you here for the cannibals. An offering, if you like. So now either get out of my sight or shut the fuck up."

With that, Cora turned her attention away from the woman, and back to the staff. They would be the most helpful of the people, the ones who knew the lay of the land and what supplies were in store.

And her verbal abuse of that particular guest seemed to have gone down well with them. They smiled to each other as they observed the woman's discomfiture. Some guests just had that effect on people, she supposed.

She'd made some allies. That, in turn, might make all the difference.

CHAPTER 11

Sabrina growled in frustration. The Compsognathus herd was doing nothing interesting, just ambling through the forest. She knew there were hundreds of natives living in those woods… but they were nowhere in sight. They must have some kind of camouflaged living spaces.

Either that or they had all climbed into the trees. There was no sign of them or of the foreign visitors from the yacht and its lifeboats.

Likewise, there was no sign of anyone doing anything in the water.

Ratzenberger had located the yacht, but it had run aground in water too shallow for Kali and Shiva to approach… and no one on the island seemed inclined to sail out where her pets could reach them.

Most frustrating of all was the fence around the resort. The thing was too tall to climb and too sturdy to topple. Maybe if, as Jermaine had wanted, they'd been able to build bigger land dinosaurs, it would have been a different story. Unfortunately, as things stood, there were a couple of dozen clueless people inside the fence who, unlike the islanders, couldn't melt into the forest at will.

Except she couldn't reach them.

"Dammit," she said, and rose to stretch and take a walk.

About halfway around the ship, an idea hit her. Moments later she was knocking on Tim Rugger's door.

"We have cell phones, you know," the logistics director said when he answered her knock. He was dressed in nothing but a yellow towel wrapped around his waist, and Sabrina thought she could discern movement on the bed in his cabin as someone tried to cover herself with the sheets. The red hair identified the woman as another of her analysts.

"I need your help."

"Can't one of my team help you?"

"With this? I doubt it."

He gave her a sour look, but they both knew that, girl in the cabin or no girl in the cabin, he had to do what she asked. "All right, give me a second." The door shut unceremoniously.

Moments later, Rugger appeared, wearing pants and a t-shirt as well as the strange cloth shoes he'd affected since they boarded the ship. He called them *alpargatas* and claimed one of the sailors sold them as a side gig and that gauchos out on the Pampas swore by them.

Sabrina didn't care, but so many people had asked him about them in her presence that she knew the explanation by heart.

"I need you to set up some rafts to float a few Compsognathus onto the island, between those fences."

He held her gaze. "No one is going to believe that those aren't putting people at risk," he said.

"That's why I'm asking you, and you'll need to bring trusted people into this only. Can you do it?"

"Of course. We already floated the main herd onto the island, didn't we?"

"Yes. But that was unguided. We let the waves take them in. We can't move in so close this time. They'll see us."

"So?"

"I don't want that to happen. Survivors can't know what happened. I want them to think that everything that hit them is native to the island."

"Between your beasties and the natives, I don't think we'll have too many survivors," he replied.

"We still can't risk it. Is there any way to guide the rafts?"

Rugger sighed. "Short of sending them in on rubber boats with people on board to steer, no."

"Then we'll do that." She hoped her tone made it clear that she wasn't looking for an argument. This was something they absolutely had to do.

"Just like that?"

"Yes."

For a moment, she thought he would argue anyway, but then he sighed again. "And how many of these creatures are we supposed to drop on their doorstep?"

"I think twenty should do it."

"Damn. Let me think about it. Give me half an hour."

"Take your time, it's still about an hour before sundown, and we have to do this at night. Remember not to involve anyone…"

"…who doesn't already know," he completed the phrase. "Yeah, there's no need to beat me over the head with it. I don't want to wind up in jail any more than you do."

He walked off to consult with his team.

***

The shadows grew longer and Cora watched them without enthusiasm. This would be her second night on the island, which was just stupid. She couldn't believe the imbeciles had no way to contact the mainland, not as much as a satellite phone. What would they do if there was an emergency? The attitude was completely insane.

Supposedly, there was a boat that had gone to Andaman to report the jet ski incident, but everyone had given it up for lost. With the monster out there, that was the only possible conclusion to explain its non-return.

She'd trained to be able to deal with the reality of finding herself cut off from the world. Being behind enemy lines without the ability to communicate due to equipment failure or having comms get compromised, unlikely as that latter scenario was. Her unit's training had put them through every scenario the brass had managed to think up—plus a bunch she suspected the brass would never have been able to have envisioned without heavyweight help from people with actual brains—and taught the troops how to deal with it, both mentally and physically.

She'd always thought that part of her training had stuck.

Well, it hadn't, at least not the psychological part. She couldn't bring herself to believe that they were actually out in the boonies with no way to talk to people. Even in the friggin' middle of the Indian Ocean, the yacht had had an internet connection, even if cell phones were forbidden for everyone but Lai to avoid overloading the wi-fi, you could still connect to the outside world.

Fortunately, the rest of her training still held firm. Stupid or not, this was the situation she had to deal with. And that meant sticking to the plan.

The plan was that there were teams of two people walking the perimeter. These consisted of the young and healthy people: the three Asian guys from Philadelphia, Sked and the thin woman with him, the resort staff, Mary—the bunny's name, of all things, had turned out to be Mary—and the ship's cook, and the remaining sailors. Lai and the Colonel had been included on their own insistence, and a couple of forty-odd-year-old guests were also added, but most of the guests had remained holed up in one of the cabins. Ten teams in all, each with instructions to yell and run for help if they saw anything at all amiss.

Now was the most dangerous time. Night fell quickly in these latitudes, and it would soon be full dark. The staff had told her that the lights would come on automatically when it was dark enough, but they weren't clear on whether that would happen on a timer, a light sensor or what.

So it was conceivable that there would be some minutes of near-complete darkness before the lights came on.

They'd find out in a few minutes.

She was paired with one of the forty-somethings, a balding guy from South America whose weeping wife had wanted him to remain in the room with them, but who'd offered to help anyway. His English was heavily accented, but with a strangely ample vocabulary.

"Do you think they'll come tonight?" he said.

"I'm sure of it. That's how I'd do it."

"But you're a soldier. These guys are like cavemen or something. They aren't even civilized."

"That doesn't make them any less dangerous," she reminded him.

"I suppose. But we have guns."

"Three of them."

She'd been surprised to learn that the Colonel had come unarmed, but unsurprised when he told her in his clipped accent that he had come to burn himself to a nice angry red color under a tropical sun, not kill insurgents in their sleep. So he'd put swimwear in the space his gun would normally have occupied. "A soldier," he said archly, "prepares himself for the task at hand."

"It should be enough. They've probably never seen one before. They'll think it's some kind of magic."

"You haven't read much military history, have you? Give it a shot sometime. You'll be especially interested in colonial skirmishes in the American West and Sub-Saharan Africa."

That seemed to fly way over his head, but he must have understood the subtext, because he shut up. She kept her eyes pinned on the shadows of the forest beyond the fence: that was where the bad guys would come from, and that was also a good way to keep her eyes accustomed to seeing in the growing darkness.

To her relief, the lights came on with an audible click. They were soft at first, but within three minutes, they had achieved operating temperature and threw up decent illumination.

Military-grade, in fact. She wondered why a resort would have such good lights.

Cora shook her head to clear it. That wasn't her problem. Her problem was to spot whoever was trying to come through the glare before whoever it was spotted her.

They completed the first lap of the complex without incident and stopped at the lobby where the older guests and the women who'd opted out of guard duty were holed up. They reported that all was well and headed out to the perimeter again.

Ten minutes into their second lap, Cora's conviction that an attack was imminent began to flag. The woods seemed quiet and peaceful as befitted a tropical paradise.

In the distance, someone screamed.

Cora and her companion turned to see if they could spot where the screams were coming from before they died out.

But they didn't die out.

"It's coming from the resort," the guy said.

Cora nodded and they sprinted for the complex. The guy must have been frantic about his wife because, chubby or not, he gained on her. She pulled her gun out of the holster as they ran.

***

Sked and Akane had been teamed up, of course. No one would have dreamed of trying to separate them.

They did their dusk patrol along the perimeter fence and checked in just as if they had nothing unusual planned.

The second lap, in the darkness, was when they would make their move.

Akane had brought a set of bolt cutters from one of the maintenance sheds and they went to work on the fence just where the beach met the water. It was the perfect spot, partly because the lights were weaker there than elsewhere, but mainly because the patrols behind them would focus on the fence in the forest, not here. No one expected the natives to attack from the beach.

So the hole they were quickly cutting in the fence might go unnoticed until the following morning.

"I feel kinda bad weakening their defenses this way," Sked said.

"See? That's the kind of thing that never would have occurred to you before. You're getting soft on me."

It was precisely the same argument she'd used to convince him of going along with her plan. Whether he truly someone else overlaid on the brain of the man she'd once known, or whether he was actually just going crazy, one thing was certain: his feelings for Akane were too powerful to ignore. He would do anything for her... and his memories indicated he'd done many of them already. Up to and including springing her from a secret Chinese detention facility.

So just double-crossing a bunch of people he didn't know wasn't a huge leap.

As they cut into the wire, he imagined alarms lighting up a panel in that bunker they'd seen in the forest and camouflaged, automated guns taking a bead on his back.

But nothing happened and, working quickly, they soon had an opening in the fence large enough for them to squeeze through.

They did so and ran up the beach, the pistols they'd taken from the hapless Triad would-be murderers drawn and cocked.

There. The lumpy shape of the Zodiac was exactly where the men had said it was, easily visible in the bright moonlight. They redoubled their speed.

And stopped dead when they arrived. The islanders had been there already. The inflatable boat was cut and pierced with arrows and the contents of the packs were scattered on the sand.

"Dammit," Sked said. "We can't use this."

"You don't say."

"I should have..." he paused and cocked his head. "Wait. Do you hear that?"

"What?"

"Listen." He remained silent for a moment.

"Oh, shit," Akane said. "Someone's screaming. Back where we came from."

"Do you think someone got in through our cut?"

"They would have had to find it in the dark."

"We need to go help," Sked said. "Are you coming?"

"I normally don't run towards the screaming," Akane said, "but I don't think I have much choice this time. Without this boat, we're better off all together."

They headed back towards the resort, at full tilt, scratching themselves on the cut fencing. Even though they were in a huge hurry, however, Sked took the time to illuminate the ground beneath them.

"I only see our prints. Whatever is going on back there isn't our fault," he informed Akane.

She either didn't hear him or didn't care, and they raced towards the cluster of cabins along the shore. Sked saw movement around the biggest building, the glorified hut where the hotel lobby functioned. His heart sank. That was where they'd left the old people and the women who didn't feel they wanted to be part of the patrol rotation.

They were pretty much helpless; and if the natives had reached them, they were pretty much dead. The whole plan revolved around not letting anyone get through the perimeter or at least getting early warning if they did.

Though he couldn't understand how, the plan had failed.

The lobby's main window was broken, so Sked simply stepped through. The lights were only half-on and the place was pandemonium.

People seemed to be crawling through the shadows at high speed. Either that or they were crouched near the ground. Was that how the natives hunted? It hadn't given him that impression from the description of the attack on the lifeboat survivors.

Suddenly, one of the forms came at him out of the dim interior and jumped at his head.

Sked reacted without thinking. He punched at his assailant with his right hand and, using their own motion against them, launched the figure behind him. Only later did he realize the thing was much too light to be an islander.

"Akane, get back!" he shouted as he began to retreat. "It's the dinosaurs!"

Akane still wasn't listening to him. She flashed past without slowing and rushed to a table where the source of the screaming appeared to be standing. Sked was shocked to realize that the Colonel's wife was up there, clobbering any of the little dinosaurs who got too close with a chair. Even though she looked quite intimidating in her elevated position, it was obvious that she wouldn't last much longer: there were just too many of them.

Sure of their kill, the creatures had grown overconfident and neglected to watch their backs. With a scream, Akane was among them, kicks and a couple of shots dealing with four of the monsters and opening a path to the old woman.

The Colonel's wife grabbed Akane's proffered hand and, pausing only long enough to throw her chair at the dinosaurs on the other side with a shout of "Eff you, you buggers!" she jumped down. The two hurried towards Sked.

Now that they'd lost the element of surprise, Sked thought the little dinosaurs would mob them, but now that the woman was down from the table, the creatures seemed uninterested in giving chase. Instead, they nosed at stuff on the floor.

The trio retreated into the floodlit sand in front of the wrecked lobby, just in time to see Cora arrive, gun drawn.

"What the hell is going on here?" the former Marine asked.

"Dinosaurs," Sked said, nodding towards the broken glass. "In there."

"Where is everyone?"

It was the Colonel's wife who replied. "I think they're also in there. Dead. One or two might have gotten out in the commotion, but I can't be sure. The ones I saw went down."

And Sked understood why the monsters hadn't come for them. Why go after enemies that had shown themselves capable of self-defense when you could gorge on the corpses of those who weren't. That was what they were nosing on the floor for: easy food.

"Ugh," he said.

"You mean this isn't the islanders?" Cora asked. She blanched. "If everyone heard the screams, they're probably all coming this way... and no one is on the fence."

"So what?" Akane interjected. "We've already lost the people we were supposed to be defending. What difference does it make where we set our new perimeter?"

"Damn," Cora said. "I wish that weren't true." She seemed to deflate, which Sked found surprising. This woman had given him the impression that she would chew through barbed wire just for something to do on a lazy Sunday afternoon.

Just then, the Colonel barged in, accompanied by one of the sailors and another man, red and panting. Sked recognized him as having been paired with Cora. As the Colonel hugged his wife and received her report, the man asked, desperate, where his own wife was.

Sked just shook her head and pointed to the carnage in the lobby. While they were talking, something must have shorted out inside, because a small fire was burning. Even that hadn't scared the dinosaurs into abandoning the grisly work of gorging themselves. They could be seen clearly.

The man cried "Talia," and rushed towards the broken window.

Sked had been waiting for that, and tackled him before he went three steps. The other man might have been desperate, but Sked was a couple of decades younger and well trained. He pinned him without effort.

"If you die, she'll still be dead," he said.

"No." The man struggled, trying to free himself.

"Yes. Listen to me. You need to calm down." Then, a few seconds later, after the man had stopped struggling: "Can I trust you to get up?"

The man nodded, desperation in his eyes.

"Good." Sked released him, hoping the other man wouldn't do anything stupid, but determined not to stop him again. If he wanted to become monster food, that was his own problem.

"We need to get out of here," Cora said. "I count fifteen of those things. We might shoot every bullet we have trying to take them out."

"So let's take them out," the sailor said.

"No. I'd rather use them on the natives and let the animals take care of themselves. The natives are the real danger."

The sailor glanced in the direction of the hellscape in the lobby. He didn't look convinced.

Cora led them to the nearest cabin, and they stood behind it, intercepting the other groups as they arrived. Unfortunately, the Triad guys were next. Cora relaxed visibly when Lai showed up with the doctor.

The last to reach them were Mary and the cook, panting and red.

"The islanders are coming," she said. They're climbing the fence about two hundred meters from the shore, on the north side."

Sked swore, but he knew what he had to do.

"All right," Sked said. "I know where we need to go. Follow me."

"What about the rest of our people?" the big Marine asked.

"I can't help them. I'm going to save myself and anyone else who wants to come. They'll be here any second. And the monsters are already here. For all we know, they killed everyone else."

"Two more minutes. That should give survivors time to reach us."

"All right. I need to go get something in my room." He ran in that direction.

"What kind of something?" Akane said when they reached their door. "Are we ditching these bozos?"

"Not yet. We may need either muscle or cannon fodder where we're going."

"Now you're talking... but you didn't answer my question."

"I'm getting my equipment. We'll need to bust a lock."

"You have equipment here and you didn't tell me?"

"It didn't seem important," he said. "Besides, we were supposed to be lying low."

The venom in her look expressed her opinion of that, eloquently. But she knew he had cause to distrust her. It wouldn't be the first time she'd run on him after liberating a crapton of expensive electronics from his possession.

He chuckled. Being on the receiving end of that kind of thing every once in a while would do her good. Build some character.

"Got it. Let's go."

Chapter 12

The woods were different at night, and it wasn't just the darkness. Sked had expected darkness. In fact, if the darkness had been complete, it would have been easier to navigate using flashlights and cell phones.

What made it confusing was the way the illumination from the perimeter floodlights worked its way between the trees and cast sharply defined shadows. Since the main features of everything they could see were redefined by whether the light from the fence was making it through, it became truly difficult to understand what you were looking at.

Fortunately, the deeper they went into the undergrowth, the less light arrived, but even in the heart of the triangular woods behind the resort, one was occasionally surprised by a sharp beam and stumbled into the obstacle behind it, unseen in the pitch darkness of the shadows.

It nearly became a moot point, however, because Sked couldn't find the gap where he and Akane had pushed off the path and into the woods. The undergrowth to their left appeared to be an unbroken wall, either pitch black or bathed in actinic light.

"You need to hurry," Cora said.

"I'm trying," he replied. But the bushes seemed to have grown back to their original position, and he was not in the least tempted to push through in the dark.

"Try harder," the Marine replied.

A tiny dent in the vegetation suggested a way in, and he pointed. "This way, I think."

"Good." Cora pushed past him and began to move the branches aside. Sked followed, with Akane and Lai just behind him. If things were going according to plan, the Colonel and the doctor would bring up the rear of their little procession, fifteen people strong.

Fifteen people left. How many had there been originally? Sked wondered. Forty? Fifty? Many more if you counted all the people on Lai's yacht. So around fifty dead already, and the night was still very young.

They had three guns between them. Cora had one, the Colonel had the one Sked had taken from the Triads, and

Akane had refused to give hers up. Against what? Dozens of armed islanders who knew the terrain better than they ever could, plus a herd of small but vicious dinosaurs that could probably hunt by scent just as well in the dark as they could at noon.

The odds definitely seemed stacked against them.

He hoped they could get into the bunker and close the door behind them, mainly so they could regroup in safety. If the people inside the bunker—he was certain there was something in there—were armed, then the game was pretty much over. They would be caught between the proverbial rock and the hard place, and would be ground to dust between them.

"Fuck," Cora grunted. "You guys went through this crap? You must be a hell of a lot tougher than you look."

The Marine was right. The undergrowth ahead of them was thicker than he remembered. They were probably forcing a new path through the wall of weeds... but by this point, Sked was fine with that. The clock in his head, honed to a fine point during mission after mission and against the firewalls of hundreds of sites, told him things were about to get too hot to handle, and that they needed to punch through now. He'd learned to trust that sixth sense with his life.

If they went back now, they were all dead.

So he let Cora blaze the trail and pushed aside any stubborn plants that sprang back after she passed. By the time the Colonel went through, the gap in the plants would be wide enough for a blind tracker to find by echolocation...

But he doubted the islanders would have any blind trackers with them, and the lighting would work against anyone working by sight. They might just have a chance.

Once past the wall of weeds, the paths were as he remembered them. Fortunately, the light was much better within than it had been outside. Unfortunately, that also meant it was darker.

But there was no real need to navigate. The path here led straight to their destination, so Sked passed the scratched and cursing Marine to take the lead and ran along the barely visible path for a couple of minutes until the hulking bunker came into view. This time, instead of bypassing the entrance, he headed up the path and knelt by the keypad, illuminating it with his phone.

"Dammit," he whispered.

"What?" Akane said as she arrived.

"Industrial lock."

"Commercial?"

"Yeah, but not one I can brute-force quickly."

"If someone built this out in the boonies, maybe they hired a lazy contractor…"

"Default code?" he said with a smile.

"That's what I was thinking, yeah."

"Let me check the database." He opened the laptop and pulled up a spreadsheet.

"What are you guys doing?" Cora said.

"Opening the door."

"You brought explosives?" She sounded both surprised and impressed by the idea.

Sked rolled his eyes even though he was fairly certain that she wouldn't be able to see it in the darkness. It was a question of principles, and he hoped no one would ever mistake him for the kind of grunt who blew up doors. Especially doors they would need to keep the bad guys out after the good guys were inside.

"We don't blow doors up. We're a little more sophisticated than that."

"You can get this open?" she asked.

"I can. The main question is whether it's going to take ten seconds or an hour."

One of the Triad guys, Harold, appeared and said: "I really hope it doesn't take you an hour. Colonel says he heard something behind us."

"It'll take however long it takes," Akane said. "Now let him work."

But Sked was already working. "I have several Bharat listings here. Do you see a model number anywhere?"

"It's a MaxCode 210," Akane replied without even looking at it. He could hear the unspoken reproach in her voice, but said nothing. Akane was one of those people who believed everyone should also be a second-story man, no matter what else they might be doing in life. Which meant she expected everyone to know the model numbers on every industrial keypad in Asia on sight.

"Okay. Then type… let me see. Three hashtags, then four zeros, four nines and another hashtag."

The steel door began to whine as it lifted.

"Bingo," Akane said.

Cora jumped into action. "Get to cover!" she shouted.

"What for?"

"If there's anyone in there, you all make a wonderful target, silhouetted against the light out here."

"What light?"

"It's much less dark outside than inside. Can't you even tell that?"

"Hey, I work with stealth and surprise," Sked said, raising his arms. "This shouldn't have triggered any alarms."

"But you said they have cameras. Unless they're morons, they know we're here."

"All right." They moved to one side and waited for the door to finish lifting. It took thirty seconds.

Cora popped her head around the corner and immediately pulled it back in.

"Did you see anything?" Sked said.

"Impossible. It's dark as a billionaire's heart in there."

"I heard that," Lai whispered from the shadows.

Cora chuckled and Sked wondered about the relationship they had. It wasn't usual for a guy with that much money to treat his employees as equals, but that seemed to be how Cora saw herself.

"What do we do?" Sked asked.

"Normally, I'd recommend tossing some smoke grenades in there, and maybe hose the whole place with machine-gun fire, but since you forgot to bring any decent weapons and we can't stay out here any longer, let's try this: we'll flash every light we have into the hole and try to blind whoever's waiting for us. Then we'll go in, guns blazing. So I'll need a volunteer to run in with me and someone to cover us without exposing themselves."

"I'll go with you," Sked said. "Just get me my gun back."

Akane rolled her eyes. "He's grown a hero complex all of a sudden," she informed the Marine. "I'll cover you guys. From safety. Because I don't have a testosterone problem."

"I do not have a hero complex. But I'm the only one here who's done this kind of thing before."

"Whatever," Akane replied.

The Colonel passed Sked his gun, and Cora turned to the group. "All right, turn on your flashlights. On my mark, point them into the entry *without showing your heads*. Just put your arms around the corner." She turned to Sked. "Are you ready?"

He nodded.

"Three, two, one… mark," she whispered.

She rolled out into the center of the door, fired two shots and charged in. Sked opted for a less dramatic spring into the now-illuminated tunnel beyond the door.

Someone had used the place for storage. Dust-covered shelves and equipment with sheets over it were lumped to the sides, forcing Sked and Cora to run through a narrow corridor between the junk. Perfect targets, unless the Marine's plan to blind anyone waiting for them worked.

Following Cora's lead, Sked dove behind a large blob of machinery and sat tight for a couple of seconds before diving towards the next one.

Just as he became certain that there was nobody waiting for them, a loud bang filled the tunnel. Sked could have sworn he heard a bullet whizz by his head.

A second later, everything went dark and he realized that the people behind them had probably instinctively pulled their hands away from the tunnel opening that had suddenly begun to fire at them.

That wouldn't last. Even unarmed, Akane would soon get them organized again. And the Colonel would help.

Akane with a gun? He grinned.

Three seconds later, the light was back up where it had been. The tunnel was well-illuminated enough that he could see Cora crouched behind another unidentified pile of equipment. The stuff reminded Sked of medical equipment, but that made no sense—who'd build an underground clinic on an island no one was allowed to visit? She pointed ahead and to the left.

Sked nodded.

If there was only one shooter, he was better positioned to get close without exposing himself. If there were more than one, but they were holding their fire until they could see the whites of Sked and Cora's eyes… they were toast.

He crawled between two crates and emerged into a maze of vehicles. Tata pickups and Bobcat earth movers were parked along the wall, just as dusty as everything else.

They afforded excellent cover, and he managed to advance several yards before he had to stop and consider his next move. He sat in a dark pocket and he tried to see where he could advance without making any noise. Knocking over a can would give the game away.

Or maybe he could intentionally draw fire from whoever was waiting back there, thus giving Cora a clear field to advance and expose the shooter or shooters.

For some reason, he didn't find that option tempting. Instead, he moved carefully between a couple of canisters standing in front of him. On the other side, he found a long clear space that allowed him to advance quietly for several yards.

Brilliant. He figured that he was now actually past the position Cora had indicated, so he turned to the right and looked where she'd pointed.

Admiration filled him and he almost wanted to applaud. Cora had been exactly right, to a couple of inches. A figure huddled behind a stack of metal shelves holding a large gun in both hands and occasionally risking a look over the equipment. Unfortunately for him, there was little to be seen except for the beam of several blinding flashlights.

Sked grinned and crawled silently up to the guy. He placed the muzzle of his pistol against the back of his head and whispered, "Hi. I'll be your captor this evening. Put the gun down right now. Make a false move and you're dead."

Sked had no clue if the guy understood or not, but the gun lowered slowly. Sked grabbed it and moved a couple of feet back. "All right. Nod if you understand me."

The man nodded.

"Good. I want you to sit on your hands now. That's right. Now one more question, and this is the one which defines whether you live or die. Is there anyone else waiting for us?"

The man shook his head.

Sked shrugged. He had no choice but to trust the guy.

"Cora," he called, "target is secure. He claims he's alone."

An instant later, Cora rolled to a position a few feet away. She must have been making her way through the clutter, and Sked, even though he'd known she was out there, hadn't noticed her. She was really good.

Cora nodded. "Nice advance. Good takedown. I'm impressed," she said. "Up until a couple of minutes ago, I was convinced you and the thin girl were just a couple of amateurs playing soldier. It seems I owe you guys an apology."

The praise filled him with pride; it wasn't often that one of Sked's operations had witnesses. His clients normally didn't know how much skill was involved in getting the results they paid for. And Akane, who'd seen his ability firsthand, would rather die than say she thought he was any good.

But Sked would have been the first to admit that, had the showdown been between himself and the Marine… he would have been dead.

"What do we do now?" he said.

"Let's get everyone inside and get that door closed."

"What about the people in here?"

"We'll deal with them if we need to. We need to take it step by step."

Sked ran back to the opening and gave the order to get inside, then looked for the interior door mechanism. To his delight, he wouldn't need to enter any codes. A big red button worked the door from the inside.

He gave the captured gun to the Colonel, who glanced at it and then, with practiced ease, slid the magazine out to check the number of bullets. "This is filthy," he said. "Whoever you took this from isn't a soldier."

"I agree. He's just some fat sweaty guy. Want to meet him?"

"Not in the least, but I suppose I must."

Cora was questioning the prisoner when they arrived. Flashlights up close revealed a dark-skinned man who spoke English with an accent Sked couldn't quite place. If pressed, he would have guessed he was from Latin America, but it could easily have been an Arab, a Central Asian or a man from Southern Europe. His grey t-shirt had damp patches under his arms and he had a scraggly beard halfway which ended down both cheeks.

He looked like an office worker. Pudgy and stooped.

"He says there's four more of them in there," Cora reported.

"Are any of them dangerous?"

"They are doctors and scientists," the man said. "Not dangerous. They work here. For a salary."

"What is this place?"

"Readjustment facility," he replied.

"What kind of readjustment?"

"I don't know," the man replied.

That earned him a prod from Cora's gun. The man recoiled. "I really don't know. They do science work with people. People come in, they stay here a few days, then they go out. I fix the doctors' computers and their equipment."

"What kind of people?"

He looked uncomfortable for a moment. "Mostly women," he said. "Some men. I don't talk to them."

"And weapons?"

"Some. I don't think the doctors know how to use them. They're in a room."

Sked spoke up. "Do you have a connection? Phone? Internet? Anything?"

The man, who'd shown every sign of being a nervous wreck to that point, actually laughed. "Of course not. We work here until they take us away. No one in this place ever communicates with the outside world."

"Why not?"

He shrugged. "The bosses don't want anyone asking questions."

"Well," Cora said, lifting him by the collar, "I'm someone, and I'm asking questions. What the hell is happening in here?"

"I told you. I just fix the computers."

Damn, Sked thought. He'd seen this kind of thing before quite often. The guy wasn't refusing to answer their questions because he'd suddenly grown a backbone. He was more scared of whoever ran the place than he was of a gun in his face. "Leave him," he said. "We'll go look for ourselves."

The man stood and Cora said: "Lead the way." She prodded him in the back with the gun.

The tunnel was shorter than it had appeared when they were expecting to be shot in the face. Just ten meters further on, it ended at another door. This one was carpeted in grey.

"I guess we can rule out a WWII storage bunker," Akane said.

"I guess so." Sked turned to their prisoner. "Anything we should know before we open that door?"

"No. It's just a door."

"Think carefully, because if you tell us it's safe, we're sending you through first."

He hesitated, but finally nodded.

"All righty, then," Sked said. "In you go. And if you run for it, I'll shoot you in the back."

They opened the door carefully. The room beyond was carpeted in the same grey and held four cubicles with shoulder-high partition walls. Though anything could be hiding behind one of those, the prisoner appeared unconcerned as he advanced towards the back of the room.

Sked and Cora took no chances. They crouched to the cubicles and checked each one.

"Clear," Cora said when they were done. Akane and the Colonel led the rest of their team in.

The man led them to another door in the far wall. This one opened into a circular room about fifty feet in diameter, with a high, domed roof. It was lit like an operating room.

The four people who met them inside fit the surroundings perfectly. They wore white lab coats and the tall one in front was pale to the point of looking albino. All four were men, but the other three were Asian.

"What is the meaning of this?" the pale man asked. His English was near-perfect, the accent Germanic.

"We need shelter," Cora replied.

"Well, you can't have it here. This is private property. I must ask you to leave right now."

"Well, I'm afraid that's quite impossible," Cora replied. "We go out there, we die. So we're staying here."

Akane moved up beside him and whispered in Sked's ear. "Tattoos," she said.

Sked cursed himself for a fool. The three Asian men each had a red flower inked on their neck. Even the white doctor had a hint of petal sticking out from beneath the white of his lab coat. It was the sign of Blood Orchid, a smuggling and white trafficking organization that held sway east of Istanbul.

The tall man spoke again. "You really don't want to be here. You have no idea who you're messing with."

Akane laughed. "Oh, yes I do," she said. She rolled back the sleeve of her left arm to show another tattoo: a two-by-two grid with ideograms in each square. "This is my code from when I was being readjusted."

Then, without another word, she lifted her gun and shot the Asian doctor standing to the left of the tall man. The bullet caught him right between the eyes and he collapsed backward.

"Hello, Dr. Suzuki," she said. "I told you I'd find you and kill you."

She spat on the body and walked off.

CHAPTER 13

What the fuck was that all about?

Cora watched the woman walk away, gun in hand. She looked to Sked to see if he gave any clue, but as none was forthcoming, she turned back to the pale scientists. That wasn't the way she would have handled the initial greetings, but one thing was for certain: Akane had gotten their attention. These guys would be receptive to anything they said from this point on.

"As you can see, we aren't particularly worried about you or your superiors. In fact, you need to start thinking of why we would leave you alive to rat us out once we're gone. It might be healthier for us if you're dead. I'll let you think about that for a little while." She turned back. "Colonel, do you mind keeping this group covered for a moment? I'd like to speak to Sked."

"Of course. Tell me what he says, afterward."

The Englishman's eyes burned with a fury she'd never seen there before, and she understood the rage: you didn't just shoot an unarmed prisoner in the head. Not without a good reason. He knew exactly what she wanted to discuss with the hacker: what the hell was up with Akane?

She hoped Akane had that reason, because she didn't want to spend the rest of their stay on this island keeping those two away from each other. Though Akane didn't look like she would be much in a fight, she was dangerous in her own way. And the Colonel? He might be twenty years past his prime but he was well-trained and experienced.

It would be better if they got along.

Sked was already walking beside her when she realized one of the Asian men from the resort had joined them. Cora raised an eyebrow in Sked's direction. He nodded and she shrugged. This should be interesting.

They sat at a perfectly normal table in a nook about ten meters from the rest of the group. It was a four-person table with a white plastic surface surrounded by white plastic chairs. The nook was perfectly normal, obviously a cafeteria space holding two more tables, a marble tabletop holding a microwave and a refrigerator. It could have served as the break room for pretty much any corporate office on the planet.

"I presume one of you can tell me what the fuck happened back there."

Sked and the Asian guy—she thought his name was Harold, but he hadn't spoken in her presence as far as she could recall—exchanged a glance and then Harold said: "Blood Orchid. These guys are bad news. Creeps of the highest order. Dangerous, too."

"Criminal bad news or state sponsored?"

"Oh, most definitely criminal. Not even the North Koreans would touch these assholes."

"Do tell."

Harold nodded. "They're the guys your mother warned you about. They supply the stuff that most criminal organizations don't want to get involved in. The lab-built drugs that give you a high unlike anything else, but that kill you quicker than anything else, too. Sex slaves for the high-end trade, girls and boys willing to do anything, and to do it with anyone, with a smile. I heard a rumor they'd set up a studio somewhere that would, for a budget of a million dollars per body, film all the snuff you could ever dream up."

Cora swallowed and looked around. "Is this…"

Sked shook his head. "I don't think so," he replied. "This is a medical center, so…" he glanced over at the three well-lit operating tables in the center of the room, "Organ harvesting?"

Harold shook his head. "I don't think so. The fat, sweaty guy said this was a reprogramming center, didn't he? So I'd say this is where they make the dolls."

"Dolls?" Cora said.

"Human sex toys," Sked responded with a smile. "This is where they break the personality. They mostly do it with drugs, but I know they also do surgery, prefrontal cortex stuff. That's why you have tables and doctors."

She recoiled at the idea. "So, what you're saying is…"

Harold cut her off: "Screaming, scared kidnap victims come in and purring, happy sex toys go out. Mostly women, of course, but enough pretty boys to keep everyone happy."

"Motherfucker." Anger radiated from her gut. She wanted to go back and kill the three bastards that Akane had left standing, and the IT guy for good measure. Then something hit her. "Wait. Akane said she knew that guy. Was she one of the…?"

Sked nodded. "She never talks about it, but she definitely went in and came out, and they worked her over." He smiled. "As you can see, it didn't take, but she spent at least a little time in a house in Thailand."

Cora leaned back in her chair. She didn't want to think about what someone who ended up in a brothel after coming through a place like this might go through, so she changed the subject. "You guys both seem to know a hell of a lot about this kind of thing."

Sked shrugged. "I'm a freelance hacker with a background in field work for a couple of different governments. I work on the edges of the law. I need to know about the kind of stuff I might get dragged into if I'm not careful."

Harold snorted.

"And sometimes a little bit past the edges," Sked admitted. "The further you cross the line, the better the pay. But I don't take the really wet and sticky jobs. Akane takes those, usually against my advice and against her own best interests. But there's some stuff no one will touch unless they're really desperate. This is one of them."

Cora nodded and turned to Harold. "And you? Another hacker? You sound like you're from the States."

"Yeah. Philly." He sighed. "I guess you'd probably call me a member of an organized crime family, except we're not Italian. You ever heard of the Triads?"

"Of course."

"I work for them."

"In Philly?"

"Yeah."

"A little out of your jurisdiction, aren't you? Did you come here on vacation?"

"Not much vacation in my line of work. We came to put a hit on Akane." The shock she felt must have showed because he held up both hands. "Look, I know you chicks stand together and she was in the whorehouse and all of that so you'll defend her. But don't let the past fool you. Akane is bad news. She's on so many shit lists that I might probably have gotten medals from the governments of the US, Russia and China if we'd taken her out. Not a lot of people can unify the world that way."

"And she knows this?"

"We have a truce."

"I'm glad to hear it. But as soon as the truce ends, are you sure she won't shoot you in the face?"

Harold shrugged. "I don't think so. What you just saw back there, it was personal. With me, it's just business. We keep our side of the bargain, everyone walks away."

Cora just stared at these two guys. They acted like everything they were saying was perfectly normal, that criminals and hackers were just in business, and that a murder could somehow not be personal. She stood.

"Sked, I need you to keep an eye on the prisoners while I explain that murder we just saw to the Colonel. And then I'm going to see where Akane has gotten off to."

***

The Colonel proved the simple part of the equation. When Cora explained what she'd learned, he reacted exactly the same way she had, but with more self-control. He didn't look as if he was about to kill the staff of the place as soon as she got out of his sight.

Finding Akane proved more difficult until Cora noticed a small door leading out of the main room into a corridor built of bare concrete.

About five feet in, Akane sat on the floor, sobbing.

"Go away," she said.

Cora thought about obeying, but only for a moment. "No. If you don't want to talk about it, that's fine. But you're not staying here alone with that gun. I'm trying not to lose any more people."

"I'm not one of your people."

"You are to me," Cora replied.

The red-eyed woman looked up. There was gratitude in her eyes, but also something else: a deep-seated mistrust. Cora suspected no one would ever get past that barrier: it was integral to her need to protect herself. "Whatever," Akane replied. "But it's not me you need to worry about. There's a woman in the third cell over. Get her out. I tried, but that cell…" She began sobbing again.

Cora gave her a look, trying to see if anything about the woman in the fetal position on the floor indicated that she was about to do herself harm. It didn't look that way, and trying to take the gun might do more harm than good. So Cora walked down the corridor towards the indicated door.

The hall was as filthy as the room outside was immaculate and corporate. The passageway actually smelled of human waste, and the floor looked like it hadn't been swept in years. The walls and floor were of roughly-finished concrete, jagged to the touch. The only illumination came from an incandescent bulb suspended from its own wires hanging from a hole in the roof.

The third door was rusted and slick with slime. The only part of it that wouldn't give you tetanus—or worse—was the bolting mechanism. That was shiny and sturdy. No one was breaking it away.

But there was no key. All you had to do was to slide the bolt aside and the door would open.

Cora gripped her pistol, tensed and slid the bolt aside. She pushed the door inward.

Nothing happened. No one jumped her.

At first, she thought the disgusting cell on the other side was empty, holding nothing but a tiny cot and a bucket.

Then she realized that what she'd thought was a pile of ragged blankets in one corner was a person. A woman.

She was covering her face and trembling.

"Hello," Cora said, not sure whether it was safe to approach. The figure made her think of the very definition of the word 'cornered'. "Can you hear me?"

Her only answer was a soft whimper, barely audible even in the silence of the hall.

Cora stepped into the cell. The floor was wet and it smelled worse than the corridor.

"It's all right. I'm not going to hurt you," Cora said.

A face looked up at her. Thin to the point of emaciation, skin so pale a network of veins could be seen under it. Bags under her green eyes. Delicate features, but too thin for Cora to call her beautiful.

The woman didn't speak.

"I think you need a doctor," Cora said.

That got a reaction. The woman pressed herself even harder against the wall and screamed, a short, hopeless sound.

"I'm not going to hurt you," Cora said. She stuck her head out the door and called out to Akane. "Go get the doctor."

Akane looked up with a dazed expression.

"Do it now," Cora repeated. This time she used the special sergeant's bark she reserved for wet-behind-the-ears recruits that were moping and feeling sorry for themselves. "This woman needs help!"

Akane actually stood with an alacrity that made Cora think she would snap off a salute.

Of course, that didn't happen—she suspected Akane was incapable of that particular gesture—but the hacker girl was back in less than thirty seconds with the Indian doctor in tow.

The man took one look at the cell, cursed under his breath and walked straight up to the woman on the bed without even asking if it was dangerous. That guy was truly amazing.

The woman on the cot tried to shove the doctor away, but the man delicately—but firmly—pushed her arms aside and took her head in his hands. He looked at her eyes and then took her pulse.

"Open your mouth," he said.

Completely in his power, the woman complied.

"All right. You can close it." The doctor turned to Cora. "It should be safe to move her to one of the operating tables. Whoever did this knew what they were doing. She's not in immediate danger."

"No. Please. No. Not the operating table. Please. You promised." The woman's voice was a hoarse whisper laced with desperation.

"Can you help me pick her up?"

They hauled the feebly protesting woman out of the cell and into the main room, where every pair of eyes followed their progress. As they laid her on the soft surface of the bed, Cora realized the woman was crying.

"Can we clean her?"

"Yes. But not yet. Find something for her to drink. Water first. Clean water. And then find some juice, too. They'll have it somewhere because their intention is for their victims to live."

"You've seen this before?"

"It's a standard breaking procedure for women bound for the... houses of ill repute. They starve them and keep them in filth, so they're grateful to get the luxury of the... houses."

Had the situation not been so serious, Cora would have laughed at the doctor. He'd shown himself to be both fearless and dedicated... but he wouldn't talk about whorehouses.

It made her like him even more.

"I understand what's happening, doctor. Stay here with her."

She went straight for the fridge in the break room, where she found both bottled water and an Indian brand of orange juice she'd never heard of. She opened the container and found it smelled all right, so she took it along.

When she arrived, the doctor had the woman sitting on the bed, and was asking her questions in soft tones.

She drank the water without question, trying to get too much down at once. "No. Go slowly," the doctor said.

The woman nodded, but when he tried to take the glass away from her, she clutched it close.

"We're going to clean you now," he told her.

"Not you. Her," the woman whispered, pointing at Cora.

The doctor nodded. He lay the woman down again—glass still clutched in her hand—and took Cora aside. "There are other... aspects... to the torture. It's normal that she wouldn't want a man with her. Can you do this?"

"You bet your ass," Cora replied. "I don't care how dirty she is. Just get me some water and some sponges or something."

The doctor nodded, and Cora began to pull the privacy curtains around the operating area shut. Moments later, the doctor returned with a big bucket and an armful of white towels. Cora was unsurprised to see Akane with him, but she was utterly shocked to see the bunny from the boat. She'd changed out of her Union Jack bikini, but still looked like a low-class bimbo.

Damn. Old habits were hard to break. This one had already proven herself to be at least as good as anyone else on that yacht, and yet Cora still couldn't get past her prejudice.

"Oh, you poor thing," the woman said, advancing towards the woman on the bed. "What have they done to you?"

That pushed Cora into action. She closed the curtain behind Akane and got down to helping the emaciated girl.

But Akane pushed her aside and grabbed the woman's chin.

"What's your name?" she asked roughly.

"I am a Blossom of the Goddess of Love."

"No. Fuck no. Your real name."

"I am a Blossom of the Goddess of Love."

"I won't hurt you for not saying that. Tell me your name. I want to know your name. Look." She showed the woman her arm, the tattoo that matched the one on the woman's own skin. "I was what you are once. I saved myself. But you need to say your name."

"I…" the weak voice petered out. She stared hard at the tattoo for several moments. "Ania. My name is Ania."

"Good," Akane said. She hugged the woman. "I'll save you, Ania. I'll save you from everyone."

***

Once they'd gotten her cleaned and gave her some orange juice—the doctor also found an IV for her—Ania slept, fitfully at first and then deeply.

"That's a good idea," Cora said. "I'm going to get some sleep. Who wants first watch?"

"What do you mean? We need to figure out what we're going to do next," Sked said.

"We're safe for now. Neither the villagers nor the dinosaurs are going to be able to get in that door. See if you can get our prisoners to tell us where their bosses are, and when they expect them back. I want everyone who isn't on watch getting some sleep. We'll plan after we've rested."

"But…"

"She's right," the Colonel said. "I'll take first watch."

Cora knew the staff had to sleep somewhere so she searched for the dormitories. She found one, and was probably asleep before her head hit the pillow. It was easy to do, knowing the Colonel would bully people into getting some shuteye.

She woke hours later and entered the larger chamber to find almost everyone still asleep. The doctor was on watch.

"Where are the prisoners?" she whispered.

"Over there." He pointed to several white lumps piled in a corner.

For a second, she was confused, but then the doctor pointed to another pile of debris.

"And their heads are over there. If you want my professional opinion, the murder weapon was a watermelon chopper. They only woke me up to patch up the technician."

"Patch up…" she was numb.

"To stop the bleeding. But between you and me, he will never sing bass in the men's choir again."

"Holy shit. Who did this?"

"I promised not to say, but there were enough of them in the group that woke me that I can tell you it was a majority decision." He grabbed her forearm as she turned to go. "This isn't the army, Sergeant. They don't have to obey your orders." He said it softly. "They wouldn't have obeyed mine. Or the Colonel's. Or your boss'. This was going to happen."

"Akane…"

"Was asleep when they woke me. She's still asleep and will be for a couple of hours more." He smiled. "She needed to calm down, and she shouldn't have trusted anything any doctor gave her, because doctors are sneaky bastards who slip stuff into your drink. She didn't do it."

"We needed their information."

"We have it. They didn't die quickly." He pointed to a sheaf of neatly written notes. The top sheet was spattered with brown droplets of dried blood. "And the tech guy, who was in charge of communications, will live. He isn't happy right now, but there are still painful things to cut off if he doesn't cooperate."

She gave him a hard look. "You sound like you approve of what they did here."

He returned it without flinching. "I don't. But I don't disapprove." He hesitated. "That woman sleeping on the bed was at the resort. The manager and a couple of other men asked me to look her over. She seemed to be drugged, but otherwise all right. I told them to let her rest and to call me if she had difficulty breathing. I never saw her again. I asked about her the next day, and the manager told me she was feeling better but didn't want to stay on, so she'd taken the morning boat off the island. It got me to thinking how many other drunk girls I'd given a clean bill of health to send to hell. So I won't harm anyone myself, but I'll let them torture that bastard over there, and then I'll stitch him back together so they can do it again…"

"You never did tell me your name, Doctor."

"So you can send me to jail later? It's Prakash. Doctor Pendalai for the criminal records. You'll find me registered in Sri Lanka and at the resort, if any of the records survived."

She sighed. "I don't like what's happening here, but if I've learned one thing from this clusterfuck, it's that you don't deserve to go to jail."

"You should do what your conscience tells you. I will follow mine."

"I believe you," she said.   With that, she squeezed his hand and walked off to gather her thoughts.

CHAPTER 14

Sabrina growled as she watched the footage again. The first part was fun: those old women in the resort lobby had fallen to her Compsognathus without much of a fight. No matter what happened next, she would be able to use that footage to sell the product.

Even with that in mind, what happened next truly sucked.

The little dinosaurs went on a feeding frenzy, diving into the corpses with relish and losing track of the rest of the resort's inhabitants.

Then, when they did get back on the trail, the scent disappeared into what seemed to be some sort of concrete storage locker built into a hill, complete with a solid curtain door. In the jumpy footage, it looked like a bunker, and she knew there was no way twenty little theropods were going to beat down that door. Besides, the Compsognathus weren't remote controlled, so she couldn't order them around. The way they worked was that you put them somewhere and let their instincts—hunger and self-defense—do the rest. The bunker wasn't edible and they wouldn't see it as a threat… so they'd ignore it.

But even that wasn't the worst of it. As the little creatures milled around, unsure of what to do now that they'd lost the scent of fresh prey, arrows rained in from the forest and took down four or five—it was difficult to make an exact count—almost immediately.

The only thing that kept it from being a complete massacre is that the wind shifted and the dinosaurs caught the scent of their assailants.

The rest was literally a blur. It was impossible to truly see what had happened in the unfocused, jumpy night-vision images, but from what she could piece together, the remaining Compsognathus charged at the islanders hidden in the underbrush. She counted three or four definite kills against the natives… but at the cost of the entire complement of dinosaurs.

She consoled herself with the thought that gathering data like this was why you tested, and she could conclusively state that the little ones weren't something you'd send after armed opponents, but Sabrina still ground her teeth to think that these bastards had murdered her babies.

The final insult came next. Instead of licking their wounds and counting themselves lucky to be alive, the natives got to work chopping down saplings, tying each carcass to a pole and carrying them away, presumably to be eaten. Every single camera was still working, and she watched them pull the poles over the fence and drag them out to a clearing where they were dumped among what looked suspiciously like dead human bodies.

What the hell had been going on on that island? she wondered.

Whatever it was, the savages were going to die, even if it meant flooding the entire place with little dinosaurs. Hell, she had plenty of them to send. She couldn't take them back… getting them through US customs was a non-starter.

She smiled. "I hope you little savages have said your prayers to whatever insignificant tribal god you worship. Because I'm going to send you to meet them as soon as I deal with the jackasses from the resort."

***

Everyone was awake, and Mary looked around the room. There were some grim faces in the crowd, men and women who appeared ready to take on the Galactic Empire, or whatever those guys in the skull masks from the movie were, singlehandedly. Hell, with the way they hadn't been able to shower in two days, most of them even looked scruffy enough for the roles.

She giggled to herself, even though she knew it was completely stupid… but there was no one else to talk to. Every one of the girls she'd come on the trip with was missing, most likely dead, and the cook… well, he was a great guy, but he looked like, had this been a movie, he'd have been the first to pick up one of those laser rifles.

It was hard to believe they couldn't see how ridiculous they all appeared. A bunch of tired people playing soldier. They had the slim dark woman, the mysterious guy with unusual skills, two big, straight soldiers—one of them was even a woman, for diversity's sake—and the old billionaire. She had to admit she'd always thought Lai looked wise, but then she'd always thought elderly Asian men looked wise. So they had their wise man. Not green with pointy ears, maybe, but an old Asian would work in a pinch.

They even had three criminals helping them try to solve the problem and seek whatever absolution was on hand.

It was straight out of central casting, and if their situation hadn't actually been dire, she would have said so.

But the situation *was* dire.

And it was worse that she was now at least a witness, probably an accessory to four murders and a mutilation. She'd finished making love with Marco, the cook, and she was going to the fridge to see about getting a drink, when she noticed five people around a table. The Chinese guy with the big square knife and the American accent had invited her to sit with them, and had told them exactly what they did to people—both men and women—in that place, how they transformed them from pretty but clueless young people into commodities that could be sold on the worldwide sex-slave market.

He told them that he knew a woman, back in the States, who'd been in this network. Blood Orchid had used her up and discarded her when she became too old to work. She'd almost died from the drugs, but eventually had managed to pull herself together and become a nurse.

That woman had found the man with the knife bleeding in an alleyway and applied the tourniquet that had saved his life.

Once ambulatory, he'd tracked her down and given her a lot of money. In exchange, he heard her story.

Finally, he looked around the table, drained his glass of water in a dramatic gesture and said: "Which is why I hope you won't mind that I'm going to cut those bastards into little pieces. It's for her, and for every boy and girl like her that will come up."

Mary had gone back to the niche she shared with Marco and started another round. She didn't want to hear what was coming next.

Now, she listened to them and counted heads. Fifteen people left from the three groups whose lives had collided so strangely. Plus Ania, the woman they'd found in the cell. The one that had been half tortured to death. She shuddered to think about it. Except for Ania, who was staring off into the distance, they all seemed to be discussing what to do next.

To her surprise, Mary spoke. "What about this place? Is it part of the hotel? We already know they brought people in on the hotel boats, but didn't anyone ever see them leaving?"

They all looked at her like she was a dumb bimbo, a look she'd learned to simply weather over the past couple of years, until Cora of all people, came to her aid.

"That's a pretty good question. Did anyone see anything?"

The only hotel employee remaining, a tiny guy whose blue shirt was nearly shredded, replied: "I don't think anyone knew. The boat leaving the island would be gone by five in the morning. We were either asleep or making ourselves scarce, because if they caught you out and about, you might get drafted into loading the thing."

"So who did the loading?"

"The manager, mostly. And the ship's crew." He looked pensive for a moment. "Come to think of it, it was kind of weird. The resort's cargo ship always seemed to have way too many sailors for such a little boat."

The hacker who could shoot, the one who called himself Sked, looked up. "A more interesting question might be who they bribed to get this parcel of land? From what I read, North Sentinel Island was pretty much off limits to everyone. Off limits in the sense that the Indian Navy would send a cruiser after you if you so much as came within five nautical miles of it. And suddenly, here we have a little boutique resort. Sure, it's a crappy one not worth much more than a couple of stars... but the fact that it's here says something. And if I were anywhere near an internet connection, I'd find out exactly what."

Lai waved his hands. "If anyone actually cares once we get off this island you can look into it to your heart's content. Hell, I might give it a shot myself. But in the meantime, the question remains: does anyone have an idea about how we should leave?"

For some reason they all looked at Mary. What she wanted most was to fade into the background, but she had to say something. So she blurted the first thing that came into her head: "Whatever happened to the other lifeboat?"

Cora shook her head. "It's on the other side of the island. We'd never make it."

"All right." She began to sit, but Lai spoke again.

"But it's the only working boat we know about. Maybe we can send a crew to get it and drive it around the island to the resort. Someone who can do the jungle."

"Aren't you forgetting Godzilla?" Cora said. "I don't want to look that thing in the teeth again."

The doctor spoke. "It's not Godzilla."

"Who cares?"

"Actually, we all do. That thing isn't some kind of monster from a movie. It looked like a very large aquatic reptile, but I noticed something about it that is pertinent. Like a lot of aquatic creatures, it doesn't have earholes. Or at least none that I saw... and I saw it really, really close. I think it has enormous membranes, one on each side of the head, which act as ears."

"So it can hear really well underwater. So what?"

"But that's exactly the point. I think we can use a boat, as long as we don't activate the engine. An engine must be like a beacon to something like that. And possibly a challenge."

"So what? You want us to row?"

"If necessary. At least until we put some distance between ourselves and the island."

Cora spoke up. "We may not need to go far. I saw a container ship out there. It wasn't moving, maybe it's still there."

Lai didn't look convinced. "Container ships need to earn by the hour. You can't just leave one in the middle of the ocean. That costs the owners tens of thousands of dollars a day in missed profit and operation costs. Not a good way to earn your money back on the kind of investment a big ship entails."

"Then we just need to row a little further. And then we activate the beacon."

"Didn't we do that last time?" Dr. Pendalai said.

"Yes," Cora replied.

"So what if I'm wrong and it's not the motor but the beacon that attracts the monster? Maybe we shouldn't turn that on."

"Good point."

"Maybe we shouldn't do this at all," Lai said. "No matter what we do, it will be risky."

"I know, but it's the only real chance I see."

"What about just sitting tight? An entire resort can't just go off the grid. Someone has to come looking for it, right?"

"No dice," Sked said. "This resort was never on the grid. It seemed weird to me at first, but now I understand why. No one can stumble over the island's dirty little secret and transmit it to all the world. And even if someone did find this place, they could be captured, disappeared and then explained away. No one arrives and no one leaves without the owners of this lab allowing it."

"So no one's coming," Cora concluded.

"Exactly."

Just as she was wondering why Lai was being the stumbling block, that worthy spoke again. "All right then. I think we should go with Cora's plan. It seems to be the only workable solution." Then he winked and smiled at her.

"Except," one of the Chinese guys from Philadelphia said, "you don't call the shots here."

"Of course not," Lai replied softly. "We should take a vote."

Everyone voted for Cora's plan, including, sheepishly, the Triad guy who'd objected. Even Mary raised her hand; it was better to do something, even something dangerous, than just to die of hunger in a tunnel. The only abstention was, predictably, Ania. She didn't seem aware of anything around her.

"All right," the man said. "I guess we do this. But how? Are you proposing we just walk back out there and climb the fence?"

Akane laughed. "No wonder no one's ever heard of the Philadelphia Triad," she said. "Not only do you not think like humans, you don't even think like criminals." She gestured to the large room around them. "Do you really believe anyone would build this James Bond villain lair and not provide it with an escape tunnel? Hell, I'll bet you that not only is there a tunnel, but that the far end will drop us on the other side of that fence."

The man gave her a long look and grinned. "And now I see why you're on everyone's kill list. But I guess you're right."

They split into groups and searched the place. Unsurprisingly, the group containing Sked and Akane hit paydirt before the rest: they found not one but two separate escape tunnels.

"We need to see where each of these goes," Cora said.

"All right. I'll take this one. Sked, you take the other one," Akane said.

Mary wondered if Sked, obviously competent in his own right, would bristle at taking orders from his girl. But he didn't seem to mind—he just adopted an amused expression and disappeared into the hole exposed by the false panel on the wall.

Ten minutes later, he returned, shaking his head. "This one opens in the resort, in the false back of one of the ovens."

"Let me guess," the resort employee said. "The one that never worked and they never got around to repairing."

Sked grinned. "I have no idea, but that sounds like the right way to manage this. After all, escaping into a tunnel with the cops hot on your heels just to be broiled in the oven could ruin your whole day."

Akane reappeared moments later with a smile on her face. "Harold, you owe me five bucks," she called to the room at large.

"I never said I'd take the bet," came the response from the break room area.

"Pussy," she called out.

Harold responded with an obscene gesture, but by that time, no one was paying attention. They all crowded around Akane.

She smirked. "This one goes straight on for about a couple of hundred yards and appears under a dirt path in the woods. It had a bunch of loose rubble on it, which is why it took me so long to get back, but it's definitely on the other side of the fence. I could see it just behind me."

"Could you see the beach?" Cora asked.

Akane shook her head. "No way. Looks like dense jungle, except for the path through the trees."

"All right. Who's on the recovery team to get the boat?"

"All of us," Sked said.

"That's insane. It's dangerous as hell."

"I know. That's why we need to do this in one shot. If we start crossing the jungle just so we can sail around to retrieve people, the natives are going to turn us into appetizers. We need to use the element of surprise while we still have it. And that means one strike, as fast as we can make it out there, and get everyone on the boat. Then we run for open water."

"How long do you think the surprise will last?"

"Longer than if we try to do it your way," Sked replied.

"Colonel?" Cora asked.

The older man stepped forward and held up a hand. A look of intense concentration crossed his features before he finally sighed. "I think Sked's right this time. I just don't think we can run a complex operation, not even at night. I think we move after nightfall—that will give us ten more hours to lick our wounds—and do it all at once. Either we all make it or we all die trying. I know you disagree with this plan, but you're critical to its success. Can I count on you?"

Cora straightened. "Yessir!" she said.

"Thank you. Now, the castrati over there," he gestured in the general direction of where they'd left the IT guy, "mentioned there was a cache of weapons. If the one he had is any indication, they will be badly-maintained and as dangerous to us as to anything we might encounter out there... but it's better than nothing. Let's see if we can find them. Once we do, I want everyone to get plenty of food, plenty of liquid and plenty of rest. Get it all now, because I don't know how long this will take and I don't want anyone carrying food in their pockets. Remember that the natives are only half of our problems. Those dinosaurs can probably smell food a mile off."

He left them to try to locate the cache of weapons. Mary, who'd never fired a gun, didn't join the search. She just sat there, thinking that the Colonel was probably right that the dinosaurs could smell food from a long distance.

What he hadn't mentioned to the group at large was that *they* were the dinosaurs' food.

CHAPTER 15

Sked had drawn the rearguard position, so he waited patiently while everyone else filed into the tunnel. In theory it was the safest spot because you could see if everyone else was getting massacred before stepping out into the open. Of course, that situation reversed itself immediately as soon as you got out of the tunnel. If you got hit from behind, you'd have to run over everyone else in order to get the hell away.

And if you did, they'd probably be mad at you for running from the rearguard spot. You were supposed to die a hero.

Cora led the group into the little door, with two of the Triad guys and a sailor—looking much more confident now that they had guns again—following. Behind them came the noncombatants, which was to say everyone who hadn't been issued a gun. They included the rest of the sailors, the Colonel's wife, the cook from the yacht and his girlfriend.

After them, surprisingly, came Akane. She'd foregone her role as part of the combat team—but still kept her gun—in order to take Ania under her wing. The woman they'd rescued still looked dazed, but was slowly coming to understand that this actually wasn't some new form of torture, that the people around her were trying to help.

But the only one she responded to was Akane. He didn't know if it was the fact that she'd shown the woman her tattoo, or whether she'd told her that she'd shot one of the doctors, but for some reason, the woman understood that Akane was her fiercest ally. And Akane had taken the responsibility to heart. Sked suspected that, if it came down to saving his life or the woman's, Akane would choose the woman.

That hurt like hell, but he would think about it later.

Crazy Eddie followed Akane in, watermelon chopper at the ready. Then, just ahead of Sked, the Colonel. Before going in, the bluff Englishman squeezed Sked's shoulder. "One way or another, we're nearing the end of this," he said. "Good man." Then he disappeared into the tunnel.

Sked looked behind him one last time to check that they weren't forgetting anything. He had his gun, and he had his laptop and other electronics stuffed into a backpack. There was nothing else he really needed.

They'd abandoned the castrati IT guy tied loosely to one of the hospital beds. He should be able to work loose after a few hours, and if he didn't, Sked really wasn't going to lose much sleep over it. They were pretty much in the same line of work—freelance experts in the tech field—but you chose which assignments you took. For this one, you had to be a real creep, no matter what the money was like. He played the innocent, but there was no way he didn't know what had been going on, what he'd been supporting.

If he got out, he deserved to be monster food.

Satisfied that nothing of value had been forgotten, he entered the passageway and almost immediately bumped into the Colonel.

"Sorry," he said.

"Think nothing of it. Looks like traffic control up there hasn't had their morning tea yet. Still sluggish."

The Colonel seemed completely calm, which contrasted with Sked's thumping heart. Of course, this guy probably went into quite a few of his missions by jumping out of an airplane at night into enemy territory. That had to be sheer terror. Sked, on the other hand, got a jolt of adrenaline from walking through a darkened tunnel—quite a few of his bloodier incursions had started out exactly this way.

Finally, the group ahead managed to get itself moving and, within minutes, word was passed down the line that Cora was about to open the door.

He tensed and waited, but other than the line advancing slowly towards a slightly lighter patch up ahead, nothing indicated they'd entered a new phase in the operation. Another few moments later, his turn to leave the relative safety of the enclosure arrived.

The night was warm and silent, with wind rustling through the trees. For a single second, he felt a sense of cognitive dissonance. Fragrant nights like this one should have been dedicated to drinking caipiroskas and dancing in a tropical sweat, without the sense of imminent death.

The group came to a halt and Cora circled back to talk to him and the Colonel. "It's a pretty long line. If we get separated, take whoever is with you to the lifeboat. I calculate you need to head to the northern tip of the island and once there, walk on the western coast. You shouldn't need to go too far."

Sked patted his pocket, where they'd put one of the three compasses the team had liberated from the Blood Orchid base. Evidently, without access to cell towers or satellite phones, the white slavers had reverted to archaic means of finding their way through the woods.

He nodded. "Are we taking the path?"

"Yeah. I would actually prefer not to, because I assume it's for the use of the natives, but we'll never get everyone through this tangle if we try to go through the trees. Try to keep them as close as you can."

"I'll try," Sked replied. The truth, however, was that he was concerned about the survival of exactly one person: Akane. That probably meant he was going to have to take care of the woman they'd pulled out of the cell, but that was it. He'd help get the group to the lifeboat exactly as long as Akane was part of it.

He smirked. She would be proud of him, thinking he was returning to his old personality, becoming the bastard she knew and loved again, but it was more a question of prioritizing. He didn't know these people; he wouldn't risk Akane to save them.

They advanced over the path in a hushed silence that still managed to seem noisy. Though the march had been uneventful, he still wasn't relaxed five minutes after exiting the tunnel.

For good reason.

His position in the rear allowed him to hear the attack coming up on them seconds before it arrived. But that was too late.

Small figures darted out of the woods at high speed. By the time he realized it was the dinosaurs, several had already shot past him.

One of them bounced off the Colonel and fell to the ground. The only sign the enormous man gave that he'd felt anything was a muted "oof."

Up ahead, screaming began as the group realized what was happening.

Sked ignored everything else and rushed to get to Akane. He pushed her against a tree, helped Ania into position beside her and tried to see where the creatures had gone.

It was too dark to spot anything, and the sudden panicked trampling from the front of the line made it impossible to hear. It sounded like a troop of elephants stampeding, trumpets and all.

Then there was a lull, a few seconds of relative quiet as the people making noise moved farther away. It was broken by a high-pitched screech that echoed to their right, just before Crazy Eddie emerged from the darkness. He carried his phone in one hand for light, and the head of one of the creatures in the other. His watermelon chopper hung from his belt, black where it was stained with blood. He grinned maniacally when he spotted them. "One down," he said. "A lot to go."

"Too many to go." It was the Colonel's voice. The man joined them as if he'd just materialized out of the jungle. Had he been an enemy, Sked knew, they would all be dead. "We won't be able to push through that many. They're strong for their weight."

Sked studied him. The Colonel was covered in blood, black in the dim light. Bleeding gashes scored his chest, but he didn't seem overly troubled by the injuries. His jaw was tight, and it didn't take a genius to guess what he was thinking: his wife was out there.

"Did you see where everyone went?" Sked said.

"No. They scattered when the creatures came."

"So what now?"

The Colonel hesitated, but when he spoke, he did so with a dull voice. "We need to head north. That's where we'll find survivors. There's no way we can mount a rescue operation in these woods in the dark."

"All right."

They headed north, moving through the underbrush about five yards from the path, trying to stay in the shadows.

"No good," the Colonel whispered after a few minutes of that. "We're losing so much time and making so much noise that we're not gaining anything by not being on the path."

Sked pushed a branch out of his face. "Yeah. And we're also wasting a ton of battery life just trying to keep ourselves from tripping over the bushes."

The group stepped back onto the path, watching for enemies, human or animal. Nothing appeared, so they made their way up the path with the Colonel in the lead, shooting down the path at an accelerated clip. Though the big man made no sound, he also made little effort to allow them to keep up. He'd likely die before admitting it, but Sked guessed he was desperate to know where his wife was, whether she was alive.

Crazy Eddie scrambled into position directly behind the Englishman while Sked let Akane lead a whimpering Ania ahead of him. He brought up the rear, knowing if they got separated from the Colonel, it would be up to him to bring them home.

He had the compass, but he wouldn't be surprised if the old officer at the helm could find his way on the winding path in the dark by dead reckoning.

The moon shone through the trees, bright enough that, by staying on the well-trod sand, they could move without using the cell phones or flashlights to show the way. They were also moving relatively quietly.

"Careful here," the Colonel's voice came from the front of the line. "Casualty."

Seconds later, Crazy Eddie cursed.

The Triad guy who wasn't Harold lay in the path, very much dead. Sked expected him to have been bled to death by their dinosaur pals, but that wasn't the case. An arrow protruded from his neck, straight up into the air.

Ania yelped at the sight, but other than that, gave no sign of life. She was keeping up with the group, but Sked watched her shuffling steps and suspected that she was too weak to keep it up much longer. The woman wouldn't have made it this far without leaning on Akane.

He stepped in and supported the weight of Ania's free shoulder. Akane gave him a surprised glance that promised questions if they made it out, but he simply said: "We need to get moving. You're slowing us down. Come on."

They pushed through the undergrowth and found themselves on the beach. The moon reflecting on the water was almost as good as daylight.

"Try to stay low. We'll be silhouetted against that," Sked whispered to Akane.

She chuckled. "That's not going to be easy."

"Just leave me," Ania whispered. "I'm slowing you down."

It was the first time Sked had heard her speak. Her accent seemed more German than Polish, which was where he'd pegged her as being from, considering her name. Interesting, but not unexpected. The kind of people that captured women for the sex trade were particularly fond of grabbing people who didn't quite belong. Children of migrants were an old favorite, and the Polish girls scattered over Europe with no safety net were popular in Asian and Middle-Eastern markets.

"Absolutely not," Akane said.

"I'll carry you if I have to," Sked replied.

With those words, Ania broke down and began to cry, but she redoubled her effort, as if trying to justify his concern.

"There's the lifeboat," Akane said.

A few yards ahead on the beach, the Colonel had stopped dead. They could see their objective up in front, but none of their companions had made it there yet. Though they'd been at the back of the line, they were the first to arrive at the lifeboat.

"I just hope this one isn't full of arrows as well," Sked said.

When they reached the lifeboat, it had obviously been disturbed, but appeared to be otherwise undamaged and seemingly seaworthy.

The Colonel motioned to the sand behind the boat. "Stay here. If the rest of the group arrives before I get back, leave without me. Understood?"

No one answered.

"Understood?"

Sked nodded.

And with that, the Colonel ran across the beach and disappeared back into the woods.

***

When the dinosaurs hit, Cora dove to one side, sheltered behind a tree, and grabbed anyone who ran into range in the blind panic. To her relief, Lai was one of her catches. Mary and the cook landed a few moments later.

It took all her training to keep from rushing blindly into the trees when the sound of someone being torn to pieces by the dinosaurs reached her through the night. Normally, she would have ignored all the tactical advice about knowing the numbers and the terrain before rushing in, but this time, the training held.

She'd just spotted one of the natives.

It was just a glimpse, only for a second as he crossed a moonlit gap between the trees. He'd disappeared from sight immediately but she knew better than to question what she'd seen. There was at least one native out there.

And if she'd seen one, there would be a dozen under cover, using their intimate knowledge of woods they'd roamed since prehistoric times to remain hidden from even trained interlopers.

So she stood perfectly still, in the dark, just watching and listening, barely breathing. Lai and the rest took her lead, either because they were smarter than she expected or because they were scared completely shitless.

She knew the shock would only hold them motionless for so long, so she reinforced the message by catching each of their eyes and putting her finger over her lips, receiving a nod from each in turn.

Cora held them in place for five minutes, each goddamned second lasting an eternity. She heard movement in the trees, screams, grunts and screeches in the distance. But with no way to understand who was a friend in need of help and who was an enemy just waiting for a clear shot with an arrow, she had to stay where she was, hating every second of it. The grinding of her teeth sounded loud in her head, but she had no capacity to stop herself. Not moving was as far as her self-control took her; to ask for more would have been inhuman.

Only when both her senses and her instincts told her that the coast was clear did she turn to her companions and whisper, "Follow me."

"Where are we going?" Lai said.

She knew what he was asking. He wanted to know if they would be charging off to ambush the dinosaurs and the islanders and save whoever could be saved. He probably wanted to do just that. "To the lifeboat," she replied through teeth she still couldn't quite unclench.

Lai nodded, the gesture just visible in the dim light. He didn't like it any more than she did, but he wasn't going to argue the point.

Not that Cora was about to let him. The only thing she'd succeeded at thus far was keeping Lai alive. That would change over her dead body.

"This way," she whispered.

They headed away from the path, at right angles to their original trajectory and then, after walking for a minute or so, turned back the way they'd been moving. That would take them in the same direction the path went, but it should allow them to avoid the three-way fight brewing back where they'd come from.

The going was hard enough that Cora almost led them back to the path, but then she heard the sounds of... something... approaching from that direction. So instead of being able to return to the course of least resistance, they pushed further into the tangle.

The maneuver did nothing to throw off their pursuers. Whatever was out there appeared to be matching them step for step.

She held up a hand and her tiny, ragged band stopped behind her—almost like real soldiers. But the rustling in the night kept up.

"Move!" she said. No point in being quiet anymore. Someone or something knew they were out there. Cora grabbed Lai's wrist and tugged him at high speed through the trees, trying to bear the main brunt of the whipping leaves herself. The objective wasn't to outrun whatever was chasing them. Instead, she wanted to open up a few dozen yards of distance while the element of surprise was on their side, then choose a place to make a stand and shoot it out.

As if echoing her thoughts, the crack of a gunshot sounded off in the distance. It was too far off to have anything to do with their own predicament, but she instinctively turned her head in the direction of the sound.

That proved a mistake.

A large, white object on the ground sent her tumbling into the weeds with Lai flying over her and the cook and Mary only managing to stop in time.

"Oh my God," Mary said. "It's the Colonel's wife! Oh... I think she's dead."

Cora spared the body a glance, and it was more than enough. She was full of arrows.

That told her exactly who was following. It was the natives... and she'd led her team right into the place they were waiting for her.

Another failure.

Cora nearly gave up then and there, but then remembered her life, growing up in the *barrio* and everything she'd had to go through to reach the place where she was. She'd never given up. She didn't even think she was capable of giving up.

More gunfire in the distance told her others weren't giving up either. She stood and hauled Lai to his feet, too.

She selected a pair of trees growing together for cover and, still dragging her employer, she hunkered behind them. They seemed to be correctly angled to allow her to face the people coming for her. She had little hope of surviving... but she would take some of them to hell with her. Her pistol felt right in her hand.

The first native charged in, and she shot him in the head. It was a silly thing to do, but she was pissed, and he was stupid, running in the light, so she risked the low-percentage shot.

Then she hid behind the tree as an arrow thunked into the trunk.

"Screw you!" Cora yelled. Out of the corner of her eye, she saw that Mary and the cook were hiding behind the next tree over. How they'd gotten there was beyond her: she'd lost track.

She broke cover to fire, but couldn't get a clean shot.

Nevertheless, the movement saved her life. An arrow impaled the tree where her neck had been just a moment before.

It had come from behind them.

Cora turned to confront the new threat, already aware that they were dead. Surrounded, outnumbered soldiers didn't come home.

The five islanders facing her, arrows already drawn, knew it as well as she did. They didn't crow, just studied her for a moment. She would be dead before she raised her gun.

A shot exploded from the left and the nearest of the natives fell. The rest scattered, spooked, to be replaced by a large figure in white.

The Colonel, panting like an overworked horse, glared at the woods where the natives had scattered. Then he turned to Cora.

"Where is she?"

Cora just shook her head. "Behind us. She didn't make it."

The Colonel nodded. "Where?"

"Ten meters down our trail."

"Thank you. I'll hold this place. Get to the lifeboat. You're almost there. Straight the way I came."

"I'll..."

"Don't argue with me. Go now."

"Yes, sir." This time, she did salute before grabbing Lai again and thundering into the trees.

Behind her, she heard another gunshot. And another.

The lifeboat sat on the beach precisely where the Colonel had said it would be. Four faces looked out from behind the boat, and she felt gratitude that someone else had survived.

Another shot rang out from where the Colonel had been as they reached the boat.

Another fired while they began to drag it into the water.

Then two more.

And then nothing. The jungle was silent, almost as if it was empty.

Cora knew better.

"Do you think anyone else is coming?" Sked asked

"I doubt it. It's a mess in there," Cora replied.

"Eight of us?"

"Yeah."

"All right. Let's get the hell out of here." They began to push it back into the sea.

CHAPTER 16

It's a good thing the waves aren't very big, Cora reflected, because Akane never seemed to have heard of the basic principle of pointing the ship's nose into the breakers. It took them nearly five minutes, buffeted from the side, to push the lifeboat to where they could climb aboard and row.

There were only four oars in there. Lai, Cora, Sked and Crazy Eddie grabbed one each. After three pulls, Mary yelled.

"Wait! Someone's coming out of the forest!".

They stopped rowing and turned to look. At first, all Cora saw was a group of natives... but then she saw that the natives were actually running after two figures already waist deep in the water.

"Turn us around!" she called to Akane.

The subsequent maneuver would never be taught at any of the great military colleges. At one point, the current was pushing the boat away from the desperate swimmers faster than they could advance.

But in the end, they managed to drag a panting and spluttering Harold aboard. He fist-bumped Eddie as the crew rowed towards the black dot that marked the position of the other survivor. His head bobbed up and down in the water about fifty yards from the lifeboat.

"Come on!" Cora shouted. "Pull like men, you pussies."

For a moment, just one single second, she was a Marine again, working as part of a team to help a comrade in trouble. All the problems, and the questioning, the failures of the past few days were forgotten as she pulled with body and soul.

Mary and Harold, not on the oars, dragged the wet man aboard. He collapsed onto the floor of the boat and hyperventilated for thirty seconds before pushing himself to his hands and knees.

Cora was too preoccupied rowing the hell away from the shore and the natives to check on him. The important part was that he was out of the water.

Besides, there were more important things to consider. As she watched the beach recede, it became very clear that the only thing that saved them was that the islanders seemed unwilling to wade further than about knee-deep into the water, and they hadn't shot any of their arrows. Perhaps they only shot them when they were certain they could recover them later. Maybe they thought the sea would finish off the interlopers.

Which meant they knew about the monsters.

Finally, after rowing forever, she felt safe enough to take her eyes off the beach and contemplate the man they'd saved.

She let out a guffaw, a sound of pure delight and... relief? "It figures," she said as Doctor Pendalai looked up at her. "I'm starting to wish we'd had you around back in my days in the service. It's always nice to have at least one soldier in your platoon who just can't be killed. Not by monsters and not by bad guys. I would have sent you on every suicide detail ever, secure in the knowledge that you'd come back."

The doctor grinned, but there was more relief than humor in the look. "I was pretty sure I wasn't going to make it this time. My arms are still weak from yesterday." He pulled himself onto one of the empty seats. "And I can't really say I'm delighted to be here. Last time I was on one of these, it got chomped by a huge dinosaur thing."

"We can throw you back," Akane said.

Another smile. "Thanks, but I think I'll risk it for now."

"Okay. Just let us know. The rowers would thank you for lightening the load."

Cora scanned the water, looking for any signs of the monster in the moonlight. She pushed the question of what she felt for the doctor, why she'd been so happy to see him, off to one side. For now, she would simply write it off as admiration for a person she respected, combined with the emotional stress of the last few days.

Because a middle-aged Indian doctor definitely wasn't the kind of guy she would ever fall for.

"Does anyone still have their compass?" she asked. Her own had been smashed when she dove for cover in the initial dinosaur charge.

"Here," Sked said.

"All right. Does anyone know which way we need to go?"

"East," the doctor replied. "As true as we can keep it, and we'll hit Andaman. We really can't miss. It's only about ten kilometers and the island is quite long, stretching north and south. We should actually be fine, unless..."

His voice trailed off. There was no need to clarify the 'unless'. Everyone knew what he was referring to, except for Ania, who looked unsure about what was happening. She just sat on the floor beside Akane's pilot chair, one hand on the hacker's thigh, as if the human contact between them was the only thing that kept Ania believing that she had actually woken from her nightmare.

"That's a long row," Eddie said.

"You want to turn on the engine? Doc says that's what caused the monster to hit us last time," Akane interjected.

"Then you row and I'll steer. Shouldn't these things have emergency beacons? I mean, if you're shipwrecked, you'd want to tell as many people as possible, right?"

"Except," the doctor said, "that I'm not sure the monster can't hear them. When we went out in the other lifeboat, we were attacked just after we turned it on."

"I thought you said it was the engine."

"I said I thought it might be. The truth is that we don't know, and I'd rather not test it."

Eddie grunted, but said nothing more.

"Guys," Mary said, "I think I see something."

"What kind of thing?" Cora asked, craning her head.

"Something big. With a red light on it."

"Huh?" Finally, almost directly behind her, Cora spotted what Mary was referring to. "It's the container ship!" she said.

"Son of a bitch," Lai said. "It's still there? Someone is going to take a huge loss this quarter. Either that or a huge repair bill for ship engines."

"Should I steer towards the ship?" Akane asked.

"You bet your ass," Cora responded. "They should be able to get us some help. Worst-case scenario, they'll have a radio, satellite phones and internet access."

Mary looked worried. "Unless it's a ghost ship," she said.

Cora laughed, but not as heartily as she usually would have. The way things were going, it wouldn't have surprised her at all to find an army of the walking dead waiting to eat her brains when they arrived. "Not likely. Ghost ships don't have working lights."

"I suppose you've been on several dozen ghost ships in your lifetime," Eddie snarked from his oar.

Cora gave him the finger, but was smiling inside. That was almost exactly the way this conversation would have played out on a Marine vessel, right down to the final single-digit gesture. They were all nervous, and they all tried to mask it under a veneer of moronic banter. She was home.

"Whatever. At least we know one thing," she said. "No monster is going to be sinking that ship."

"I dunno. From what you say, those things are pretty big."

"Not that big."

"And what if the ones you saw already were just the babies, and mommy comes out to play?" Eddie asked.

"Then, for all our sakes, I hope you're really good with that straight knife of yours, because I don't have any answers."

Eddie grinned. "Don't worry. I'll slice it into lizard sushi."

"Cool. I'll watch."

The dark bulk of the ship loomed ahead of them. Cora realized that every eye on the lifeboat was focused on the container vessel, and most faces were rapt, as if expecting God himself to reach out a hand from the large vessel.

She didn't fall into that trap. There were still several hundred yards to go, and they already knew what kind of thing swam in these waters.

Cora scanned the waves for any sign of monsters.

***

Sabrina leaned against the railing. The lifeboat approaching the ship had sailed inside the interdiction zone where the ship's sonic defenses kept Shiva and Kali away, which meant they were safe from getting eaten. She cursed and turned to Dieter Ratzenberger. "If you'd told me about this earlier, we could have herded my babies and taken them out."

The Mosasaurs could be directed using the same sound generators that the ship used to keep them away. All they would have had to do was to nudge one of the creatures into the correct area and then watch. Once in place, they pretty much had only one reaction to something the size of the lifeboat, and that was to establish territorial domination.

The problem would have disappeared. Instead...

"I don't want anyone to see them boarding. Clear the deck of the crew and all the analysts. If they argue, tell them we're doing a pirate boarding simulation, and if they still argue, toss them in the dinosaur pens. Then get these people on board and lock them somewhere without internet access until I decide what to do with them."

Dieter gave her a tight grimace. "Thank you so much for telling me how to do my job. Should we also escort them aboard with a minimum of fuss or should we frighten them and make them panic, so they scream a lot? We're trained professionals, Sabrina. We can handle this."

"Then handle it." She refrained from asking him if he was going to be as ineffectual as he'd been when attempting to monitor competitive activity. No need to antagonize him yet. But if he messed up again…

Men in black jumpsuits clustered around Ratzenberger. Sabrina could see others sweeping the passenger deck of the *Stern Liberia*. They could do nothing about anyone watching from the bridge, but she wasn't too concerned about that: the crew had been told that there would be some unusual comings and goings, and part of their contract was that they weren't to be curious about it. As long as they didn't get close enough to see anything or hear the conversations, she was fine with letting them watch from afar.

One small blessing had been the bright moonlight. Had the moon been down, or the sky been clouded, their lookout probably would have missed the tiny lifeboat until the people on board were knocking on their hull. In that case, containment would have become a nightmare.

She wasn't qualified to assess whether Ratzenberger was any good at his job, but he certainly gave every indication of competence as he coordinated the onboarding efforts. First, he assigned two of his men to guide the lifeboat in using light signals. Then he had other men throw down a rope ladder while a little group held innocuous items like blankets and a first aid kit. She didn't think any of the resort guests—or the survivors of some playboy's yacht disaster—were going to board the rescue ship looking for trouble, but if they did, their minds would be set at ease when they saw those preparations.

Sabrina grunted in grudging recognition. Maybe he knew what he was doing after all. Then she joined him at the head of the rope ladder.

He nodded and looked happy to see her.

That was a first. She would have thought Ratzenberger would want to do everything himself. But then she remembered an anecdote she'd heard from a guy who used to work for a tech startup in Latin America. He'd told her that the recruiting team, male and female, were assigned female names and email addresses when in the hiring process. The reason was simple: having a woman coordinating things made it seem more legitimate and less intimidating, especially for female candidates. And since the company this guy worked for had a tiny office with no meeting room and had to hold all the recruiting interviews in cafés, they wanted all the legitimacy they could get.

She'd angrily asked him if that wasn't sexist as hell, and he'd shrugged and said no one cared, because it was true.

Dieter apparently shared that philosophy, and thought it would be good for the rescues to see a woman's face, so Sabrina lined up beside him and gritted her teeth for her closeup. She hated being around people she didn't know, and this encounter promised to stretch her social skills to the limit.

She contented herself with the knowledge that it would only be for a few minutes and that, after they were safely contained, she'd feed them to her Compsognathus families. They would undergo a marvelous transformation from useless witnesses to usable nutrients. "Hello, dinosaur food," she whispered as the lifeboat clunked against the hull of the *Stern Liberia*.

Dieter shot her a look that was half amused grin and half warning to control herself.

People began to climb up the ladder. The first to come up was a young woman in awful makeup, followed by another, equally young but much too thin, who refused all offers of help and stood apart, flinching away from everyone, even the man who offered her a blanket.

Dieter's people led the two women off to a conference room that opened onto the deck and which had been chosen not only for its proximity but also because the door was a nice thick bulkhead-type door, complete with one of those round locking mechanisms that she associated with submarines. They'd removed the one on the inside.

Weirdly, the lost-looking tourists that the first two girls represented perfectly were soon replaced by a much tougher-looking crew. The next person up the ladder was another woman, almost as thin and pale as the second, but covered with tattoos. She didn't look frightened as she emerged onto the deck; instead, she looked around with a sharp eye that seemed to take everything in at once.

Sabrina forced a smile. "Would you like a blanket?" she said, trying to look concerned.

"It's a hundred degrees out here. Who the hell needs a blanket?" the woman replied. "Where are Mary and Ania?"

"We put them in a room with refreshments." It was true. The table in the room they'd prepared held soft drinks and cookies, the only thing they'd been able to scrounge up on such short notice, but another link in the chain of deception.

"Show me."

"It's that door right there," Sabrina replied, pointing.

The woman marched straight in.

Next came a bunch of guys, each harder-looking than the last. An old guy with steely eyes. Two Chinese-looking men who seemed almost too relaxed for her comfort, as if they were used to controlling larger numbers through intimidation. The following two men were more nondescript, but the last guy, though not big, exuded an air of competence that chilled her. Like the second thin woman, he seemed to take everything at a glance, but unlike her, Sabrina could almost see his thought process. He counted heads and shrugged. Then he went where he was told.

The last person up the ladder was a woman a full head taller than Sabrina and who looked like she could beat Ratzenberger's team up singlehandedly. She saw Sabrina looking down the ladder and grunted. "I'm the last one. Ten of us made it off that island. That's it."

"What happened?"

"It's a long story. Do you have an internet connection?" The big woman held up her phone. "I'm not getting anything, and I have to make a shitload of calls."

"We should be able to connect you inside. If you step in that door over there, we have some refreshments set up, and you can tell me your story. It sounds absolutely incredible."

The woman headed for the door. Unlike the guy before her, she seemed unconcerned with Dieter's troops standing around. Even holding blankets and first aid kits, they looked anything but innocuous.

Sabrina turned to Dieter and whispered, "Sink the lifeboat."

He gave her a sardonic smile. "Thank you, Captain Obvious."

She snorted and walked to the room holding the survivors. She stuck her head in the door to see that they were beginning to relax, drinking from Styrofoam cups. Some had even sat in the chairs around the table. One of the Chinese guys was munching a cookie.

She pulled her head out of the door and nodded to two of Dieter's men who immediately swung the thick metal door shut and spun the wheel to seal it.

"They can't get out?" she said.

"Not unless they can chew through metal," the man closest to her replied.

"Good."

She walked off to think about how she could feed them to her dinosaurs without anyone else on board being any the wiser. If she had Dieter kill them all, it would be easy, but her poor babies cooped up on the ship needed their exercise. Hunting live prey would be ideal.

But how to make it happen?

CHAPTER 17

"Subtle," Sked said.

"As a plane crash," Akane replied.

"What are you guys talking about?" Cora said.

"The way they locked us in," Sked replied. "They weren't very concerned with making the reception committee believable in the least."

"Nope," Harold, the Philadelphia Triad leader said. "But they were smart enough to split us into groups of two when we boarded. With all the guys they had patrolling the deck, there wasn't a hell of a lot we could do to fight it. Besides, they had cookies." He finished stuffing one into his mouth. "That has to count for something."

Cora studied each of the speakers in turn. "Are you saying the people on this ship aren't what they seem? That their welcome was fake?"

"Try the door," Sked said with a nod in the appropriate direction.

He was amused to see that the big Marine actually walked all the way to the thick iron plate and studied it intently.

"There's no handle."

"I know. It should be a big metal wheel. Someone took it out before they closed it from the outside."

"What the hell?"

"Precisely what we said," Sked replied. "They don't want us in the way, from which I surmise that these guys aren't thrilled to see us."

"No wonder they could afford to park an expensive boat in the middle of nowhere. They're probably smugglers or pirates," Lai said. "Now it makes a little more sense."

"What they're doing doesn't matter," Akane said. "I would like to know what they're going to do with us."

Sked winked at all of them and pointed to his ear, signaling that the crew of the ship could very likely be listening to every word they said. "I wouldn't worry about that. They have been really nice to us, so I guess we owe it to them to trust them. Maybe they'll keep us confined here until they can drop us somewhere, but we're much better off than back on that island."

"I suppose you're right," Akane said, playing along.

While they spoke, Sked rummaged in his backpack and pulled out a small black box. He turned it on and walked around the room, holding it out towards the walls. He'd already done a visual check and was pretty certain there were no cameras in the place, but the black box would rule out any really small or well-concealed cameras or listening devices.

He finished his lap of the room and chuckled. "Either these guys are total amateurs or they're so good we're screwed anyway. I can't find anything."

Akane pulled a chair out and sprawled on it. "So what now?"

"Now, we find out what's going on."

"That should be a neat trick," Crazy Eddie said. "My phone is saying there isn't a single network in a million miles, so unless you've got something in that bag of tricks that can get you through a steel door, we're out of luck."

Sked smiled. "There's no need for anything that drastic yet. All we need is a better antenna than your phone has. I'll bet you anything you want that there's a network on this ship, but that the nodes near us are off. If our hosts are planning on dropping us off somewhere, we don't want to antagonize them. If there's something more sinister going on… I'd much rather know what it is than jump out the door and run into it." He paused, wondering how much he should say openly, but then sighed. He hadn't been joking earlier: if there was someone listening, despite his precautions, they were already screwed. "We have one advantage: these guys were so preoccupied with putting up a good guy front that they didn't frisk us for weapons." He glanced at Cora's holstered sidearm, displayed proudly on her right hip. "Although I don't think they could have missed yours. Fortunately, the rest of us are a little… less accustomed to showing off our guns in public. So they'll be expecting one gun at most. How many do we actually have?"

Harold and the cook from the yacht raised their hands.

"So, five guns plus Eddie's chopper. That's not bad." He grinned at Akane. "Yeah, I'm also counting yours. You never gave it up, so I know it's still on you somewhere."

She stuck out her tongue but didn't deny it.

"Now it's time to get to work."

He pulled out his laptop and powered it up. The charge was near 100%, which meant that, unless he decided to use full processor power by running 3D rendering software or something equally stupid, he had several hours to work with. Good. He might need them.

"Akane, could you slip this wire through a crack in the door?"

"Antenna?"

"Yeah. We probably won't need it, but I would feel better knowing there's no chance of my connection going down in the middle of trying to get us hooked into the system."

Akane knew what she was doing, but still had a little trouble with the thick door until she finally managed to find a crack between the door and jamb that allowed the thin wire through.

Even before she was finished, Sked was scanning the air around the ship for electronic traffic.

"Bingo," he said.

"What do you have?"

"Ship's wi-fi. It's a weak signal, but I can probably get in. Unfortunately, I'm going to have to brute force it, because they're not using the manufacturer's defaults."

"Won't someone be watching?" Akane asked.

"I doubt it. They're using Nexxt routers without any kind of encryption." Akane nodded, knowing as well as he did that it was the kind of equipment a regular family might use, hoping the password they chose was enough to keep them safe. Normally, it was, as someone had to be specifically interested in the household to get close enough where they would actually brute force the router through the wi-fi signal. People who had something to hide or a lot of money would use better protection.

"How long?" Cora asked.

"Could be ten minutes. Could be thirty. Definitely won't go over forty for this kind of router, and it will only go that high if we're really unlucky."

"Won't it detect the failed attempts to get in and sound an alarm or shut down or something?"

"Not this stuff. Hell, the fact they're using wi-fi this open makes me think we might have misjudged our hosts. Maybe they're just afraid we might be pirates and are calling the Coast Guard."

He left the computer running and walked to the table. The first thing he did was to check the Coca-Cola bottle on the table. One of his few clear memories from his time in Latin America was getting caught out with a sugar-reduced 'regular' Coke. The locals had explained that, in an effort to pretend to be European socialists, the government had not only applied an imbecilic sugar tax but also forced any foodstuff with a high energy content to put a black mark on their labels saying that the product might be unhealthy. Though his contact hadn't been able to explain whether the government was simply brain-dead or fishing for bribe money, Coca-Cola had caved to the pressure and introduced a version of the original flavor with 'less sugar' and zero-calorie sweeteners. The sneaky part was that, other than the fact that it said 'Original Flavor – Less Sugar' on the label, it looked exactly the same as the real thing.

Until one had the misfortune of drinking it. It tasted like cow piss.

Worse, when he went to ask for something else, his friend had laughingly explained that the other companies had caved even harder, and there was not one soft drink remaining that didn't contain the recycled-puke taste of artificial sweeteners.

"Yo!" Cora said. "Shouldn't you be watching the computer instead of reading the labels on the bottles? It's a Coke for Crissakes."

"Nah. It's going to take at least a few minutes before we get any results." Unable to understand the label, he shrugged and poured himself a glass. It tasted okay; apparently the insanity hadn't reached Asia.

"Shouldn't we be doing something else?"

"If you think that would help, go ahead. I can't get us through that door, but I can probably get us onto the ship's network in a few minutes." He sipped the drink slowly, more to make the time pass than because he wanted to exude an air of calm confidence. The truth was that he *hated* waiting for brute-force password-cracking systems to work, and he was just as anxious as Cora for the results.

"And what are you going to do once you get in?"

"First, I'm going to look around very carefully to see if there's anything nasty, security-wise, lurking on the system. Once I'm confident there isn't, I want to do two things: send the video in your phone out to a couple of people I trust to handle it correctly," he nodded towards Cora, "and find out what ship this is, who owns it and what it's carrying."

"This ship is the *Stern Liberia*," someone said.

Sked didn't immediately recognize the voice and turned to see if someone from the ship's crew had suddenly appeared in the doorway to make the dramatic proclamation, but the door was still solidly shut, so he scanned the people nearby, finally settling on the ship's cook.

"How do you know that?" he said.

The guy shrugged. "I read it on the side. I never board a vessel without first knowing what I'm getting into. It seems like a perfectly legitimate ship. I see Stern containers all the time in port, and Liberia is one of the classic flags of convenience. I was expecting to be getting drunk with the crew tonight, not getting locked in a conference room." He shrugged. "It's still better than monsters and cannibals."

The woman with him, the only other survivor from the yacht apart from Cora and Lai himself, giggled as if he'd said something inordinately funny. Sked rolled his eyes and walked back over to the computer which, as expected, still displayed a sign saying that the password-cracking process was still under way.

But the incident gave him pause. Even though he had more experience in the field than most professional soldiers, his overriding instinct was to hack his way out of any problem digitally. The cook had reminded him that there were other ways to get things done, even gathering information didn't absolutely have to be a matter of going online.

"You know what," he said to Cora, "you're right. We should also be looking for another way out of this room. Check the floor and the ceiling for ways out. Check to see if we can find any vents that we can squeeze through."

"I'm not exactly built for squeezing through vents," Cora said.

"Doesn't matter. If one of us can get outside that door, all that person has to do is spin a metal wheel and the vents become academic. Besides, right now we're just looking; no one is going anywhere until either I have a sense of what's going on or I'm convinced that security is too tight to crack."

It would be a gigantic oversight for these people to have left a major escape route uncovered, of course, but it wasn't impossible. After all, they'd only had a few minutes to react between the time their boat changed course for the container ship and the time they were being ushered aboard. Even removing the inner door handle would have been a challenge in that timescale.

But the rest of the team went at it with verve, pulling up the awful brown carpet that looked like it had been laid in the 1970s and poking at the ceiling while standing on the table. Everyone was checking nooks and crannies except for Ania, who was eating a chocolate-filled cookie with an expression of wonder, lost in her own world, and Akane, who was still lounging on the same chair and raising eyebrows in his direction until he couldn't help but notice.

"We've got something," Lai said.

The billionaire was unceremoniously standing on a chair they'd put on the table itself, legs scratching the veneer finish. They'd pulled out a white foam ceiling panel and Lai's head was lost in the wiring above the false ceiling.

"What?" Cora said.

"Air vent. Not big, but maybe big enough for me to squeeze through."

Akane tsked. "If you can squeeze through, so can I. And I can probably shoot straighter."

"If we have to shoot at anyone, we're screwed," Lai retorted.

"No. If I have to shoot at anyone, *they're* screwed," Akane replied. "I don't miss."

"I mean if you start shooting, the whole ship will know what's happening. And container ship crews know how to deal with unfriendly boarders."

A shrug. "So I'll shoot them all. Pretty sure Cora will help out if you guys are too afraid."

"And then you'll be taken in and tried for piracy. Pray that it's the Indian Navy that grabs you, because you don't want to be taken by anyone else."

"What's another death sentence? I've been there, done that and I used to have the t-shirt, but they take that away when you get the tattoos."

"Guys," Sked said. "We're in."

Everyone crowded around the computer.

"Not going to work that way," Sked informed them. "Give me some space. Besides, only Akane will even be able to understand what I'm looking at, so there's no need to suffocate me." They moved back, ushered along by Cora and the doctor.

He began to type in commands, tentatively probing the ship's internet access.

"Pretty standard MSI," he said.

"And in English?" Cora demanded.

"Sorry. Maritime satellite internet. It's internet for ships." Finding nothing unexpected in the setup, he took a risk and accessed the information about different wi-fi routers. Only one of them caught his eye, a node grafted into the system via a cable connection. It likely meant that someone had brought their own router and piggybacked onto the ship's system. Those people would likely be sending encrypted traffic and their security would be professional grade both in detecting threats and blocking them. With the current setup, there was nothing Sked could do about breaking into something like that.

But he wouldn't need to. There were plenty of computers on the ship that he now had access to. No one expected someone to hack into your wi-fi at sea, after all, so security was anywhere from basic to downright silly on some of the devices he had access to. He ignored the obvious cellphones and tablets—why hack into the porn stashes of a bunch of bored sailors?—and also the navigation and propulsion systems—he had no interest in steering the boat off course, anyway.

"Bingo."

Everyone crowded around him again. This time he let them.

"Full points to you, sir," he said to the cook. "This is, indeed, the *Stern Liberia*, and we're carrying a load of biological specimens from San Diego."

"Zoo animals?" Cora asked in a puzzled voice.

"By the size of the load, it can't really be anything else. Half of the tonnage was loaded there." He scanned the rest of the manifest. "Ooh. Naughty. Mr. Lai was right. There's also a couple of dozen containers full of air conditioners on their way to Singapore which are ten days overdue already. Someone is going to be sending the shipping company a very sternly worded letter."

"More likely a very large debit note," Lai sneered.

"So a bunch of zoo animals and some household appliances. And if I'm reading this right, the ship is stopped here because they want to be here, not because of any mechanical failures. At least they didn't mention any to the Indian Navy when asking permission to halt for a couple of weeks."

"It makes no sense," Lai said.

"Agreed. And that leaves just one place to look if we don't want to get into some very serious hacking. The passenger manifest."

He clicked a few times. Either the admin computer he was accessing was extremely slow or the distant wi-fi router signal was very weak. It took forever before the names of the passengers began to appear on-screen.

None of them rang any bells, but there were a lot. He glanced at the cook. "Says here there are about sixty paying passengers on the ship. Is that normal?"

"On a container ship in the middle of the Indian Ocean?" He thought for a second. "Depends. They might be migrants heading to South Africa or something for a major infrastructure project. In that case, I wouldn't be surprised. Sometimes people pool their money to negotiate a room like this one for a passage."

"Nah. These guys are mainly American. A few Euros in there, too. Oh, and they all work for the same company. A company called ZooDef."

"Never heard of it," Cora said. "But it sounds right if they're transporting animals."

Akane spoke. "Ask the Buddha," she said.

Everyone looked at her. "Who?" Cora asked.

"Sked knows."

He did, and he also wished Akane knew how to keep her mouth shut. Especially when she was right.

He dashed a quick query to a one-time address from the list he'd been given to speak to the Buddha under non-secure conditions and, while he waited for an answer, turned to Cora. "Want to send out that video?"

It took forever to upload even a short clip and by the time he was done, an answer from the Electric Buddha was sitting in his inbox.

I'm glad you're alive. I was starting to fear the worst when you didn't contact me for so long.

ZooDef is a gene-modification company developing biological systems for defense applications.

If you are interested, there is a large fee offered for information regarding their current level of development.

There is also a job for Akane, if she wishes it. It concerns a passenger called Sabrina Williams. There is an even larger fee offered if she is unable to continue her research.

Sked looked around hastily, but since he'd been doing boring video upload stuff, they'd all drifted back to the table and to studying the air vent.

He cursed under his breath.

The bastard Buddha had known what they would find on North Sentinel Island all along. Both the white slavery operation and the crazy monsters. And he'd sent them there anyway.

In fact, the Buddha had probably sent everyone except Lai's yacht and the slavers themselves into the operating theater, knowing that if they damaged each other, he could get paid for all of it. After all, the Triads spent half their time at war with Blood Orchid, and the contract figures at the bottom of the email made ZooDef a very tempting target.

He sent us all here to kill one another. Son of a bitch.

Or maybe not. Maybe the Buddha had figured that Sked would find a way to contact him from the island, and therefore be able to give him instructions. Hell, that was what he, himself, had expected.

It hadn't worked out that way. Blood Orchid had been extremely smart to completely cut the island off from the net. That the Buddha had found out about it was typical of the man... he just seemed to know everything.

Which meant that he'd actually sent Sked and Akane to do a job. Blood orchid was probably part of the job. And this was definitely part of the job.

He erased the message and whispered in Akane's ear. "You up for an assassination assignment? Pays six zeroes."

"I'm stuck on this ship," she replied warily.

"So's the target."

CHAPTER 18

"All right, everyone, listen up," Sked said.

Eyes focused on him again.

"We've come to the conclusion that the people on this ship aren't friendly." He waited for groans, curses, signs of disbelief, anything to show the frustration the group must have felt at his words. None was forthcoming. Instead, they regarded him with resignation. "So we're going to bust out of here. Akane will attempt to open the door from the outside. She'll go into the ventilation."

"And if there's a guard?" Cora said.

"That's his bad luck," Akane replied. Agile as a cat, she jumped onto the table, balanced on the chair and disappeared into the guts of the roof. Sked smiled to himself, inwardly relieved to see the wonders that a few weeks of R&R had done for her. There was no sign of the way she'd been brutalized by the Chinese.

"Remember that you only need to go as far as the next wall," Cora called after her.

Akane's voice echoed back. "Of course. The shorter the better. Crawling around in filthy vents is not my idea of fun. This looks like it hasn't been cleaned since 19-oh-whenever this piece of crap ship was launched." Her voice trailed off, making it hard to understand what she said next, but it sounded to Sked that it wasn't useful information unless you were trying to expand your vocabulary when it came to terms describing obscene bodily functions.

Though he was never going to fit into a ventilation shaft—it was the one problem with being wide-shouldered—Sked stuck his head in, illuminating the claustrophobic tunnel with his cell phone. Akane had disappeared around a bend in the metal tubing.

A clanking sound reverberated through the pipe, followed by some muted cursing and then silence.

"I think she's out," he told the group. "Be ready to run."

"Why?"

A gunshot sounded, clear as day, on the deck outside.

"Because she isn't in the mood for subtlety. I hope Mr. Lai has good lawyers, because we might all end up on trial for piracy after she's done with these guys."

He tensed at a metallic sound from the doorway. What if the guard had seen Akane first?

But when the thick iron bulkhead door swung open, Akane's familiar smirk appeared. "One down," she said.

They poured out into the night, dead still and heavy with moisture in the depths of the small hours before dawn.

"Now what?" Sked asked Cora.

"We should hide."

"Where?"

"Under the lifeboat coverings."

The cook groaned. "That's literally the first place they'll look," he said. "Everyone tries that. It's stupid."

"So where would you suggest, genius?"

"I would go between the container stacks. It's dangerous as hell in there if you don't know what you're doing, plus, except along the edges, you probably won't have any security cameras like that one." He pointed up at one looking down at them from the corridor. "So they won't be able to find us immediately. It might take them five minutes."

"Dammit," Cora said. "We're fucked."

"Not necessarily," Sked replied. "There's a lot of people on this ship, and we think the bad guys and the crew aren't necessarily sharing information with each other. Even if the crew is monitoring the cameras, they might not even realize anything is wrong. They might think we're with the dudes in black."

"Your girlfriend just shot this guy," she kicked the corpse beside the door, "in the face. I kinda suspect they'll know that's not a good thing."

"Crap. Well, hopefully no one is watching too closely. No real need to watch while anchored in the middle of the ocean, after all. Help me toss him in the room."

He and Eddie dumped the corpse unceremoniously under the table in the room they'd just vacated, deep enough to hide him from a casual glace and then spun the wheel closed. There was nothing they could do about the pool of blood on the floor, but maybe, if whoever was watching the security monitors hadn't been very vigilant, they might get away clean.

Not that it would be much help. The people who locked them up would be back to relieve the guard at any moment. They wouldn't miss the blood... and the hunt would be on.

Under those conditions, Sked would have opted to be far, far away when they started looking for him.

That was not an option if they stayed on the ship.

And swimming for it was worse.

***

Sabrina watched the group from the island walk forward along the walkway and grinned. She switched to the next camera as they got out of range of the one before.

The crew, she knew, would not be monitoring the feed, not at that time of night, which made it even better. No one else would know what was happening, or how badly Dieter had messed up. All she had to do to remove him was to send the videos of the escape to Jermaine with a little note explaining the gravity of what having those particular people loose on this particular ship meant.

She'd do that, of course, but first, she had to get the situation under control. Witnesses were unacceptable, and besides, this was a great opportunity to test her Compsognathus herd under slightly more industrial conditions and gather some good video. The island had, she suspected, given all the advertising material it could, and most of ZooDef's clients weren't going to be releasing weaponized animals on remote islands. A ship was much more like a mall than a jungle was.

The witnesses had decided to hide in the container deck. Perfect.

She sang to herself, a few bars of Abba's *Dancing Queen*, and walked out of her room. For a moment she considered calling Tim Rugger to help her identify the right containers, but that wasn't necessary. She could find them by herself, and Tim wouldn't share the credit.

The ship was dark. She encountered no one on the way, which proved that Ratzenberger was incompetent. Had he been any good, he'd have known something bad had happened and had his people tearing the ship apart. But the halls were deserted, silent.

The container deck was huge, but that didn't matter. Most of it consisted of commercial freight she didn't give a damn about and the large, empty tanks they'd used to transport the Mosasaurs. She ignored all of that and headed straight for the Compsognathus area.

Most of the containers on the upper levels of the stack were empty now, which was fine by her.

She simply went along the ones on the ground floor of the pile, keyed in her override code that unlocked the outer door and the inner boxes and left the door ajar. Her beasties would come out eventually, and she hoped she'd have time to get out of the way before they did.

By the time she finished the bottom row, she calculated that there would be a little over 120 Compsognathus on the container deck by the time they all emerged, which should be quite fun.

She hurried back to her room; being on this deck would soon be unhealthy.

***

Flavia pulled her t-shirt back on and gave Johan a peck on the cheek. "That wasn't bad."

"Yeah, I could tell it was just okay by the way I had to put my hand over your mouth to muffle the screams so the entire ship wouldn't hear us," he replied.

"I wish you had a cabin to yourself," she said. The diamond pattern on the deck metal was probably permanently imprinted on her back.

He looked around. "Why? This place is kind of cool."

She shuddered. The stacks of containers around them looked like socialist worker housing, brutalist and rectangular, but infinitely more likely to topple. Except in the throes of ecstasy, she spent most of her time wondering if a big swell wouldn't knock the entire pile down on them. She grinned evilly in the knowledge that if they ever got a decent place to have sex in, he wouldn't be able to stop her screaming with just a hand.

But even though she couldn't relax completely, it was still better than sitting in her cabin watching Marion play one game after another of solitaire on her computer, and get shushed every time she wanted to start a conversation.

They started towards the back of the ship—she never bothered to learn the nautical name, even though some of the other analysts kept on about prows and bows and poops. "I should probably see what Hans is up to," Johan said. "He knows about us, but he'll be pissed if I leave him alone his entire shift."

"What's he doing?"

"Guarding some drifters we picked up. Boss says they're refugees of some sort, and we need to hold them until we can turn them over to the Indians."

Flavia grunted. His whole world seemed to be some macho fantasy about strutting around keeping order. Now that he had actual people to keep contained, he would be unbearable. Hell, she was surprised he'd even bothered to meet her that night. What was sex compared to prisoners?

Their footsteps echoed in the thin canyons between the piles of containers. The deck was mostly covered in the oblong boxes, but they were stacked together in approximately cubical formations five containers wide and five high with spaces between them enforced by metal grids high above. He was right... it did sound like her screams would have carried all the way back to the cabin area if he'd let her.

Suddenly, Johan stopped. "What was that?" he said.

She swatted his chest. "Don't start with that. You know as well as I do that the only thing we have to guard against on this ship is rats. And if it's rats, you won't be able to keep me from screaming no matter what you try."

He laughed and they began walking again. This time, she heard the noise, some kind of rustling up ahead. She'd been kidding about the rats, but it definitely sounded like there were some up ahead. She let him walk in front of her. Rats didn't actually frighten her, but why be with a big, hulking oaf if you couldn't use him to scare away rodents?

They approached an intersection between two piles of containers. Something flashed through the gap and she hugged him close.

"That's too big to be a rat," she said.

"What is?"

"Didn't you see it?"

"There's nothing there." He walked forward, laughing. She didn't want to approach whatever she'd seen, but she wanted him to leave her behind in the dark even less. The motion-sensor-activated lights were few and far between, placed every twenty meters or so. She cast long shadows.

They reached the intersection. They had to turn right to reach the stairs that led up to the main deck.

"Oh, shit!" Johan cried.

"What?"

He never answered her, and she never found out for herself. Her next impression was that the hallways were suddenly filled with a rancid odor and teeth. Millions and millions of teeth.

But that wasn't her last thought, or even the next-to-last. Her next-to-last last thought was that whoever was screaming now was certainly being heard upstairs. It was the scream of pain unimaginable.

Flavia's very last thought was the realization that the scream was hers.

***

This time, Cora saw them coming and fired first. A dinosaur fell to her first shot, the neck exploding and severing the head, which rolled off into the shadows of the containers.

"Lucky," Eddie laughed. He stood beside her with his strange square blade in the air and a look of eager anticipation on his features. "I thought that one was mine for sure."

"You'll get your chance," she replied grimly.

The tactical situation wasn't as bad as it had been on the island. The straight canyons between the container groupings were an infinitely superior place to fight a swarm of carnivores than the jungle. Not only was the lighting much better, but the terrain was straight and flat, offering no cover except for corners. It was like fighting in a city, except you didn't have to worry about snipers on the buildings.

The thought caused her to look up nervously. What if the dinosaurs had somehow gotten up there and were even now waiting to jump on them from above?

Cora shook her head. They had enough problems without adding terminal paranoia to the list.

"Fall back a bit. Let's find a spot we can defend," she shouted. "We're too exposed."

They moved along the endless, ruler-straight canyon for a few yards until they reached an intersection with one path that dead-ended at a wall. Every instinct screamed to avoid it, and Cora hesitated at the crossroad. She didn't like having her back to a wall, even if it made perfect sense from the tactical perspective of being able to hold out forever. It tasted too much of a desperate last stand.

Harold paid the price for her indecision. He was in the left arm of the crossroad and saw a group of dinosaurs heading their way. He fired at the leader, downing it, but the pack kept coming.

"Watch out!" he shouted.

Following Cora's lead, everyone else packed into the corridor she'd selected… everyone but Harold. He stood his ground, trying to take down more of the creatures to cover their retreat. Sheer numbers pulled him to the ground.

Then the dinosaurs did something she hadn't seen from them before: they dragged the screaming Harold down the corridor and out of sight faster than a person could run, moving with unexpected coordination.

Cora wanted to run after him, but Sked restrained her even as he used his other hand to grab Crazy Eddie. The dude was stronger than he looked, even though he looked plenty strong. "Nothing you can do. There's too many of them."

She turned on him and snarled. "So what do we do? Just sit here and let them pick us off one by one until there's nothing left but chewed-up bones?"

"We can hold here. They can only come at us from one direction."

"They just did that and still got Harold."

"But now we have a better proportion of guns to targets," Akane said. She was holding up Harold's pistol, which he'd dropped when they dragged him away.

"What good is that? Did you see how many there were? We'll be out of bullets in the middle of the next charge. We might as well go down swinging."

"Too late." Those words, surprisingly, came from Ania, who'd been silent the whole way. She pointed straight ahead, and then to each side. Bright points of eyes, reflective in the dark like the eyes of cats, shone back at them from all three directions. The ones in the jungle hadn't done that, either. Or they'd been too busy running to notice.

"Back!" Cora shouted, all thoughts of attack suppressed.

"Shouldn't we try to hold the entrance to this one?"

"No. We'll use the canyon as a killing field."

She was just thankful that they'd been forewarned this time. Just before the little bastards appeared, screams had sounded somewhere in the distance, terrified sounds that ended as abruptly as they began.

Cora didn't know about the rest of them, but she immediately put two and two together and guessed their sharp-teethed pursuers were somehow on the ship.

Or maybe that was the wrong way to think about it. Logic said that the little reptiles had been on the ship all along, and the ones on the island had arrived there from here. These were the people who'd built the things.

They retreated to the back of the corridor. It was the perfect place to defend against an enemy without ranged weapons: long and narrow. Every bullet would hit a minimum of one target, probably more.

"Make them count, boys," Cora said.

The team cocked their guns and awaited the charge. Eddie held his watermelon chopper at the ready. She tensed as the seconds—probably the last seconds of their lives—ticked into minutes.

Gunfire erupted, but not from them. It was automatic weapons fire, unmistakable staccato bursts. Somewhere, a man screamed.

The dinosaurs blocking the exit to their tunnel disappeared to be followed moments later by a group of black-clad humans firing machine guns. They sprinted across the intersection without looking their way.

Sked sprinted to the crossroad and popped his head out. He turned back towards them. "Time to go," he said.

"We're not going to find a more defensible position than this one," Cora replied.

"But we might find one where we can actually survive. Do what you want, I'm getting out of this death trap while the soldiers are distracted."

Cora cursed but rounded up the rest of the group and followed. Sked led them straight towards one of the stairwells on the side of the cargo deck.

They sprinted up and ran along a corridor until they came to a door that led into a room full of boxes and shelves.

"Kitchen stores," the cook said.

"It'll do for now," Sked replied.

The group filed in and the hacker faced Cora. "Akane and I are going to go have a look around. This boat is full of bad guys, so it's best that you stay here."

"Why should you go out there?"

"Because this is the kind of thing we do for a living. We know how to move around industrial areas—and ships, I suppose—without being seen."

"We've already been seen. Someone sicced the dinosaurs on us."

Sked considered that. "Yeah. But I want to know why the dinosaurs are fighting security. I have a suspicion that the left hand has no idea what the right hand is doing. Maybe we can work with that. Either way, we'll find a safe place to hunker down while we figure out what to do next."

They disappeared out the door into the pre-dawn glow. She hoped they knew what they were doing.

Because if they didn't, she sure as hell wasn't going to be able to hide this lot.

CHAPTER 19

Dieter was enraged. Sabrina could tell by the way his eyes flashed, something she'd always thought was a figure of speech. She studied him with the eye of a veteran biologist. Maybe 'flashing' wasn't the right word, but they certainly bulged and caught the light differently, wide open as they were. Also, a very unattractive vein protruded on the upper left corner of his forehead.

"That's enough, Dieter," she said. "You really shouldn't shout English insults with that accent. You sound like a Nazi in a bad movie."

He stopped mid-word, mouth hanging open, unable to believe she'd actually said what she'd said.

Sabrina had to stop herself from sniggering. He was like a cartoon character.

"Are you out of your mind?" Dieter said.

"Of course not."

"Then why is this ship overrun with dinosaurs?"

She noted the hesitation between the words 'is' and 'this'. It was quite clear that Raztenberger had been about to say 'my ship'. He always felt that the mission should have been his to command despite the fact that he brought absolutely no useful skills to the party. "Because our job is to get data about how well the dinosaurs work and footage that we can use to sell them. Showing them in action in a ship environment is a good step in that direction." Sabrina almost had enough self-control to leave the answer at that, but fell at the last hurdle. She couldn't stop herself from adding. "And also because you are a bumbling fool who hasn't been able to do anything right since this trip started. If you'd contained our prisoners, I wouldn't have had to hunt them down."

He turned purple. Interesting. That couldn't be good for his blood pressure. "The only people you've managed to hunt down so far are two of my guards and one of your own analysts, and now the things are running all over the ship. Dozens of them," he said.

"That's not true. The Compsognathus pack also got one of the people from the island. Would you like to see the video?"

"No, I don't want to watch your stupid video. I haven't got your snuff fetish."

"It's not a snuff fetish," she replied. "I am a scientist, and these videos are the best data humanity has ever had regarding the hunting behavior of small carnivores from the Jurassic period."

"Hell, there's no real need for it. We can watch it firsthand as those little monsters hunt us down one by one. How stupid do you have to be to pull a stunt like that?" He shook his head. "I will be informing Jermaine about what has been happening here, I'm afraid. He will be most unhappy."

"I'm sure you're right, but there's no need for you to trouble yourself. I sent him an email a few minutes ago. It went into your failures in excruciating detail." She smirked. "And yes, he's most unhappy."

Dieter swallowed and exited her room with a final glare, presumably to run off and try to kiss some CEO butt.

She didn't care. Unlike that jumped-up security guard, she had important things to do. Things like figure out where the nine survivors had gotten off to, and how to lead her pack to the exact area.

Unfortunately, the security cameras had chosen this exact moment to start acting up, and none of her creatures had caught sight of them over the past half hour.

She returned to what she'd been doing before Dieter so rudely interrupted her: thinking.

***

Sked grinned. "I'm good," he said.

"You're not that good. These people are total amateurs," Akane replied.

"You gotta be good to fleece the amateurs."

"Whatever."

He'd thought getting to the bad guys' control area would entail a struggle against high-end security protocols followed by a mad dash to beat surveillance camera coverage. Instead, it had been child's play to completely ignore the hardened area of the network, that single high-security node, and work through the ship's control computer, which appeared to be from sometime in the 1980s.

Whoever owned this ship wasn't concerned about getting hacked, probably because there was very little worth hacking on that particular mainframe unless you wanted to attack the ship's accounting software and take away their ability to know how much money they'd made and spent on the last thirty years of trips. He estimated the software was at least that old.

A traditional hacker would find nothing worth his time in the digital corridors, but for Sked's purposes, the system was a godsend. He simply turned off the security cameras and then installed a patch that would immediately turn them off again if anyone bothered to restart them. After that, he simply matched the areas that had been rented out for passengers with a map.

"The biggest area that the customers are using is over here, a storage locker about twice the size of the room they put us in. It was probably where the crew stored their supplies, which explains why Cora and the rest of them are stashed in a regular room full of boxes of macaroni. If they have a central control room, that's where we'll find it."

"Which way?"

"Follow me, oh princess of digital mayhem." He headed towards the ship's stern.

"I swear, as soon as I get back to civilization, I'm going to plug myself into a computer and never come out again. I'll never depend on you for technology again."

"If we get out of this, do whatever you want. Meanwhile, I'm not letting you get anywhere near my devices. Last thing I want is to discover you installed something evil in there just when I'm trying to do something delicate."

She snorted. "Delicate? You're a blunt instrument, Sked. Skilled, but blunt."

"Says the kettle to the pot."

"Huh?"

"Never mind. It's up the stairs, first door on the right."

They halted beside a door. This wasn't one of those big bulkhead doors like their former prison, but a regular door with a handle. He could hear people talking on the other side: at least one male and one female voice.

He tested the handle; the door was unlocked. They shrugged, exchanged a glance, brought up their pistols and entered.

The long, dim room was full of computers and screens showing numbers and graphs. Four young people—three women and a man—sat in front of screens. Two of them appeared to be playing some online game, the other two, seated next to each other, were chatting over a couple of cups of coffee. No one looked up to see who'd entered.

Akane shrugged again, turned the lock on the door—a simple unit like the one you'd expect to see at a home bathroom door—and said, in a loud voice, "Hi there, graveyard shift. This is your pre-dawn pirate attack. Please step away from your computers and raise your hands like a well-behaved group of mass murderers."

They did so, but one woman, the nearest to them, glared. "What the hell is this? You're pirates? You don't look like the kind of pirates we'd expect in these waters." She was pale and round-faced with bottle-red curly hair that reached just below her ears.

"Nope. And that's the only guess you'll get. I don't make nice with people who kill innocents. Especially not when you're covering for white slavers."

Sked grinned, but only to himself. For all of her genius in finding the angles for a job, Akane had never been much of one for piecing together clues in a mystery. She tended to lump everything together and jump to amazing conclusions.

But in this case, it was fine. Sometimes shaking the tree to see what fell out was the best approach.

"What are you talking about? We're here on a zoological research expedition. We're scientists. I don't have to listen to this shit." She advanced two steps towards them and Akane, without blinking, shot her in the thigh.

The woman went down with a scream and the rest of the people in the room suddenly became very attentive.

Sked stepped forward, covering his shock at Akane's brutality with a look of determination. Ignoring the sobs from the woman on the floor, he spoke in a loud voice: "You work for ZooDef, a company developing weaponized monsters that everyone knows will probably end up mostly in the hands of terrorists and insurgents. None of you are innocent of anything. We represent a faction interested in keeping the peace, and I need you to show me where the central data store is."

"Central data store?" the guy asked. "You mean the hard drive where we store our findings?"

"Yeah, whatever."

"Right here." He pointed to a computer at his feet, a regular black tower desktop.

"A hard drive? Really?" Akane said. "Are you guys for real?"

"At least we're not industrial spies."

Sked was about to argue that one, but thought better of it. He didn't know who the end buyer of the data he would take was, but he was pretty sure it wasn't the Boy Scouts or the YMCA. The genetically-modified monster field was becoming quite crowded, and some heavyweight players were getting involved. When that happened, what the wise hacker did was to make one big score early in the game and then stay the hell away from the inevitable turf war.

With practiced ease, Sked pulled the computer out from under the desk, disconnected every cable running into it and began to unscrew the casing with a screwdriver he pulled from his backpack. A number of monitors went blank as soon as the computer was disconnected.

"Bastard," the guy said. But he didn't move, and Akane's gun never wavered.

Five tense minutes later, he held a Hitachi hard disk in his hand, warm from recent use. He'd have time to figure out if there was anything useful on it later.

They backed toward the door. "Now," Akane said, "I'm going to ask you a question: Are any of you Sabrina Williams?"

Three heads shook. Akane gestured to the woman moaning on the floor. "What about her?"

"No."

"Good. Where does Sabrina Williams sleep?"

No one answered.

"Do you really want to be shot as well?"

Footsteps pounded on the metal decking outside the room. It sounded like a complete squad of the security team.

"Help us!" It was the woman on the ground who screamed. "We're in here."

Sked's hand was just in time to deflect Akane's gun. The bullet that would have taken the injured woman's head off instead ricocheted around the room and buried itself into a monitor. "No more killing. We don't know if these people are actually guilty."

Akane glared at him. "They look guilty as hell to me. This is where they control the monsters."

Someone started pounding on the door. "Open up in there," a deep voice commanded.

"No. Don't come in here. We've got a little fire. We'll open up in a second."

"Don't listen to them. They're lying!" the woman on the floor screamed. "Break down the door."

Akane kicked her in the head, hard. She went down, limp. "Happy? I didn't kill her."

"That door isn't going to hold them very long," Sked noted.

"Then we go out the other way," Akane replied, pointing to an exit at the opposite end of the room.

They charged between the workstations.

To Sked's surprise, the single man in the room, a pimply, bespectacled guy of maybe twenty-five, tried to block his way. Sked simply lowered a shoulder and sent him flying over one of the desks. After the frustration of running and skulking for a couple of days, it felt inordinately good just to rear back and *hit* someone, even if it was a completely uneven contest.

The door splintered behind them.

"Duck!" Akane shouted, but Sked was way ahead of her. He dove under the last desk before the door.

Gunfire raked the surface above him, causing equipment to explode, glass to shatter and stuff to spark.

Sked crawled under the desks a couple of meters, hidden from view of the trigger-happy security team at the door. When he was a decent distance from where he'd gone under, he risked a quick look.

One guy stood at the door with an automatic rifle which turned towards him when he was spotted. He dove back the way he'd come as another desk exploded into splinters.

"Stop it, you imbecile!" a woman's voice screamed.

"What? They're over there."

"That thing you shot up was the sonar control."

"What the hell does that mean?"

"It's the only thing keeping the Mosasaurs from attacking this ship. Oh God."

Ignoring the gunfight going on around her, one of the tech girls walked to the desk under which Sked had initially taken cover. "This is ruined," she said. "We need to get another one up."

The guy Sked had shouldered aside grunted. "Not sure we have the parts. And if we do, they're buried in storage somewhere."

"Well, find them, genius."

"I'm not moving until the people with guns leave."

Taking that as his cue, Sked took advantage of the distraction to crawl to the back door.

"Open it," Akane said.

"I prefer not to get shot."

"Wimp," she replied. But even the impetuous Akane didn't make a move for the doorknob.

"You!" the woman shouted at the guard in the doorway. "With the metallic dick extension. Get out of here so my colleague can rebuild the transmitter. I don't care if you have orders to catch the people in here. If we don't get this up and running, we'll have much bigger problems."

"Yeah. Literally," the tech guy said from the floor, his voice conveying his conviction that he'd just made the world's funniest joke.

Sked risked a look. The other doorway was temporarily vacant, so he went for the knob on the one he'd arrived at. It opened easily and he rolled into an interior corridor, with Akane a heartbeat behind.

He peered back into the room they'd just left, thinking their escape would cause some sort of commotion, or at least comment, but the three techs still standing ignored them. The man rushed out the door, while the two women poked worriedly at the wrecked equipment on the desk. They spoke in muted tones that Sked couldn't make out.

That worried him. What worried him even more was that no one was bothering to check on the woman Akane had shot in the leg and then kicked into dreamland. Either no one liked her... or the machine they broke was really, really important.

"You coming?" Akane said, tugging on his sleeve.

"Where?"

"I'm going to open every door on this corridor until I find out where that Sabrina woman is."

Sked sighed. She was going to be pissed. "No need for that. I know where she is."

"You do?" her voice was dangerously quiet.

"Yes. It was on the manifest. From here it should be the... let me see... fifth door on the left." He hesitated and went on. "I wanted to see if we could figure out what was going on before you went ahead with the hit."

"Well, are you convinced now?" Ice was warmer than her tone as she advanced in the direction he'd indicated.

"I still don't know. But I'm sure there's something very bad happening here. I won't stand in your way."

"What gave it away? Was it the fact that guys with guns locked us up or the sudden appearance of the monsters we'd been running from?"

"Let's talk about this later. This is the door," Sked said.

They stood beside it, one on either side. Sked noted that Akane had picked up a new, better gun somewhere, probably from the corpse of the guy who'd been on guard duty. Knowing her, she probably had the other one on her person somewhere, as a backup.

"Break it down or try the handle?" Sked asked.

The knob was the better option. He knew it. Akane knew it. The only reason he asked was to align themselves before she did something impetuous.

"I'm not in the mood for handles," Akane replied, and did something impetuous.

The door, a cheap item of thin wood veneer similar to the one leading to the control room, burst inwards.

Sked followed Akane inside. A woman looked up from a computer: fortyish, with some grey strands. She looked as if she hadn't slept in a few days, with dark rings under her eyes. The screen showed the feed from a security camera, a black-and-white image. Either the woman was a hacker or she had her own security system... Sked was sure he'd turned the ships cameras off conclusively.

Akane raised her gun and pointed it between the woman's eyes. "Are you Sabrina Williams?" she asked.

The woman smiled. Her hand on the keyboard pressed a letter. It was a subtle thing, the barest flicker of movement.

But it was enough. Two cages, one on either side of the door, opened with a hiss and a small something hit Sked at waist height, just as he recognized the image on the screen: that was the corridor they'd just walked up.

Sked reacted instantly to the attack. He'd seen enough of the little dinosaurs over the past couple of days to know exactly what was happening. He twisted to one side and felt the cloth of his pants tear at thigh level. Pain shot up his leg and he grunted.

The creature's momentum took it past and it slammed into Akane, who was already busy with her own little monster. She was bashing it over the head with the butt of her pistol.

Sked joined the fray. He kicked one of the things in the chest hard enough to lift it a foot into the air. When it fell to the ground he jumped on its elongated neck. It squished and held, leather resisting his weight, until, finally, something inside gave out with a wet pop.

Akane was losing her fight, though. Through instinct or luck—or simply to immobilize the hand that had been beating on its head—her creature had bitten onto the gun, just above the muzzle, and was attempting to tear it from Akane's grip.

Sked pressed his own gun against the creature's back and pulled the trigger. It dropped away.

They turned back to Sabrina and found that she was gone. An open window told them she'd made it out onto the deck.

"Dammit," Akane said. "I'm going after her." She climbed onto the chair and out the same window.

Sked sighed and followed.

CHAPTER 20

Eddie knew the big Marine broad was going to be a bore about it. He didn't care.

"Where are you going?" Cora said when he pulled open the door.

"Gotta take a leak," he replied. "Thought I'd piss over the side."

"Can't you hold it?"

"Nope."

He stepped onto the walkway and closed the door behind him. It was cool to see the sea stretching out into the distance. Darker now. The moon had gone down at some point. He hadn't noticed when, but it was gone now. It didn't matter on the ship because there were lights every few dozen yards. Not enough to read by, maybe, but enough to see where you were going.

He hadn't lied to the nutso soldier woman. He really did have to pee… and the rest of them probably did, too, but they were too chicken to come out here and do it.

Once done, he didn't head back to the storeroom, however. He didn't feel like it. The air in there was thick and smelly. Too many people. Too many boxes of food. It might have been a decent-sized place once, but now it was like a rat's nest. The walls were too close.

He looked out over the sea and simply enjoyed the feel of the tropical wind over his skin. He'd always been a man of simple pleasures: food, sex, violence. He liked to know he was alive, and the feeling of the night on his skin certainly counted. There was no incentive to return to the room where his companions were packed like sardines.

Besides, he had business to attend to.

"Harold. We're gonna send you some servants for the afterlife. Hope you like lizards."

He supposed Harold didn't believe in any of that crap. As far as he knew, his friend had been an atheist. But it didn't matter. Eddie needed to give his tribute and the lizards were going to pay for what they did.

Also, he wanted to find the body and toss it overboard. Burial at sea and all that.

Eddie wasn't dumb. He knew he was probably dead meat.

But why go out of his way to avoid it? Without Harold, the Philly Triad was dead, and the Philly Triad was his life. They might put in another boss, but everything would change. There was no real need to go back.

He'd had a good run. If his time was now, it would be epic.

Eddie pulled out his watermelon knife and let it catch the hallway light on its blade. Though it seemed that way, he knew the blade wasn't perfectly rectangular. It had a slight curve, fattening towards the business side, which hadn't been there when he bought it. It was something he'd done to the blade without meaning to, sharpening it countless times to remove nicks from when it had caught in bone.

The memories of his entire professional life were in that blade, defying his attempts to grind them out. The curve of the blade, the way the handle fit his hand perfectly, worn where he gripped it hardest—at little finger height. It was as much a part of him as his arms and legs.

And it held, he was certain, the spirits of those whose life-force it had drained. Nearly two dozen people he'd killed with that knife, countless others he'd only relieved of a digit or two, or sliced up a little.

He spoke to those spirits now:

"I know you guys didn't want to die. Hell, you're probably still pissed at me for cutting you up. But that was a while ago. You should move on. I need you to help me now, to guide the metal you live in. Add your strength to mine and we'll do something cool together."

He waited to see if the metal would respond, show some sign that his request had been accepted by the gods, a glint of blue light or something. After a few moments, Eddie decided that no response was forthcoming.

"Doesn't matter. I know what I have to do."

A burst of machine-gun fire sounded from the front of the ship and he smiled. It was like a beacon, telling him where he should be heading. Security guys firing automatic weapons meant dinosaurs… and dinosaurs meant revenge.

It was about more than just the Triad, of course. Harold had been his mentor, his older brother, the guy who'd taken a wild kid who was getting more and more lost by the second and focused those energies into something that could be used for the good of the organization.

Eddie knew they called him crazy. He'd come by the nickname honestly, by being completely out of control, never stopping to think, just charging forward and doing things. He'd been on the path to an early grave, and everyone knew it. It was so obvious that they hadn't even bothered to come back for him after the River Gang had cut him up. If it hadn't been for that nurse...

And after that nurse, Harold. He'd been in the pen for his part in the altercation, and when he got out, there was Harold. Waiting. Another Chinese face, and a man who knew how to break the ice: instead of offering his hand, Harold offered a cigarette.

"You want to live?" Harold had said.

"What's it to you?" Eddie had responded. That was the kind of guy he'd been back then.

"I think you have talent. I work for people who can always use talent." Harold was younger then, just starting to make his way up the ladder. Promoted from punk to guy allowed to run a crew. That crew had started with Eddie.

"What's it pay?"

"You mean apart from keeping you vertical a few more years?"

"Yeah, apart from that."

"More than you'd ever see with the gang. Plus, you're getting too old for that game. No more juvie for you." He nodded towards the prison Eddie had just emerged from. "Next fuckup and you're looking at doing real time."

"Speak your piece," Eddie replied.

That had been fourteen years earlier. Since then, Harold had kept him on the rails more times than Eddie could count. He'd cleaned up after him, buried bodies, provided airtight alibis, bought beer.

Now Harold was dead, food for a pack of wimpy little lizards. If he was going to be killed by a dinosaur, it should have been a big one, something that could bite you in half without even trying.

The first of the creatures he encountered was limping along the walkway in front of him. It looked like it had been in a fight, with a lame leg, a crushed tiny arm and a deep gash along its side.

Eddie didn't wait for it to turn. He simply sneaked up behind it and, with a practiced swing of the blade, sent the ridiculously tiny head, the size of a large, misshapen orange, bouncing along the path and into the water.

He snorted. Revenge wasn't about facing enemies honorably. Fuck that. Revenge was about body count.

Onwards.

The stairs leading down onto the container deck came into view. He stopped for a second to contemplate the piles of steel boxes towering overhead. Eddie wondered if he could somehow climb down them to come at the creatures from above.

He discarded the idea. It would take too long. Dawn wasn't far off, and he wanted to get the work done before then. After daybreak, the guys with machine guns would be able to see him a mile away. Not much you could do with a knife if that happened, no matter how good you were.

But there was still an hour of darkness left; he could worry about visibility if he lived that long.

The steps were slick. He looked down to see drops of slick liquid, black in the dim light, scattered in some places with small pools in others. The dinosaurs would likely be massacred by the machine guns, but if the bloody footsteps on the stairs were anything to go by, they had at least managed to take a few of the security guys with them.

The bottom of the stairs presented him with three options. The first two were corridors that ran along the wall of the container deck, one backwards towards the rear bulkhead just one container-length away, another forward, disappearing into the distance.

The third option led into the warren of passages between the containers, into the unseen middle of the mound, the center of the ship.

Eddie chose that one, moving at the fastest pace he could maintain without making too much noise or winding himself. He passed a couple of intersections and, when he judged himself to be approximately in the middle of the container deck, he turned towards the bow.

He should eventually come up on... something. He just hoped it wasn't the security dudes and their tommy guns. At least not at first.

"Blood soon," he promised the blade in his hand. "Very soon."

Something flickered under a light about a hundred feet away. She smiled; it was too small to be a human.

"Here, lizard, lizard, lizard," he whispered. "Come to papa."

The creature had stopped right outside the pool of light, half in the shadows. If he hadn't seen it move, he probably would have walked right into it.

But he had and, knowing where it was, he could see the darker shape that gave its position away. He advanced openly, daring it to come meet him.

"Not so tough without your friends, are you? Harold would have kicked your asses if you'd only come after him one at a time."

The lizard didn't move. He was twenty feet away. Ten. He could smell it, a rancid, animal odor.

Now, the dinosaur backed away, never taking its eyes off him.

He didn't slow. It wasn't moving fast enough to escape.

He raised the watermelon knife.

The creature must have realized that the gesture meant danger. It skittered back against the wall, its claws clattering against the metal floor.

"You should have run while you had the chance," Eddie said. Even though the monster was nearly out of range, he lunged at it.

It twisted aside, but not quite fast enough. The knife bit into flesh and one tiny claw fell to the deck, irrigated by monster blood.

That enraged it. It hissed, lowered its head and charged.

Eddie was expecting that. It reacted exactly the same way untrained humans did in a knife fight: letting the pain take over and charging blindly.

He stepped aside and took its head off with a mighty blow.

"No wonder dinosaurs went extinct," he said. "You guys are too stupid to understand that your necks are long and thin and easy to chop through."

He turned to walk again, to search, but the need had disappeared.

"Oh, hi guys," he said. "You want to be cut, too? Bring it, then."

Ten or twelve of the little bastards had appeared out of two cross passages. Maybe they'd been attracted by the other one's hiss, maybe they'd been waiting in hiding while the other one scouted. Eddie didn't care. This was the fight he'd come looking for.

The dinosaurs began to fan out, looking to flank him.

"No, no. Fuck that," he said. Then, without hesitation, he screamed loudly and charged into their midst.

The dinosaur in the middle definitely wasn't expecting that. All it managed to do before Eddie closed the gap was cock its head in a surprised fashion. Then the blade bit into its neck.

The angle wasn't right to lop the neck in two as he'd done with the others, but the dinosaur still fell to the ground, twitching.

He wasted half a second pulling the knife free, and that almost cost him. A second dinosaur went for his leg as he was struggling to release the blade. He knew that if they hamstrung him, he was toast, so he reached down with his left hand and pushed the monster's face away.

It snapped at him, and he pulled up a hand missing the tips of two fingers.

"Oh, you bastard," he shouted.

He closed on the retreating form and, ignoring the pain in his bloodied hand, he grabbed it from behind the head, and then knelt on it, falling with all his weight. He heard ribs crack inside the small creature. Then he stood and stomped on it, leaving it alive, but mortally wounded.

In his rage, he didn't register the one now biting his thigh until standing straight brough a bright flame of pain. He hacked at it until it let go.

Now, the rest were all over him. They'd abandoned the old wolf tactic of snapping at his rear and had come at him all at once while he was butchering their friends. One of them took his already mangled left hand in its mouth and tried to drag him to the floor. Another scratched at his back. The rest tore into his legs.

Eddie lopped off another head. How many left? Seven? Five?

He buried his knife into another, causing a river of blood to spurt. "Die, you shit."

It obeyed but, as he was pulling the knife out, he felt something give in his leg. Hamstring. The bastards had finally torn it out.

He screamed in frustration and agony as he toppled over onto his back. Heads filled with razor teeth nicked and gashed. His left hand was pretty much chewed to pieces, and that left only his knife hand to fend off the mouths.

"Gotcha, you fuck!" he said with satisfaction as another head rolled off to join his collection. The remaining number almost seemed manageable.

If he'd been in good shape, he would have kicked their scaly little asses.

But he wasn't. He was on his back, bleeding out. Too weak to move his good arm away when one of them closed its jaws around his forearm.

That ended the fight. The next one went for his neck and tore it open.

He was going to die very soon, he knew. He'd expected that.

What he didn't expect was the way he went.

A sudden jolt rocked the ship, a massive, unexpected impact. Eddie could still see clearly as one of the containers at the very top of the pile was knocked out of place.

With a deafening screech, it slid off its perch and ground its way into the corridor space between the piles.

Then it screeched all the way down.

It wasn't moving very fast when it reached Eddie and his opponents.

But it didn't need to move very fast to crush a few living creatures into pulp.

Eddie died with the satisfaction of knowing his tormentors perished with him.

CHAPTER 21

The sudden jolt threw them violently towards the left of the ship. Cora slammed into a shelf laden with bags of rice which collapsed onto the next shelf over with a resounding crash. As shelves toppled like dominoes, she was peripherally aware of her companions being thrown around like dolls.

"The fuck was that?" Mary asked, all pretense of being a high-class, dreamy-eyed bimbo gone as she groaned on the floor.

"If felt like we hit something," Lai said. He'd worked himself back into a sitting position. Blood flowed down his cheek from a new cut just above his eye.

Cora reflected that they were starting to show the wear and tear of several days in hostile territory.

A groan ahead of her alerted her that someone was under the mess of collapsed shelves. A quick headcount told her that everyone was accounted for except Ania and the cook. She looked back to where Ania had been sitting: she was still there, looking around in alarm. Being seated had saved her from getting thrown around like the rest of them.

Mary was already on her feet. "Help me get him out!" she said.

They hauled the bags of rice into a pile in the far corner and then, once enough of it was out of the way, Cora, Mary and the doctor lifted the heavy metal rack off the man trapped beneath. They'd found the cook.

His arm lay at an ugly angle, and he was breathing wheezily. He suddenly coughed and blood dribbled down.

"Move over," the doctor said. "I want to have a look."

Taking care not to move the man's arm, Dr. Pendalai pressed his head against the cook's chest and listened to him breathing. He looked up at Cora, and she was dismayed to see that the normally composed doctor looked alarmed. "This ship has to have an infirmary. I need to know where it is, and we need to get this man there now."

"Why? What's wrong with him?"

"He was crushed pretty badly, so I can't know the extent of the internal damage. What I do know is that a rib broke and punctured a lung. It might collapse, it might fill with fluid. Neither case is a good outlook. We need to get him stabilized."

"What am I supposed to do?" Cora shot back. "Walk up to the Captain and request the use of his facilities?"

"You're the soldier. Figure it out. We need to move now."

Cora growled at him. The guy acted like brass, even though he'd probably never worn a uniform in his life, much less been an officer. "Give me a minute."

"Hurry," the doctor replied. Then he turned back to his patient, ignoring Cora as she left and Mary who wept at his shoulder.

Cora walked out onto the deck. The ship was enormous; how the hell was she supposed to find one specific room here? Sked would know... but Sked was nowhere to be found. He and that lunatic girlfriend of his were probably stealing anything not nailed down.

Then it hit her. Screw maritime law. The one place on any ship that was always easy to find was the bridge. Its windows looked out over the entire expanse of the vessel... and anyone on deck could pretty much locate it by looking up.

She looked up, spotted the nearest staircase that appeared to lead in the correct direction and started climbing.

After a couple of flights, with the sun just about to rise and the eastern sky ablaze with pinks and oranges, Cora found exactly what she needed. A slim man with ebony skin wearing sailor's garb—the sailors on this ship didn't wear uniforms, but she'd spent enough time at port to recognize the way the civilian merchantmen dressed—descended the stairs two-by-two.

He didn't recognize her as a threat, merely giving her a nod and a distracted "hello" as he hurried past.

Correction. As he tried to hurry past. Cora's arm around his throat stopped the man's forward progress, and her gun against his temple attracted his undivided attention. "I need you to take me to the infirmary," she said. "And if you pretend not to be able to understand English, I'll kill you right now and find someone who does. Nod if you'd like to live."

The man nodded.

"Good. We're going down these stairs. You ahead, I'll follow. Try anything, and I'll shoot you in the head. I won't miss."

They reached the storeroom. The doctor took a look at the sailor and seemed to grasp the situation immediately. He said: "Take his legs. I'll take his arm. Get us to the infirmary now."

They walked along the ship, out in the open. It was impossible for a group carrying a wounded man to skulk effectively.

Worse, whatever had happened to the ship had woken everyone. Dozens of people roamed the decks: sailors, young people she assumed to be the passengers, even armed security forces in black. All of them were heading forward or to the other side of the ship.

None of them gave the group a second glance.

"I don't like this," Cora said. She addressed the sailor. "What's going on? What did we hit?"

"We didn't hit nothing," the man replied in an accent she couldn't place, perhaps Western African by the way his English sounded like he should be French... but wasn't, not quite. "We aren't even moving. It hit us."

"What did?"

"One of the monsters."

"But they're tiny.... Oh," she said.

"One dem big ones from the tanks," the sailor clarified.

"You brought those here? The big ones?"

"Scientists bring them. We helped unload. This the hospital. I can go now?"

"Help me get him onto that bed," Dr. Pendalai said.

They lowered the cook gingerly and the doctor opened a number of cupboards.

"I can go now?" the sailor repeated.

"I suppose. I'm sorry I pulled the gun on you," Cora replied.

"I understand." The man nodded toward the bed. "He in a bad way. Not breathing good. Hope he okay later."

With that, the sailor disappeared towards the bow. Whatever was going on was happening up there.

"Doc," she said. "Do you need me for anything?"

"No." The man didn't even turn to look. He was collecting an assortment of paraphernalia, and Cora turned away. She didn't like medical equipment, it looked unpleasantly medieval to her.

"Then I'm going to see what the hell is happening up there."

"We could use that gun of yours," Mary said. "Ania and I can't shoot. And I think Lai can't either."

Cora considered for a moment but shook her head. No one seemed to be interested in what the group was doing, so taking her gun was a small risk compared to flying blind. "We need to know what's happening here. Most of the things that happened to us can be directly traced back to the fact that we keep getting into situations where we don't know what's going on. I want to fix that."

She sprinted towards the bow of the ship. Even though she crossed paths with half a dozen of the security guys who'd locked up her group, not one of them spared her a second glance.

***

Sabrina watched in delighted shock as Shiva tried again. Mosasaurs weren't built to move on land, and they weren't built to climb onto the decks of large ships.

"Go!" she shouted. "You can do it!"

It wasn't immediately clear what the creature's objective was. Was the Mosasaur trying to board so it could feed off the scurrying figures? One man who got too close as he emptied his machine gun into her baby found out just how quickly the neck could snap to one side and the jaws could slice a man in two.

Of course, there was no need to bite him. Shiva could have swallowed the man, and ten more, whole.

The ship rocked back and forth. Understanding came to Sabrina.

"Oh, you bright little thing," she said. She would have clapped, but she needed both hands on the railing to keep her feet.

The dinosaur wanted to capsize the ship. It didn't know it was a ship, of course, it just knew it was an enemy that it couldn't attack because it had armor on the side it could reach. So it wanted to get it turned around and attack the soft parts.

Unfortunately, the attempt was doomed from the beginning. This ship might not be modern, but it was built to withstand the rocking of millions of gallons of water hitting it in waves. A single Mosasaur, no matter how unexpectedly intelligent for its kind, was not going to be able to do more than rock it a little.

In fact, it had done much more damage when it had rammed it earlier. The energy in a moving body was much better applied than mere weight. That was what had caused the ship to really move. It had even managed to overbalance a couple of piles of containers. The layered bone plates in a Mosasaur skull were more than strong enough to withstand use as a battering ram.

Just as she thought of that, the ship shook again. Sabrina thought she'd been holding on hard, but the impact knocked one of her hands away from the railing and dropped her to her knees. She looked out over the containers to realize that the Shiva was still propped on the railing, trying vainly to capsize the *Stern Liberia*.

So Kali was the one making all the noise.

As she stood, a flash of movement on the deck one level beneath her caught her eye because it wasn't a bunch of Dieter's security goons trying to get down to the monster or one of the sailors running an errand. It wasn't even one of her own analysts trying to find out what happened.

There was none of the hectic desperation that she'd grown accustomed to seeing over the past few minutes. Instead, the movement was slow, measured, furtive.

Sabrina crawled along the railing to get a better angle.

"Damn them," she said when she recognized the two people who'd invaded her quarters earlier. Whoever these two were, they didn't seem to have been too badly damaged by her pets. She hated the thought that they'd hurt the Compsognathus she'd had in her room, but she was getting used to the pain by now. She'd known before they'd sailed that none of the small dinosaurs would be coming back with her.

She turned around and spotted a fire extinguisher clipped to a drainage pipe with cable ties and quickly cut it off the wall. Moving carefully—Shiva might not be able to capsize the boat, but it was definitely rocking—she positioned herself above the interlopers and dropped the heavy fire extinguisher on their heads.

At least that was the plan. Just as she was about to release the big red cylinder, Kali decided to slam the ship once again.

Sabrina was thrown back, rolling along the passageway, and she never saw if the extinguisher landed true or not.

***

The ship lurched and saved Sked's life. He landed on his face and one second later, a fire extinguisher landed right on his left buttock. It hurt like hell and pain shot up his side.

"Ow!" he screamed.

"What?" Akane said. She was still on her feet.

"Just got hit in the ass with a fire extinguisher." He probed the area, ignoring Akane's much-too-knowing smirk. "Wait. What?"

"You should have been paying attention," she replied. "The Sabrina bitch was the one who threw it at your head."

"Why didn't you warn me?"

"I didn't want her to know I'd spotted her. Oh, come on, don't look at me like that. She's worth a million bucks dead. Besides, I would have pushed you out of the way if the ship hadn't suddenly jerked around."

"Yeah, right," Sked replied.

"I mean it. I've gotten used to you… so I'd hate to see your head get crushed."

Sked rose gingerly to his feet. He would have the mother of all Charlie horses tomorrow. He probably wouldn't be able to sit for days. "So what are you waiting for? Why haven't you gone after her?"

"I need your help." She pointed to the staircase leading to the balcony above them. "We need to box her in, and there's another staircase just like this one on the other side. Can you go up that one, and make sure she doesn't try anything ambitious?"

Sked nodded and limped around the metal walls of the bridge tower. He climbed the stairs, each step an exercise in agony. About halfway up, he heard two shots in quick succession from the opposite balcony. Nevertheless, he forced himself to hurry, though he would probably be late to the action. The smart money was on Akane having carried out the hit with two shots to the head before he even arrived, but he still wanted to get there quickly in case their quarry had any tricks up her sleeve and Akane was in trouble.

He needn't have worried. Akane stood with her gun poised over a female form. Sked recognized the woman from the room.

But Sabrina wasn't dead; she was crawling, using her elbows to try to pull herself away from Akane. The woman's legs dragged behind, leaving a trail of blood along the metal deck. The back of one thigh sported a large exit wound, blood just now staining the pink flesh.

"You didn't kill her?"

Akane shook her head.

"Why not?"

"Because I decided I don't like her," Akane replied. She showed no emotion, but her blank expression chilled Sked's blood more than a rictus of hate would ever have managed. That woman was definitely going to die, but when Akane took things personally... it might take the woman a long time to do so.

Of course, if she actually was responsible for putting the little dinosaurs on the island, she was a mass murderer and, though he wouldn't necessarily condone whatever Akane might be planning for her, he really couldn't argue either.

Sked looked away just in time to see Cora striding along the lower deck. Even though her gun was out of its holster, she walked like she owned the place. He hissed at her and she pointed the gun at him.

Recognizing Sked, Cora lowered the weapon and he motioned her to come up.

"What the..?" Cora said when she saw Sabrina crawling along, not making a noise, with a grinning Akane standing over her, occasionally kicking her in the ribs. "That woman needs a doctor."

Akane looked up. "You don't say," she said, before turning her attention back to Sabrina.

Sked took Cora's arm and pulled her around the corner. Cora came reluctantly, but she came... which was the only reason he managed to budge her.

"There had better be a really good explanation for what I just saw," Cora fumed. "I've just about had enough of that girl. What the hell does she think she is? Judge, jury and executioner? I know she had a rough time of it. That sucks. But at some point, it's just got to stop."

Sked let the big Marine finish, then tried to keep his voice level. "That woman created the monsters."

"What?"

"She took lizard DNA or something and built the dinosaurs. The little ones and the big one that munched your lifeboat. Unless I'm mistaken, that's the one that's trying to board the ship over there."

Cora looked dumbly out at the enormous creature attempting to capsize the *Stern Liberia*. "She did that?"

"Yeah. And she's the one watching the camera feed from the little monsters eating everyone."

"I didn't see any cameras."

"They're small, on collars. We just got a chance to study a couple of the things in a place where we didn't have to run from them… and they were both wired for video."

"Are they like robots? Was she controlling them?"

Sked thought about it, but then shook his head. "I doubt it. No one I've ever heard of is that far advanced in integrating digital components and nervous systems. And I'm in a business where you'd hear the whispers if someone was working."

"So she just dumped them on the beach and let them eat whatever they found?"

"Yup. And she was probably the one who opened the doors to all the cages on this boat. The security guys don't seem thrilled to be overrun with dinosaurs." He held her eyes for a couple of beats. "Akane might be a bit of an extremist, but I've never seen her get medieval on anyone who doesn't deserve it. She lives and lets live, but she's got a serious anger about what this woman did."

"And what's she going to do with her now?" Cora inquired. "Live and let live?"

"Not likely. This woman is going to get a slug in the back of the head. But Akane's in no hurry."

"Over my dead body."

"Don't let her hear you say that," Sked said quietly. "She is seriously against anyone interfering in her plans."

"Is she American?"

"Who, Akane?"

"No. I couldn't care less about Akane. I hope I never see her again in my life. I mean this scientist woman. If she's American, I'm taking her back with me when we get out of here, and I'm turning her in to the authorities to stand trial."

"People like her don't stand trial. They disappear into the Pentagon to keep developing their weapons."

"I don't care."

Sked sighed. "We need to work together to get out of here. How's this: don't say anything about this until the situation shakes out. We'll decide once we're safe."

"I don't like it."

"Be reasonable," Sked pleaded.

"Reasonable? I don't want to be an accessory to a sadistic torturer who plans to murder her victim."

"If we kill each other, it's moot."

"If I shoot her in the back right now, it's solved," Cora retorted.

"I won't let you do that," Sked said.

"You think you can stop me?"

"You think you'll survive if you kill me? Even if Akane doesn't shoot you before I hit the ground? We need to work together."

"Fuck," Cora said. "All right. But I have two conditions." She held up her hand and counted on her fingers. "The first is that we get that woman to the doctor right now. She'll bleed to death otherwise."

"I suppose I can talk her into that. What's the second?"

"If it looks like your psycho girl is about to shoot her, the agreement is cancelled."

"If that's what it takes."

"That's what it takes."

Sked explained it to Akane, who agreed readily enough to make him suspicious.

But in this situation, a yes was a yes, and he wasn't going to question it too closely.

Moments later, he and Cora had a shoulder under each of Sabrina's arms and they assisted the woman to the infirmary. Though she must have been in excruciating pain, she never made a sound.

Sked, on the other hand, complained of his bruised butt all the way. It was that or tell the two crazy women to shoot each other and leave him alone.

CHAPTER 22

"Something's not right." Cora felt the floor shifting under her feet. By now they'd become used to the back and forth swaying and sudden shaking of the *Stern Liberia* as one monster attempted to capsize it while another seemed intent on beating its brains out against the hull.

But this was something different. The ship was heeling. Seriously leaning.

She stepped out of the infirmary to try to see if she could find out what was happening. She wasn't concerned about running into anyone: the crew hadn't paid them any attention, and the security people who'd originally locked them up only spoke to them once, when they dropped off a severely injured man that the doctor had taken one look at, shaken his head and shot full of painkillers. He'd stopped breathing a few minutes later.

Everyone seemed much too busy to care who they were or what they were doing on board. The little dinosaurs were spreading all over the ship from the container deck. An occasional terrified scream told Cora when someone encountered one.

One of the sailors rushed past. Actually, he tried to rush past, and Cora recognized the man she'd press-ganged earlier.

"Hey," she said.

"You again?" He didn't seem thrilled to see her again.

"Yeah. Sorry about before."

"No problem, I guess. How's your friend?"

Cora shrugged. "Still unconscious. Doc says he really can't do anything more with what we've got here. And now he's got another patient."

"Sorry to hear that." He seemed in a hurry to get on with whatever he was doing, but obviously didn't want her to pull her gun on him again. Furtive but obvious glances towards her gun in its holster gave the man's fears away.

"Look, I don't want to detain you, but I need to know what's happening. Are we taking on water?"

"Oh, yeah. Lots and lots of water. Captain says we need to find a spot to beach."

Cora groaned. The only place she could think of was the fucking island. Was there no way to escape the cursed place?

The man fidgeted. "Can I go?"

"Yeah, sorry."

She returned to the infirmary. Doc had finished pulling the bullets out of the woman's legs and bandaged her up. He'd probably done some stitching, too, but Cora hadn't stayed to watch. She hated watching medics at work.

They'd put the cook off to one side. She had no idea what the doc had done. The dude was still out, still pale, and breathing only a little better than before. The bunny was in the corner with him, holding his hand and sobbing. For a woman who'd had her sights on landing a rich executive just a few days ago, she'd certainly fallen hard for that tough little Filipino. It looked bad for the guy, though. Cora didn't need to see Mary crying to know that much. She'd been around enough death to know what it looked like when it was close.

"Listen up," she announced. "The ship's taking on water. Not sure how long we have, but the Captain thinks it's sinking."

To her surprise, the scientist woman, sitting on the bed, smiled. "Kali," the woman said.

Cora ignored her and continued. "Apparently, the crew wants to beach on the island. Now I don't know about you, but I'm in no hurry to go back there. I propose we steal a lifeboat and go back to our original plan of rowing to Andaman. It's the perfect time to do it: everyone's too busy fighting monsters to pay any attention to us."

A sudden silence descended on the room as everyone's eyes turned to Mary and the cook.

"We can't move him," the doctor said quietly.

Mary met their collective gaze. "I'm staying with him."

"This ship is going back to the island."

"I understand that. I'm not stupid. I'll take my chances. He saved me several times, and I owe him this much." She wiped away a tear. "But you should definitely go. I'll lock the door behind you. The little monsters don't use doors."

Cora almost called the whole thing off. It was as good as sentencing them both to death, which would mean that the only person she'd managed to save from the yacht was Lai. If they'd made her choose, he was the one she would have taken... but knowing how many people she'd failed completely was a terrible feeling. Still, better to save one than to doom them all.

"All right. Are you with us?"

Everyone nodded, even the doctor, which surprised Cora. The cook must really have been beyond help for that stubborn bastard to abandon him.

"Good. Let's go."

Sked and Lai stood, and Akane grabbed the scientist by the hair, pulling her off the bed.

"Leave her," Cora said.

"Make me," Akane replied. She pulled the stumbling woman along, apparently unconcerned about whether the violent motion would burst the newly sewn stitches and cause her to bleed out. Cora had never been so close to shooting someone in the back as she was at that moment. Akane just made her grind her teeth.

Ania, ghostlike as always, paused before joining them. Then, in a rush of motion, she hugged Mary hard. "Thank you," Ania said.

Then she followed the others out the door.

Lai and Sked nodded towards Mary before leaving Cora alone with the English girl. She wanted to beg her to reconsider, to leave the guy behind; he was dead anyway. But sometimes a person knew what they had to do. Cora nodded her respect and stepped out. "Don't forget to lock up behind us," she called over her shoulder. "Maybe block the door, too." The infirmary had one of the thick doors, which closed with a solid clang as Cora pulled.

She joined the group on deck.

"Any suggestions?" she asked Sked. At this point, he was the only one she really trusted.

"There's a lifeboat on each side of the container deck," he said.

"Which is stupid," Lai added. "That's the place where they're most likely to get damaged when the ship gets loaded and unloaded. There should be more of them aft of us, near the crew quarters."

"We don't know that," Sked said. "We should go for the sure thing."

Lai shrugged. "Lead the way."

Cora reflected on how little of the man who'd run his company with an iron fist seemed to remain. Whatever this experience meant to Lai, it certainly seemed to have eroded his sense of self-assuredness. Besides the fact that he simply gave up and let Sked do what he wanted, her boss seemed to have aged a decade in a handful of days. His shoulders stooped, his formerly flashing eyes lifeless.

She led them forward. The first few yards were fine, but when they reached the front of the bridge, enabling them to look over the container area, everyone stopped dead.

The monster that had sunk the first lifeboat was halfway on the ship. A crushed container lay beside it.

"That's huge," Ania said, her eyes wide. She turned to Cora. "I'm sorry I doubted you."

Cora stared at it wordlessly for a couple of moments. Then she turned back to the woman. "I don't blame you. I wouldn't have believed myself either."

The monster towered above the container, looking like an old Godzilla film with a guy in a rubber suit tearing through a model of Tokyo. The sense of unreality was heightened by the security team firing automatic weapons at it in a display of futile bravura. When the monster snapped its jaws around the nearest security guy, it didn't feel like a real life of hopes and dreams and plans being snuffed out, but more like being part of the audience in a theater.

Beside her, Sked pointed. "Over there. Right across from the monster. One of the lifeboats."

"It's not a monster," the scientist said. She didn't look good. Loss of blood had her pale and drawn, and the painkillers the doctor had given her slurred her words. That guy didn't mess around. "'s my baby."

"Shut up, bitch," Akane said, pulling the woman toward the staircase leading down.

They made their way along the railing on the opposite side of the ship from the monster. Cora looked down to see that the sea seemed closer than it had been last time.

A container, knocked from one of the piles by the incessant banging, blocked their path, half on the ship, half cantilevered over the ocean. Sked stopped in front of it and leaned over the inner railing, the one that separated the walkway from the container deck itself.

"We can climb down onto those containers there and then climb back onto the top level once we pass the obstacle," he said.

"That looks dangerous," the doctor observed.

Cora laughed. "Like we have a choice now. Basically, even going into one of the cabins and hiding under a bunk is suicidal. The rest is just a question of degrees."

They began to climb onto the big metal boxes, the edges of which were only about a yard below them. The collapse of the pile of containers had blocked the way but also flattened the railing for ten yards on either side, making it easier to go over the edge to clamber onto the teetering steel mountains.

They made it across without incident, Sked and the doctor manhandling the wounded scientist. Cora was about to tell them to leave the woman behind. She was slowing them down... but Cora was convinced that, if forced to leave her prisoner behind, Akane would shoot her before letting her go. So she said nothing as they hailed their bleeding charge over the gaps. The woman's stoic refusal to admit pain was beginning to break down. She moaned softly as they jostled her.

The deck widened on the other side of the downed container and they found themselves surrounded by men.

Cora was immediately alert. These guys weren't sailors. Their dress, their bearing, even the fact that they were all a bit overfed spoke against that. Worse, they all had American accents, which meant they were probably all from ZooDef.

They paid no attention to Cora, but appeared intent on maneuvering a machine that resembled a giant forklift. The thing was as long as a U-Haul truck and its lifting tines were as long as the rest of it. She realized it must be designed for the ability to lift entire containers.

Cables above it, rigged to a crane, bore witness to how the men had brought it there.

No one seemed to care that they were present so Cora was about to lead the group around the men at work when the ship shook again.

She nearly fell into the gap between the main deck and the container area. Akane landed on her ass, and the scientist she'd been holding up rolled across the floor and gave herself another nasty knock. The container which had been tottering on the edge fell over with a huge splash. Someone was going to be out a few dozen air conditioning units.

As they picked themselves up, checked for new bruises and brushed off their clothes, the doctor cocked his head. "What's that?"

They rushed to the side of the ship and looked over.

A head the size of a bus looked up at them. The monster held onto the *Stern Liberia* with a tiny clawed fin.

"You're hurt!" Sabrina said in the kind of tones you'd normally reserve for a cute puppy.

The woman was right. A huge gash along the thing's side bled copiously into the sea water, and the enormous body actually looked dented. It gave the impression that it was hanging on for dear life.

What could have caused that?

The answer was obvious. The container had dropped onto it. No matter what kind of monster you were, getting hit with a load of air conditioners bound for South Korea would quickly turn a good day into a bad one. The miracle was that it was still alive.

Alive and tensing to propel itself onto the deck with its tail.

"Back! Back! Back!" Cora shouted. She pulled the nearest of her companions along with her as she retreated from the colossal surge.

A huge wave washed over the deck. Ania was swept off her feet and into the container deck. Out of the corner of her eye, Cora saw the forklift get lifted by the water, and push most of the workers over the edge as well. That was their bad luck: the pile of containers was much lower over there... the fall would not be fun. The forklift itself stopped just short.

But that was as far as she could watch her surroundings. The water knocked her down and she had to grab onto one of the crushed railings with her free hand to keep herself from going over as well.

The remaining water rolled back off the ship as quickly as it had arrived. Cora checked to see who she'd managed to save.

"Damn. Just my luck," Cora said when she realized the person in her grip was the scientist lady who'd caused the whole mess in the first place.

"Thank you," the woman gasped, spitting out water. Then she turned to look at the ship's side and smiled. "Kali," she said. "You're magnificent."

The woman stepped towards the monster, which lay panting on the side, half on the ship, half in the water, right between the group and the lifeboat.

Worse, the ship was leaning even more than before. Cora could hear containers sliding around behind her. Off in the distance a crash announced that one of them hadn't quite held. The Captain's efforts to get the ship grounded hadn't borne fruit yet either, although she could see that they were moving a little. All that seemed to achieve was to sink them faster.

She suspected they no longer had time to get to the lifeboats at the rear of the ship.

Spotting Sked limping towards her, she pointed towards the monster. "We need to get through!" she shouted. "Can we go over the containers?"

He shook his head. "They're all jumbled up. That last hit knocked a bunch of them over."

"Fuck." She walked over to the edge and looked down into the container area. Sked was correct; there was no way to climb that mess.

"Help," a tiny voice said from beneath her feet. She bent to look, and found Ania barely holding onto the edge. Her fingers were white, bleeding where the rough metal had torn at the skin.

Cora bent down, grabbed her by the wrists and pulled her up, amazed once again at how little the woman weighed. It was like lifting a small child, despite the fact that Ania was around five-foot-eight.

With so many things happening at once, she nearly missed the movement behind her. Lai, bleeding from a scalp wound and holding his hand over his head, was weaving drunkenly towards the monster, either unable to see what he was stumbling towards or too dazed to understand the significance. Finally, he sat down against a pile of debris that had been left there by the receding water. It looked like the box an air conditioner came in.

She took two steps towards him and stopped. As soon as she started moving, the monster's head had snapped over, its enormous slitted eye fixed on her.

Cora froze in place. If she tried to help Lai up, all she'd end up doing was to draw the monster's attention to her boss. He was close enough that, if the creature extended its neck, it could easily swallow him up. The only reason he was still alive is that the monster hadn't noticed him.

"Dammit."

Worse, the creature would see him any moment even if Cora didn't do anything to make it happen… which meant she had to act fast.

But what could you do against something that size? She'd seen men pouring complete magazines into it, and the monster took about as much notice of it as it would have of a gnat. She couldn't call for air cover, and the nearest tank was probably in India somewhere.

Or was it? Her gaze fell on the forklift, humming to itself just a few yards away. The long forks... well, she thought, you could put out an eye with one of those things.

Cora sprinted towards the machine, slipping a bit on the wet steel of the deck. She jumped into the seat—the operator had either made a run for it or been washed away by the wave—and began to maneuver, trying to get the forks pointed at the monster's head.

To her horror, Lai was attempting to stand.

"Dammit!" she shouted as the forks caught on what had to be the only railing still standing. She tried to back up, but there wasn't enough room for the long vehicle. Instead, she hit the lever that controlled the tines. If this thing was designed to lift containers, the winch mechanism had to be seriously strong.

The motor's whine increased in pitch as it struggled against the steel railing. She smelled ozone.

Then, with a loud gunshot-like crack, the bolts gave way and the forklift was free. Cora turned the little wheel and pointed it where she wanted it, then adjusted the height of the near-side fork to be at eye-level with the monster.

She knew she'd only have one crack at this, but it was all lined up the best she could. She pushed the accelerator lever forward.

And was suddenly pulled back into her seat by an iron cord from the railing which had wrapped itself, unnoticed, around her chest as she maneuvered.

The pressure was awful; the cord pulled back as the forklift attempted to surge forward. Something popped in her chest, and she screamed in pain and rage. She watched helplessly as Lai staggered towards his death. Just a few more yards and the thing wouldn't even have to move in order to swallow the man.

The steel rope suddenly gave way. It must have come off whatever it was snagged on and the enormous forklift's spinning tires found traction. It sped straight towards the monster.

Cora had wanted to jam the lever and jump off, but at the last moment, she realized that the fork was off target. She moved the wheel a tiny bit to the right.

Bingo!

The fork entered the eye straight on at full speed, driving itself a yard into the monster's skull.

The thing roared. It was a colossal sound, comparable to standing beside the howitzers when the artillery guys fired them. She'd be deaf for a few days, she knew. She was already starting to jump off the forklift; she suspected the monster must be mortally wounded, but even if it wasn't, it would be distracted. She could save Lai.

The cord that had snagged was still snug against her chest, biting into her skin and compressing her. She looked down to see that it was a cord of steel cables wrapped around the roll cage of the forklift behind her.

It was going to be a bitch to get out of the thing. It seemed to have managed to tie itself in knots upon knots.

She struggled to free herself, but she could barely move.

"Guys," she called to a wide-eyed Sked watching from twenty yards away. "A little help over here."

He'd barely taken a single step when the creature roared again and twitched. Death throes or something else caused it to lift its head off the deck.

Such was the massive strength of the prehistoric monster that the forklift followed.

The monster overbalanced and began to slide over the deck.

The forklift went with it.

Cora pulled at the cable, but it was too tight for flesh and blood to move.

The monster slowed slightly as the water caught it. Driven by the weight of the forklift, the tine in its eye buried itself all the way in, bringing Cora face to face with her nemesis.

"Well, if you weren't dead before, you're definitely dead now, you ugly, motherfucking piece of shit."

Then the sea arrived, and talking was out of the question.

She tugged at the cord cutting into her flesh, but it was impossible to budge. She tried to slip over it, under it, anywhere. It was too tight.

Finally, her hands lost their strength and her lungs felt like they would burst.

Don't breathe in.

Don't breathe in.

It was her only thought. Only two lungs full of water awaited if she let her discipline slip. She needed to keep trying. There had to be a way out of the forklift.

Her fingers were no longer responding.

Her lungs were about to explode.

Don't breathe in.

Don't breathe in.

Cora breathed in.

CHAPTER 23

Sked rushed to the edge of the ship and looked into the water. The only thing he saw were bubbles. Monster and forklift had sunk well out of sight.

He waited for Cora's head to bob up, stood there looking down as dazed survivors of the wave ambled around him.

A few minutes later, a hand on his shoulder woke him from his trance. A voice beside him said: "She's gone."

He turned to see the doctor standing beside him, expression unreadable. The man's other hand was on Lai's arm, keeping the billionaire from walking away.

"She can't be," Sked said. "A woman like that is indestructible."

"No one is indestructible."

They looked out over the water for a few moments. Sked grunted and turned back.

"Where's Akane?"

The doctor pointed. Akane was visible striding along the bow of the ship, with Sabrina in tow going around the container deck. She seemed to be in a hurry, impatiently tugging on the scientist.

"What's she doing?" Sked said.

"She appears to be heading for the other monster."

"Why would she do that?"

The doctor's features hardened. "I wouldn't venture a guess."

Sked shot off in pursuit, not waiting for the doctor, Lai or Ania.

Even dragging Sabrina, however, Akane's head start was too large to overcome. He was still rounding the front of the ship when Akane stopped to face the remaining beast.

He sped up, hoping she wouldn't do anything rash.

***

Akane glared at the scaled ugly facing them.

The scientist woman was sobbing uncontrollably. Akane turned to face her. "They're not so pretty close up, are they?"

Anger flashed in Sabrina's eyes. "Of course they are. They're wonderful. I'm not crying because you want to kill me. And I'm definitely not scared of my baby. I'm crying because of what that dyke back there did to Kali."

"These things have names?"

"Of course they do. They're living, feeling creatures. Much better than the likes of you." She wiped her eyes. "But I wouldn't expect you to understand. You've probably never loved anything but yourself."

"Spare me," Akane said. "I don't need to listen to a lecture from a mass murderer."

The scientist laughed. "You people live such tiny lives. Safe in your little world where nothing ever changes, with your little phones and thinking that you're important because you have a couple of followers on your social media accounts. Even when you die, you'll never understand just how insignificant your ridiculous lives are." She pointed up at the monster panting against the deck. "I have done something that doesn't fit into your limited scope, so you need to call me names. Who cares? Do you think I'll lower myself to your level to argue with you? I don't need to. I'm not one of your obedient little members of the flock. You people who argue about politics and TV programs, who can't even see just how utterly worthless you are."

Akane studied the woman. The scientist looked like she was about to collapse. Bleeding from both legs and pale as a ghost, she should have zonked out long ago. Only her insane drive was keeping her awake. "And I suppose you can see just how worthless I am?"

"Yes!" Sabrina replied. "Yes, I can. And do you want to know why? It's because unlike you sub-humans, I can actually see the beauty in human progress. I know the wonder of having changed the world in a real and tangible way, and not because I wrote a clever tweet. People like me can see the rest of you for what you are: just wastes of space, taking up resources that could be better spent on making more beauty. The deaths on that island weren't murder, they turned irrelevant nothings into food for magnificent experiments. Dung into wonder." She turned to face the enormous monster, and took two steps towards it. "I created this. Me. By myself. The only thing I got from any of you were the resources, money I needed to make it all work. You could never have done it. This is my baby, born of my vision." Another step closer, but Akane noted she was very careful to stop a prudent distance from the jaws. "If you can stand here and tell me you don't see how wonderful this is, you're either lying or an utter imbecile."

Akane glanced at the monster. "Yes, it's very impressive," she replied laconically. "But you know what would be even better?"

"What?" Sabrina replied, naked challenge in her tone.

"Watching you take a closer look." She gave the scientist a healthy push in the back. The woman tried to slow down, but on those injured legs, she had no chance. Sabrina stumbled forward five steps.

The huge eyes locked on her and the monster struck, lightning fast, all traces of laziness gone.

Sabrina tried to scream, but all she managed was a weak yelp before the enormous teeth closed around her.

Akane turned away as blood spattered onto her face.

As she wiped away the gore, she realized she was smiling broadly. "Now *that* was beautiful," she said.

***

Sked stopped running when he saw that Akane was walking in his direction. Nearly fifty yards still separated them, but he could see her grin.

"Your girlfriend is a violent nutjob," Dr. Pendalai observed as they watched her approach.

Sked chuckled. "Is that the kind of medical terminology they use in Sri Lanka?"

"Yeah. We stopped using 'batshit crazy' because it was deemed offensive to refer to the mentally ill in that way. But that woman has some issues."

"I can't argue with that," Sked replied. "She has her good points, though."

"Shut up, you two." They both turned to see Ania, an angry expression on her face, stepping between them. "Akane is wonderful. And you two... men..." she spat the word with considerable disdain, as if it were the worst insult she could think of, "can never understand the things she's gone through. Besides, isn't the woman she just killed the one who made the monsters? Didn't she hurt a lot of people? And wasn't she just going to keep hurting people if she survived all of this? Akane did the right thing."

Then she was running headlong, and met Akane in the middle, embracing her.

Sked shrugged. If Akane didn't want to tell her new ward that the death of that woman had been ordained by a contract on the woman's life as opposed to any particular concern for humanity on Akane's part, he wasn't going to say anything. It had been a little more dramatic than Sked expected, but one of the reasons Akane was always in trouble was that she had a flair for the artistic that went beyond mere brutality. She'd fed that bitch to her monster because it was the right way for that particular woman to die.

Either way, she'd be picking up the bounty.

Sked raised an eyebrow as she came into view. "Are you quite done? The ship is sinking, and we need to get off as soon as we can."

"Whatever," Akane said. "If you were so worried about that, you should have left without me."

Sked cursed her internally. She was very sure of him, secure in the knowledge that no matter what insane stunt she pulled, he would be there like a loyal dog to pull her chestnuts out of the fire.

He turned back and began to walk towards the lifeboat without another word.

Even though it was much lower in the water, the ship seemed to be moving a little faster than before. He wondered how long that would last... he could see water sloshing around in the lower reaches of the container deck, a few dozen yards below them. And it must have gotten well distributed, because the ship had leveled out, no longer listing to one side.

He grinned. Hopefully, those little bastard dinosaurs couldn't swim. He'd grown to hate those things... even more than he hated the big ones.

Lowering the lifeboat proved simple enough. Between Sked and the doctor, they got it down without much more than a couple of rope burns.

As they began to row away, two people jumped off the *Stern Liberia* and landed with a splash in the water behind them.

"Help!" they called. "Let us on."

Sked would have left them there, but the doctor's stern visage convinced him that with a ten-kilometer row ahead of them, another couple of oarsmen would come in handy.

He was enormously surprised to see that the people they'd picked up were the man and woman from the central control room where they'd destroyed the sonic control for the big monsters.

"Funny meeting you here," he said as they boarded. "Didn't fancy going down with the ship?"

The guy responded. He sported a dark bruise under his chin and Sked vaguely remembered hitting him in the head with his shoulder. "We didn't fancy going anywhere under the command of that mass-murdering bitch."

"What changed your mind?" Sked said. He wished someone else would pick up the conversation. Rowing while talking was exhausting.

The woman replied. "We went into Williams'... Sabrina's... room and found some extremely disturbing video footage. You were telling the truth."

"No shit, Goldilocks," Akane said. "Did we sound like we were bullshitting you?"

The woman seemed taken aback by Akane's forthrightness, almost as if she expected to be welcomed with open arms for making the enormous sacrifice of admitting that someone else was right and she was wrong.

"Before you answer that," Sked said, "could you each grab an oar and row? I want to get out of range of the ship's security people. They have guns."

"I'd worry more about the Mosasaur," the guy said.

"Nah," the girl replied. "I think we're okay on a rowboat. The noise won't be enough to attract its attention in these waters. Not while the *Stern's* engines are on."

"I guess you're right."

"Will you please get rowing?" Sked growled. "My ass is killing me and the doc and I could really use your help."

They rowed.

***

A small Indian Navy vessel picked them up before the coast of Andaman came into view. Sked wondered how the hell they could have failed to find the island after rowing what seemed like forever.

The Indians were extremely suspicious of the group of people climbing the rope ladder. A couple of cadets with rifles stood on either side of the ship's Captain as he ushered them aboard.

"Have you noticed no one is ever happy to see us?" Akane said.

"Yeah. They must have heard of you," Sked replied.

She stuck her tongue out at him.

This time, they were unable to sneak their weapons aboard. As soon as they reached the top of the ladder, both Sked and Akane were patted down and the guns were confiscated. The Captain of the cutter looked through Sked's backpack but shrugged and handed it back.

They were led to the front of the ship, where an open space allowed them all to stand together in the shadow of a reasonably sized deck gun. The artillery actually made Sked feel much better than before: they would be able to defend themselves, at least.

"All right," the Captain said. "Who can tell me what's going on here?"

Sked was about to speak, but the doctor stepped forward. "My name is Dr. Pendalai. I'm the doctor at the Sentinel Island resort. We suffered an attack by the natives… and by some other things you wouldn't believe, and these are the only survivors."

"Why are you on a lifeboat from the *Stern Liberia*?"

"Because the ship picked us up, but it's sinking now, and we needed to get off," Pendalai replied.

That earned them a hard look. "Sinking? Are you certain?"

"Absolutely." The doctor seemed completely unintimidated by the Indian Navy.

"They haven't sent a distress call."

"They wouldn't want you to board them."

The Captain turned to his men and began to give orders telling them to get the ship ready.

"Don't turn on the engines!" the woman from the control room said, pushing to the front of the group.

"Unless you have a really good reason for that, Miss, we're moving out right now."

He turned away from them.

The doctor grabbed his arm. "That isn't a good idea. There's a large sea monster on that ship. Maybe two."

The Captain turned back to them. "Maybe you'd better tell me the whole story from the start. But I'm not stopping the ship unless I hear something a lot more compelling than sea monsters."

Sked spoke. "We'll tell you everything, but please arm your weapons." He nodded towards the deck gun. "We've been through much too much for you guys to get us killed now."

The Captain shrugged but gave the order. The cannons on the deck were designed to dissuade illegal fishermen, but they were a hell of a lot better than a machine gun if the monster attacked. These things could do real damage, and naval types were always ready to show them off… at least until they had to explain firing expensive shells to budget-conscious superiors.

They told the story as the tiny ship headed back the way they'd come. The Captain listened with raised eyebrows which made it easy to guess what he was thinking. He wasn't concerned about whether they were telling the truth. He'd apparently dismissed that as a possibility as soon as he heard the words "sea monster". He was probably asking himself if the group he'd picked up was stoned out of their minds, or if he'd had the bad luck to rescue a lifeboat from the loony bin.

Sked shrugged it off. "Do you guys have wi-fi?" he asked instead.

"Not for civilian use, I'm afraid," was the answer.

"All right."

Sked returned to the group at the front of the boat, wondering if he could hack the Indian Navy's wi-fi. He decided against it. It was bad enough that any routine background check they ran would turn up a few anomalies. He didn't want to do anything that might lead someone to follow up on those anomalies. If they asked Washington about him… it could lead to awkward questions at the very least.

The *Stern Liberia* came into view and Sked swallowed. The ship was much lower in the water, and it didn't appear to be moving at all.

There was no sign of the monster.

"You really need to turn off that engine," Sked told the Captain.

"What I need to do is to go see that ship," the officer replied.

Sked shut up, saving his arguments for a battle he could win. This man wasn't going to listen to reason. Meanwhile, he scanned the water, bracing for impact. He didn't think the… had they called it a Mosasaur?… was big enough to bite this cutter in half, but it could probably put a serious dent in the hull and launch it a few yards into the air.

Hopefully, he'd get thrown into the water, where the creature would ignore him while it demolished the ship.

"Look!" Ania yelled, pointing into the sea.

A hundred yards away, the monster breached, challenging this new interloper. Sked wondered how any animal could function if it felt it had to attack everything bigger than it was. He assumed Jurassic seas weren't exactly teeming with large ships, but it still felt like an exhausting way to live.

"What the hell..." the Captain said.

"This is what we were telling you about," Sked said. "Get your gunner on the job, man."

"We... we don't have a gunner."

"How can you sail without a gunner?"

The Captain gave him a look. "In ten years, I've never had to do more than fire a warning shot for an arrest. People don't tangle with the Indian Navy. Not in these waters. So we just need someone who can point the tubes up and in the general direction of the people we're trying to frighten and push a button to fire over their heads. They get the message pretty quickly."

"I don't think the monster got the memo," Sked replied. Then he sighed. This next bit was going to cause every single one of the awkward questions he'd wanted to avoid. "I can target the guns."

"You can?" The Captain's voice turned icy.

"Yes."

"And if I ask you where you acquired such a skill?"

"I'd tell you to take it up with the Pentagon. I'm not allowed to tell you. But we're wasting time."

To his credit, the Captain led him belowdecks, only pausing to warn the group behind them to get the hell away from the guns if they wanted to keep their hearing.

The gunnery console was at least three generations older than the ones Sked had trained on, but it had been updated with video monitors. The 1990's computer display told him he was looking at the firing control for an OTO 76mm gun. He grinned; Godzilla was going to have a bad day.

He quickly established distance and fired. Miss.

"I could have done that," the Captain said, deadpan.

The explosion enraged the monster. It circled a few times trying to find the source of this new and painful noise, but, finding nothing where the shell had detonated, it began to move quickly towards the ship again, fueled by its anger.

"We're gonna get one more shot at this thing before it gets too close to shoot at," Sked said as he tracked the monster on the screen.

"Make it count, will you?"

Sked fired just as the monster dove. The explosion kicked up a fountain of water.

"Did you get it?" the Captain said, leaning over Sked. The man smelled like soap and Sked suddenly felt every single minute of the days they'd been on the run land on him like the proverbial ton of bricks. He would gladly have killed for a shower.

"I don't know. The shot was good, but it dove right before impact."

Suddenly, another splash just ahead of them revealed an enraged monster that reared, almost revealing its full body. It must have been unimaginably strong to lift that mass out of the water.

Sked didn't even bother trying to find the range. He just pressed the button and the rapid-repeating gun at the front of the ship boomed.

This time, there was no doubt. Instead of a spray of water, a large chunk of the creature's lower jaw exploded outward in a shower of pink gobbets. The smell of cooked meat wafted across the ship, overpowering even the strong scent of sea.

The creature toppled backward and sank beneath the waves.

"Told you I could hit the thing," Sked said. He slumped back in his seat, drained now that the adrenalin was gone.

"Are you all right?"

"There's nothing wrong with me that a few weeks in bed won't cure."

"If you need a bunk, we've got a few free."

"Why are you suddenly being nice to me?" Sked asked.

"Because you hit the thing."

"A blind civilian could have hit it at that range."

"No. I meant the second shot. It was bleeding before it came out of the water. I think it was already dying and wanted to take us with it. If you hadn't hit it, it probably would have come at us underwater. I know that's what I would have done in its place. Good show."

"Thank you," Sked said. "I'm glad I could help." He sighed. Even the possibility of dropping on a bunk wasn't enough to inspire him to move out of his seat. He preferred to just nap there. "Now what?"

"Now, we need to assist that ship over there."

"You might want to wait until backup arrives. You'll want Marines and zookeepers."

"What?"

Sked sighed. "Ask the folks outside. I need to sleep. But don't board the ship without backup. I mean it."

Sked's eyelids grew too heavy to keep up. Sitting down on a padded chair in front of the console had been a mistake. He suspected he'd wake in an interrogation cell somewhere in a New Delhi basement.

He would worry about that later. Now, it was time to rest.

CHAPTER 24

Mary checked her map. Though Google was telling her she was on the right road, she didn't trust it, which was why she bothered with the impossible-to-fold paper item. It was one of the few times in her life in which the roads she was approaching didn't have a Street View giving a preview of what she was getting into.

But then, Digos City's suburbs weren't exactly on the beaten path. Fifteen miles south of Davao along the coast, the town looked, at first, to be a series of shacks along the Pan-Philippine highway. Only when the car she'd hired turned off on a muddy road that seemed to disappear into the jungle did she realize that here, hidden from view, lay the real town.

But she also realized that she was completely at the mercy of her driver. She would never be able to find her way out alone. The map was as useless as her cell phone.

Fortunately, the guy seemed to be more concerned for her than she was. He turned back to look at her. "Are you sure this is where your friends live?" he asked in excellent English. "This is a poor part of town."

"I know. This is the right place. Do you know where it is?" she said.

"According to the guy I asked back at the highway, it's just a little further this way."

The houses here were pretty much all built on the same pattern: cinderblock walls topped by steeply sloped corrugated roofs, streaked with rust. A style that would have telegraphed poverty anywhere else in the world was given a certain charm here because there was sufficient space between houses for dense vegetation to turn everything an impenetrable green with houses and walls and fences sticking out.

The air coming in through the car's open window was hot and humid. But things had been hot and humid ever since she arrived in South Asia. She was used to it.

"This is the house, lady."

She smiled. No matter how often she'd been addressed that way in the past year, she never quite managed to suppress the desire to respond: "Oh, lovey, I'm no lady." But once again, she kept that to herself. She didn't want any misunderstandings with the driver. Instead, she simply said, "Thank you. Please wait here until I get back."

"Of course." He got out of the car and, leaning on the fender, fished in the pocket of his shirt for a cigarette. "If there's any trouble, yell for help. I'll come as soon as I can."

"Thank you." She gave him another smile. "I'm not expecting any trouble."

To Mary's surprise, she believed what she was saying. If someone had told her she'd willingly walk into the poor part of a backwater town in the Philippines with no one to take care of her but a tiny little driver who she could probably take in a fair fight, she would have told them they were crazy.

And yet, now that she was here, she was perfectly relaxed. The place appeared peaceful. A couple of goats chewed the grass on the side of the road, luxuriating in the mid-morning sun. This scene was too bright, too idyllic to be threatening. She smiled. It would be very different at night, she thought, wondering if any of the widely-spaced streetlights even worked.

Mary realized she was stalling. The most frightening part of the entire trip was what happened next. She opened the thigh-high iron gate, rusted and repainted in the tropical manner, and advanced to the door.

A deep breath later, she knocked on the door, a blue-painted panel whose uniform finish was broken only by a black ribbon tied around a nail.

She heard a scuffing sound from within, so she waited. Just when she was about to knock again, the door opened to reveal a dark woman with grey-streaked black hair.

"Are you Mrs. Ramos?" Mary said.

The woman nodded, eyes suspicious but unafraid. "I am."

Mary sighed with relief. She'd been sure the woman wouldn't speak any English and she'd have to hire a translator.

At least now she understood why she hadn't been able to get a phone number or an email address for the woman. The house didn't look like it held such technically advanced items as a cell phone or a computer.

"I knew your son," Mary said. "Marco. He was a cook for a man I know."

"He worked on a ship."

"Yes. I knew the owner."

"He's not here. He died three months ago. Far away. I'm sorry." The woman made to close the door.

"I know. I was with him when he died."

The door stopped and, for a moment, Mrs. Ramos seemed undecided about what to do. Finally, she opened the door with a sigh. "You should come inside. Is that man with you?"

"He's my driver. I don't want him to hear this," Mary replied.

"I will offer him water." Without waiting for Mary's response, she called to the driver in Filipino. The man responded with a smile and the woman disappeared into the dark house, reemerging a few moments later with a glass of clear water. The man accepted it with grateful-sounding words.

"Your driver is a polite man," the woman said. "Please come inside."

Mary entered, expecting a house of that sort to be dirty, smelly as well as dark. But again, her preconceptions proved wrong. The house smelled of lemon, the floors were boards, not rough, but worn smooth, with no sign or scent of the damp that pervaded the rest of the country. The underside of the house must have been very well insulated.

And the darkness was only real in relation to the bright sunlit exterior. Within moments, her eyes had adapted and the house began to take shape around her, illuminated by the open window in the rear as well as the door, still open to the street.

Lai's yacht, it most certainly wasn't. The house was furnished in a potpourri of mismatched wood and metal furniture painted in bright colors. The overall effect was of a happy, colorful place. A kindergartener would have felt right at home there, but that wasn't what caught Mary's eye. Her attention was drawn to the embroidered wall hangings and the little figurines, saints and animals, that adorned the top of a rectangular dresser.

Suddenly, she was sitting in her grandmother's house in Bournemouth, on some long weekend visit, staring at the little religious icons on her mantlepiece and inventing stories for each of them.

Mary pulled herself away from the memory. She had a conversation to get through. The first part would be the hardest.

"I was with your son when he died," she repeated, not knowing how else to broach the subject.

"You were nearby? You spoke to the doctors?"

Mary shook her head. "I was holding his hand. There were no doctors. We were on a ship. It was sinking."

"The ship he worked on?" the old woman asked.

"No. A different ship."

"He abandoned his position?" Mrs. Ramos cast her eyes downward, obviously disappointed, but at the same time stoic, as if no amount of bad news could ever surprise her or beat her down completely. She gave the impression of a woman who had lived a full life. That her dead son might have been unreliable just seemed to be part of her lot.

"No. Of course not." Mary thought for a moment. "Your son didn't seem capable of doing such a thing."

"Heh. Someday you'll have children of your own. Talk to me after they grow up."

Mary felt a pang. But no, this woman needed to know how her son died before speaking of why she was really here. "Your son died a hero. He saved my life. More than once." Mary wiped away a tear. "If he hadn't been there, I would be dead now."

The woman nodded, unconvinced. "You came all the way here to tell me that?"

"Yes. I mean, I would have, even if there hadn't been other things."

"Other things." The woman's voice was flat, her expression saying that nothing good could possibly be forthcoming.

"Yes. Mr. Lai... your son's boss, that is, sent you this." She handed Mrs. Ramos the envelope containing a fat check that Lai had entrusted her with. The woman tore it open.

"There must be some mistake," she said.

"No mistake. Mr. Lai knows your son was a hero. He wanted you to have this. If you don't want it, give it to your daughters. To whoever you want."

"You don't want it for yourself?"

"No. Mr. Lai was very generous with me as well. I don't need your son's money."

"You could have mailed this. The post usually arrives."

"I wanted to bring you this myself," Mary admitted.

"To tell me my son was a hero?"

"To tell you your son was a good man."

Mrs. Ramos sat silently, thinking. Then she held Mary's gaze for a long, long moment before she said, "There's something more." Again, it wasn't a question.

"Yes." Now it was Mary's turn to hesitate, to sit silently and wonder how to broach the subject. She couldn't think of any way to circle around what she needed to say, so she decided not to try. "I'm carrying your son's baby. I'm pregnant. We were together for a few days before he died."

Mrs. Robles sat for another moment, then she got up and closed the distance between them. She knelt beside Mary and put a hand on her stomach.

"This is my grandson? My son's son?"

"Yes. You can hardly tell, but he's in there."

The old lady laughed. "Oh, I could tell as soon as you arrived. The first thing I said to myself was it's too hot to leave a pregnant woman standing outside."

Mary nodded. It wasn't the first time someone had seen it; even though even Mary herself could barely have told, one woman had gotten up in the airport and given her a seat in a crowded departure gate. Another woman had told her to skip the line at immigration.

It was always women who were able to tell, generally women over fifty.

Mary looked down into Mrs. Robles' dark brown eyes. "I came here to ask for your blessing."

"My blessing?" The ghost of a smile played on the thin, wrinkled lips. "It sounds like you already did what you wanted."

Mary smiled in return. There had been more playfulness than malice in the words. "I want to keep his memory alive. I'd like to name my child Marco Robles in honor of your son."

"Why do you need my blessing? You are the mother. You can do what you think is best."

"Because he told me about you, and made me realize how much it would mean to him that you knew about this. I think, somewhere, Marco is watching over me from wherever he is, taking care of me, and that this will make him happy," Mary said. Now the tears flowed freely. "One night, we were in terrible danger and I was scared, so he told me about the day he realized he wanted to go to sea. He told me you took him out to the beach to watch the fishermen, and that they had blue boats and green boats. He told me that he wanted to learn to be a sailor so that he could come back here and fish close to home. But he didn't want a green boat or a blue boat. He said he would get—"

"A red boat," Marco's mother finished the sentence which the crying Mary was unable to complete.

Mary nodded. "You should have seen his face when he said it."

Mrs. Robles smiled. "I saw his face when he said it as a child." The old woman put her hand back on Mary's womb. "You have my blessing. All of the blessing this poor woman can possibly bestow."

And they fell into an embrace that seemed to last forever.

CHAPTER 25

The Antonov An-12 shuddered and shook, but as far as Sked could see, he was the only person on board who looked nervous. The five-man crew, African mercenaries that Cyrano had hired to fly him in, seemed bored. One of them was actually dozing on the long metal bench the Soviet Army must have used to carry soldiers from one place to another.

Well, when this old tin can went down, the joke would be on them: Sked was the only person aboard wearing a parachute.

The window showed him nothing. The Congolese jungle was not illuminated at night except for the occasional single light in the distance, probably a mine or a military outpost. There were people down there, but the route had been specifically selected to avoid major towns and villages.

He wished he could have slept, but that wasn't in the cards, and hadn't been since he landed in Tanzania, two days before. Just getting to South Sudan had been an adventure... and that was the legal part of the trip. Once in the new nation, a place where things were still quite unsettled after the conflict that had granted it independence, he'd been met by Cyrano's contacts and whisked to an airfield where they'd waited in a hangar for night to fall.

Only after the sun went down did they wheel out the old airplane and fly south.

Though he was already tired of the whole thing and wanted to be on the ground, where the fear of discovery would banish the exhaustion he felt, there were still a couple of hours of flight time before they reached Kananga.

He leafed through an old girlie magazine stuck in the remains of the webbing behind one of the only four seats in the cabin. It was a German mag full of pale women with unlikely hairstyles that must have been at least twenty years old. A lot of it had been cut up, and several pages were missing.

"Damn this," he said, and looked out the window again. Things were still black down there.

His phone vibrated and he smiled. After the experience on North Sentinel Island, he'd updated his tech. His satellite phone would keep him on the grid—even serving as a data bridge for hacking—no matter where he went. The guys who built it for him swore that he'd have bars on his phone in the middle of the Pacific or at the North Pole.

So he wasn't surprised to be interrupted by a call on a plane over an African jungle, even though almost no one had this number.

"Cyrano," he said. "Wasn't expecting to hear from you until I got on the ground."

"You're going to be busy once you get down there, so I thought it better to tell you this before the jump. Just got a couple of pieces of the news you asked me to keep my ears open for."

Sked's blood froze. He'd asked Cyrano to find out all he could about Akane's whereabouts... and he was terrified of what he might hear. "Tell me," he said.

"The little lady is in South Korea. Seoul, to be precise."

"What?"

"Holed up in a fleabag high-rise apartment building in Dondaemun, pretending to be a working girl from Estonia. She's got another woman with her, a girl who isn't on our radar calling herself Ania." Cyrano chuckled. "Get this: she seems to be teaching the other chick to hack. Either that or Akane herself has forgotten even the basics. Some of the stuff they're doing is really crappy."

"And they're all right? No one gunning for them?" Sked asked.

"Just a half dozen people, a handful of governments and every criminal organization on the planet. The usual suspects. But the good news is that no one's really focused on her right now. If she takes care, she should be fine."

"Good. What else have you got for me?"

"I think I know who the Buddha sold your data to."

Sked had completed his assignment, turned over the stolen hard drive and told the Buddha not to call him until his anger subsided. That would take a while... they'd barely made it out alive, and knowing the Buddha had sent them in willingly made Sked see red.

But not red enough to burn bridges. The Buddha was a major player, and what he'd pulled wasn't that unusual. Every time Sked went into the field, he worked under the assumption that the client wasn't telling him everything he needed to know. The Buddha's manipulations had been an extreme case, but not a deal-breaker.

"Tell me," Sked said.

"Not that it means anything to me, but the buyer appears to be a guy named Park Sun Lee. He's a North Korean defector and his last position was working for the Russians, but he seems to have left them in the lurch as well."

"What line is he in?"

"The same line as ZooDef, apparently. He builds genetically modified animal weapons. I wouldn't swear to this, but the rumors say he's teamed up with a guy named Philippe, some kind of mad genius. I think you might know him."

Sked covered his shock. He did know the man. In fact, that guy was responsible for his new personality. But he wasn't going to say that out loud. Cyrano's job was to gather information and either sell it to the highest bidder or, as now, use it to get people to work for him. Sked's business depended on people knowing as little about him as he could. So he ignored the question. "Any idea where Park is operating from?"

"I shouldn't tell you that," Cyrano retorted. "It's valuable data."

"I don't need to know specifics. I have no interest in going after the guy. But I'd like to know which part of the world I should avoid. I've had enough genetically modified creatures to last me a lifetime. You're sure there are no monsters where I'm going, right?"

"Completely sure. You're on your way to a Finance Center built by the Chinese government. Those guys use tech, not biology." Cyrano paused. "And to answer your question, the rumors place Sun Lee in Mali."

Sked grunted. Even though the monster makers were more than a thousand miles away, he would really have preferred it if they weren't in Africa. But it made sense. That kind of project required empty space and very little government interference to be able to function correctly, and there were few places available... especially if you couldn't head for Russia. South American governments were much too nosy nowadays. And that left Africa, if you could find the right spot.

"Figures," Sked replied. "You're absolutely sure none of the monsters are going to suddenly appear out of nowhere while I'm on the ground?"

"Listen to me," Cyrano replied. "You're going to have enough problems keeping the Chinese off your ass without worrying about stuff that isn't going to happen."

"Yeah, you're right. I'm just jittery because I have to parachute. I'm always like this before a jump. Just your bad luck to call me right before."

Cyrano laughed. "Yeah. I think you're a complete lunatic to throw yourself out of a perfectly good airplane into a jungle at night just for a few hundred thousand dollars. At least the fact that you're nervous about it makes me believe you might be human after all. Is everything else okay?"

"Yeah, all good. We're actually going to be early. Pilot said we had a tailwind all the way."

"Great. Call me when you get down and have a feel for the lay of the land."

"Yeah." Sked cut off the connection.

Another one of Cyrano's quirks was that he never gave out the name of the contact in the operating theater until the very last second. Sked assumed it was because he trusted no one, not even the people flying the plane, so he wanted to be sure Sked was out of their hands before giving anything up... but the truth was that if the flight crew was compromised, then the mission was fucked already, and the Chinese would be waiting as soon as he hit the ground.

If that happened, they wouldn't dirty their hands with him, just foist him on the Congolese with instructions to let him rot in jail for a few years.

Sked didn't think it likely. The crew went about their business in the gruffest way possible, pretty much treating him the same way they would have treated a large box: he would be taken to his destination, tossed out the door, and forgotten. No one had tried to make friends with him. No one had tried to get any information from him.

He would be okay.

Besides, he had no intention of wasting away in an African prison. Now that he'd located Akane again, he would do this job, get out of Congo by land and fly to South Korea. He knew she wasn't hiding from him. When they'd parted, she'd pretty much said that she would let him know where he was... and that she expected him over as soon as she did.

Well, the fact that Cyrano knew her whereabouts meant that Akane had decided to let him follow her trail. And knowing her, she would raise an eyebrow and ask him what had taken him so long.

Sked grinned at that. After everything she'd put him through, it was only fair that she should have to wait on him for a change.

He leaned back in his chair and tried to relax.

It wouldn't work this time, either.

CHAPTER 26

Jermaine Jakes leaned back on his chair, letting the smell of soft leather waft around him. He felt his mouth open in a huge grin and a sigh. He couldn't have helped it if he wanted to; he'd earned the right to relax.

It was incredible. He actually felt the tension leaving his shoulders as he reread the email. The message was quite simple, really, and in normal conditions it would have been satisfying, but not so important. It was from the offshore department of LichtenBank and read simply:

Deposit received. $25MM. Holding for further instructions.

He'd send further instructions on Monday. But for now, he could crow. His vision had been vindicated. The Compsognathus were being well-received by potential buyers everywhere.

At a million dollars per half-dozen, they were going to be the company's most profitable product line.

Jermaine had already typed up the email to the board of directors, and it had been waiting on his computer until the deposit cleared. He just gave it a final once over before hitting send and smiled.

After three months out in the wilderness, he'd be the company golden boy again.

Those three months had been hell. The disaster on the *Stern Liberia* and that goddamned island had caused an international stink, despite the millions he'd had to invest to have most of it covered up. By the way every do-gooding human rights organization had screamed, you'd think someone important had died. Hell, even the morons in the animal-rights movement had gotten in on the action.

And it had been Jermaine's job to smooth things out. The official story was that the animals had gotten loose while being transported to a facility in Saudi Arabia. Getting people to corroborate that story had cost him. He owed the Saudis one of the Giant Mosasaurs and a hundred Compsognathus. They wanted to build a zoo or a theme park or something. It was cheap at the price, though. By "proving" that the deaths had been accidental, the company had been able to make the two analysts who'd discovered the truth and defected sound like crazy media-pandering attention seekers.

The company was going to be fined... but LichtenBank could deal with the Indian government. The fine would never be levied. The fine would never be paid. Other favors would be exchanged instead.

Of course, the board was pissed at having to exchange those favors, but they were even more pissed at seeing their company logo on the front page of every newspaper and on the top of every website.

Even so, if his only problem had been damage control, it would have been fine. He was used to doing damage control. One of his first jobs had been at Procter & Gamble where he'd been in charge of a huge detergent recall in Argentina which had nearly killed the brand he'd been working for.

Since then, as he moved up the corporate ladder, stress had been a constant companion. He could deal with a disaster if it had a management-driven solution. And since management simply meant getting results by way of other people, *everything* had a management solution.

Unfortunately, damage control was only half the problem, and the lesser half at that. The world wouldn't really worry about a bunch of unknowns who became monster food somewhere no one had heard of. It had only been news for a day or two.

The real problem was Sabrina. That she'd managed to get herself killed was a huge setback. She'd been the undisputed master in her field, but better still, she hadn't cared about anything else. Not money—despite the fact that she was being paid spectacularly well—not men, not friends, not family. Nothing but her work. He'd only ever seen her show positive emotions to the creatures in cages.

Jermaine's past few weeks had been a scramble. He couldn't hope to replace her with someone equally talented to continue her research, so he just tried to figure out who on her team was actually capable of getting the stuff they'd already designed into production so they could sell the things to clients.

Unfortunately, they'd had to move their production facility out of Arizona because the US was investigating the incident in the Indian Ocean, but that wasn't a problem.

South Africa had welcomed the factory with open arms, but getting even one cloning vat up and running had proven challenging with the personnel on hand.

In the end, they'd had to bite the bullet and reach out to get one of the Russians from Yekaterinburg to sign on. Those guys had all lost their jobs when the nature of the lab's research came into the light, but getting them out of Russia had been a nightmare. They were afraid to work for anyone else because they thought every branch of the secret police would come after them if they did.

It had required a boatload of dollars for one of the senior people to cross over, but it had been worth it. He'd beaten the soft, under-utilized team into a functional unit in weeks. So good, in fact, that Jermaine hadn't hesitated to sign the contract with the Belgians.

Of course, he knew that the final buyers weren't really Belgians but likely based in the Middle East, but it wasn't polite to pry. And now that the money for the initial shipment had come in, who they represented was no longer his concern; all Jermaine had to do was to make certain the creatures arrived where they were supposed to go. And it was easy to ship stuff from South Africa to... well, basically everywhere.

He was back on his way. The endless study, the long hours working his way up the corporate ladder, the nights and weekends... they were worth it now. Running a company from the CEO's seat was very different from getting that seat at a startup and then turning it into a viable company.

Jermaine thought about Shawna, and whether he could have done something different, if there had been some way to keep her from leaving him. But even a couple of years later, he didn't know what that might have been. She had been adamant: she didn't want to move overseas, she was content with a nice suburban house outside Cincinnati. Her dream growing up had been stability, the bourgeoise life her parents hadn't been able to afford and the acceptance that society refused to give. She'd never understood that, for Jermaine, such things weren't anywhere near enough. He'd known since day one that he had the talent and the drive to reach the very top.

And now he'd arrived.

Jermaine sighed contentedly and was about to sign off for the weekend—it was already 3:30 and there was nothing else he wanted to do this Friday afternoon—when his calendar popped up and showed a reminder.

Oh, right. The potential clients from Singapore.

As if reading his mind, the phone on his desk beeped. He hit the speaker button and his assistant's voice came over the line: "Your 3:30 is here."

"Thanks, send them in."

He heard a pop over the speaker and stared at the phone in irritation. It had been acting up lately, and he'd need to get it replaced.

The door opened and Jermaine frowned as a man in a light grey suit showed himself in. "Didn't Siena offer to show you in?"

"She did," the man replied. "I kept her from getting up. I can show myself through a door."

"Ah, good." He'd have to talk to Siena, too. She knew that ushering people was part of her job, and she'd supposedly been trained not to give them any option other Ooption. "Please have a seat."

He studied his guest. The suit he was wearing was loose around the shoulders and waist. Jermaine didn't consider that an insult. His potential clients were the kind of people for whom the very fact that the man was wearing a suit at all could indicate a huge concession to the niceties of formality.

Apart from that, the man didn't look in the least bit Asian. He was tall and blond and lithe, but that was par for the course in this business. Everyone triangulated their purchases through shell companies and intermediaries. The kind of people who wanted to buy dinosaurs that would kill people didn't exactly advertise the fact.

And that was how he opened. "Are you authorized to negotiate?"

"To the very end," the man replied. His accent was perfectly neutral. It was impossible to know where he was from.

"Good." It wasn't really a surprise. This man—or, more precisely the people he worked for—would have been vetted by both the business and security side of ZooDef's operation. Only after making his way through them would this man have been allowed to see Jermaine. "Then I'm sure we can get this done quickly. As you know, we've got favorable prices for our early adopters."

"That doesn't concern me in the least," the man said, putting a hand into the pocket of his jacket. "My employer is not interested in your price list."

Jermaine let the man speak; he'd name his conditions and the bargaining could begin.

"I represent a man named Lai bin Amir. He is Malaysian."

The man paused, and Jermaine thought about the name for a moment. Lai... Lai... he knew he'd heard it, but couldn't quite place it among the groups that might be interested in his wares. Then his eyes widened as he recognized the name of the single important person involved in the *Stern Liberia* fiasco. A man who'd survived.

"Ah," his visitor said, nodding approvingly. "I see you've placed him. He sends his regards, and says his main regret is that Cora can't be here to deliver this message personally."

"Who the hell is Cora?" Jermaine sputtered. "What message? No, forget it. I don't care. I'll have security throw you out."

"No need," the man replied, standing. "I'll show myself out." In a quick motion, he pulled a pistol with a silencer out of his jacket, aimed it at Jermaine's forehead and pulled the trigger.

The bullet hit him right between the eyes and he knew nothing more.

THE END

SEVEREDPRESS

Check out other great
Dinosaur Thrillers!

Rick Poldark
PRIMORDIAL ISLAND

During a violent storm Flight 207 crash-lands in the South China Sea. Poseidon Tech tracks the wreckage to an uncharted island and dispatches a curious salvage team—two paleontologists, a biologist specializing in animal behavior, a botanist, and a nefarious big game hunter. Escorted by a heavily-armed security team, they cut through the jungle and quickly find themselves in a terrifying fight for survival, running a deadly gauntlet of prehistoric predators. In their quest for the flight recorder, they uncover the mystery of the island's existence and discover an arcane force that will tip the balance of power on the primordial island. Things are not as they seem as they race against time to survive the island's man-eating dinosaurs and make it back home in one piece.

P.K. Hawkins
SUBTERRANEA

Fall, 1985. The small town of Kettle Hollow barely shows up on any maps, and four young friends are used to taking their BMX's outside of town in an effort to find anything interesting to do. But tonight their tendency to go off by themselves may have saved them, and also forced them into the adventure of a lifetime. While they were away, Kettle Hollow has been locked down by the government, and a portal to another world has opened on Main Street. It's a world deep below the ground, a world where dinosaurs roam free, where giant plants and mutant insects hunt for prey. It's also a world where all their family and friends have been kidnapped for sinister purposes. Now, with time running out before the portal closes, the four friends must brave the unknown to save their loved ones. Time is running out, and in the darkened tunnels of Subterranea, something is hunting them.

Check out other great

Dinosaur Thrillers!

Julian Michael Carver

TRIASSIC

After spending many years in artificial hypersleep, a handful of survivors of the exploration vessel Supernova awaken to find their ship torn to shreds. They are unsure of what happened in space or how they crashed into an uncharted planet. Upon exploration of the new world, they soon realize their destination: The Triassic, the first chapter of the Mesozoic Era. A plan is formulated to escape this terrifying landscape plagued with dinosaurs and prehistoric beasts. The survivors soon discover that there may be an even larger threat looming under the trees than just the dinosaurs, threatening to cut their mission short and trap them all forever in the primitive depths of the Triassic.

Hugo Navikov

THE FOUND WORLD

A powerful global cabal wants adventurer Brett Russell to retrieve a superweapon stolen by the scientist who built it. To entice him to travel underneath one of the most dangerous volcanoes on Earth to find the scientist, this shadowy organization will pay him the only thing he cares about: information that will allow him to avenge his family's murder. But before he can get paid, he and his team must enter an underground hellscape of killer plants, giant insects, terrifying dinosaurs, and an army of other predators never previously seen by man. At the end of this journey awaits a revelation that could alter the fate of mankind ... if they can make it back from this horrifying found world.

Check out other great

Dinosaur Thrillers!

Steve Metcalf

OBJEKT 221

Ruthless multi-national conglomerate Allied Genetics is under siege from a paramilitary force for hire. Allied calls in reinforcements and fortifies their crown-jewel property – an abandoned Soviet military facility in Crimea known during the Cold War as Objekt 221. Fortunately for the future of their research, O221 straddles a stretch of rocky landscape that hides a rift – a portal through time and space. Through this rift, Allied Genetics can travel, at will, to the Cretaceous – 100 million years into Earth's past – and bolster their genetic experiments with dinosaur DNA ... something their competitors want to stop at all costs."Objekt 221" is a story blending numerous science fiction elements such as repurposed military facilities, time travel, rogue corporate armies, dinosaurs and the hint of a super-ancient civilization.

Bestselling collection

PREHISTORIC:
A DINOSAUR ANTHOLOGY

PREHISTORIC is an action packed collection of stories featuring terrifying creatures that once ruled the Earth. Lost worlds where T-Rex and Velociraptors still roam and man is now on the menu. Laboratories at the forefront of cloning technology experiment with dinosaurs they do not understand or are able to contain. The deepest parts of the ocean where Megalodon, the largest and most ferocious predator to have ever existed is stalking new prey. Plus many more thrillers filled with extinct prehistoric monsters written by some of the best creature feature authors this side of the Jurassic period.

Check out other great

Dinosaur Thrillers!

P.K. Hawkins

THE LOST ISLAND

Scientists Dr. Eccleston and Dr. Lerner have done many routine expeditions for the Skurzon Corporation in the past, helping the company search the ocean for newly available resources freed by melting ice. They're expecting to maybe find oil at the bottom of the Arctic Sea. What they aren't expecting is a lost island that defies all scientific understanding. When something comes out of the sea and destroys their research vessel, the scientists and the rest of the crew are forced into a game of survival against forces no human being has ever seen alive. If they can survive the giant insect swarms, the man-eating plants, and the dinosaurs, they might be able to live to tell the tale. But when each passing moment reveals murderers in their midst, their survival starts to look less and less likely.

William Meikle

THE LAND BELOW

A treasure hunt into the deepest cave system in Europe takes a turn for the worst.Now rather than treasure it is survival that is at the forefront of the spelunkers' thoughts. But their attempt to escape out of the dark deep places is thwarted. Men are not at home in the depths. But there are things that are, pale terrifying things. Huge things.Things red in tooth and claw.

www.ingramcontent.com/pod-product-compliance
Lightning Source LLC
Chambersburg PA
CBHW071502170626
46811CB00007B/2690